THE
GENTLEMAN
FROM
FINLAND

ADVENTURES ON THE
TRANS-SIBERIAN EXPRESS

D1111716

THE GENTLEMAN FROM FINLAND

ADVENTURES ON THE TRANS-SIBERIAN EXPRESS

Robert M. Goldstein

Published by Rivendell Publishing Northwest
Seattle, Washington

Printed in the United States of America
Library of Congress Catalog Number 2004098986

Book and cover design by Liz Kingslien
Cover photo property of Robert M. Goldstein

Publisher's Cataloging-in-Publication
    Goldstein, Robert M., 1955-
        The gentleman from Finland : adventures on the
    Trans-Siberian Express / Robert M. Goldstein. -- 1st ed.
        p. cm.
        Includes bibliographical references.
        LCCN 2004098986
        ISBN 0-9763288-0-1

    1. Railroad travel--Russia (Federation)--Siberia.
    2. Goldstein, Robert M., 1955---Travel--Russia (Federation)
    --Siberia. 3. Velikaia Sibirskaia magistral.
    4. Siberia (Russia)--Description and travel.   I. Title.

DK756.2.G65 2005   915.704'854
                           QBI04-200531

Table of Contents

Acknowledgments

This book could not have been written — nay, the adventure experienced! — without the generous help I received from Ken Olsen and Carol Williams, who somehow managed to pry a visitor's visa and train tickets from the Soviet bureaucracy for me. In addition, I am indebted to them for the generous hospitality they extended to me during my stay in Moscow. Ken, using his new-found Russian language skills, spent countless hours in line on my behalf, trying to wrestle train seats and reservations from the Soviet bureaucracy. The idea of the book languished for thirteen years before I dusted off an early draft of the chapter titled *The Colonel* and fed it to a newly formed writer's critique group I had joined. I stuck with the group, and the core group stuck with me. Thanks to Lisa Schnellinger, Mike Warlum, Adrienne Ross, Dan Becker, Caroline Ullmann, and Steve Nicholas, who were honest and forthright in their criticism and praise. The writer's group, as we called ourselves, shaped the work into its present form, a process that took three years. Another three years elapsed before it actually became a book.

A special thanks to Dan, Caroline, and Caroline's husband Mike Ullmann, who continued to serve as critical readers even after the writer's group had dissolved. Mike, a long-time friend, and another friend, Mike Merritt, provided critical assistance in getting my coveted visitor's visa from Seattle to London just before I left for the Soviet Union. Ashley Hulsey, who came into my life late in the development of the project, gave additional insight and encouragement. My cousin Bernie Rubin provided the key evidence regarding our family's link to Finland, while my aunt Frances Baumgarten provided details about my family history, and her husband, my uncle Aaron Baumgarten, helped with a few translations of Yiddish and Russian. Thanks to Lara and Vladamir Iglitzin, old Russian hands, who checked the manuscript for dialog and other details. My friend Ron Lovell, author of the Thomas

Martindale mystery series, provided much needed encouragement, as well as advice for marketing and publicity.

Lastly, I want to thank my late grandmother, Angela Ubiarco, for the pinstriped engineer's hat, which seemed surgically attached to my head during the early years of my life, and my parents, Morey and Magdalena, for the wooden trains, the Lionel set, and for indulging me in countless train rides during my childhood.

Dedication

To Nonny and Bubba

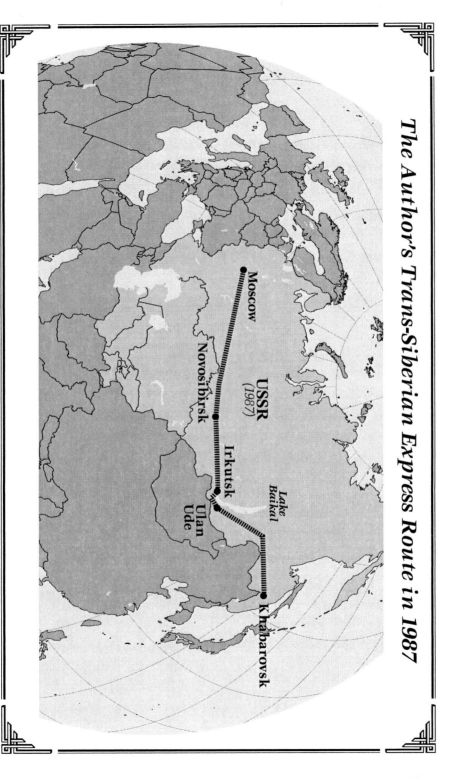

The Author's Trans-Siberian Express Route in 1987

Prologue

Somewhere between training wheels and Tinkertoys®, I fell in love with trains.

As a child, I watched in fascination as the commuter and freight trains thundered down the Southern Pacific railroad tracks near my home in Santa Clara, California. In my bedroom, I never tired of rearranging the layout of my wood block trains, courtesy of the local Goodwill store. Until I started kindergarten, I couldn't be separated from my gray-blue, pinstriped engineer's cap.

One telling bit of family memorabilia that chronicles this growing obsession is preserved in an 8 mm film shot by my father. The scene is by an old steam locomotive, which was displayed in a park located somewhere along U.S. Route 99 between the turnoff to the Bay Area and Los Angeles. In those days — the early 1960s — we made frequent trips to Southern California to visit relatives. In the film's opening sequence, an elfin figure dressed entirely in railroad pinstripes and hat, with a red kerchief tied smartly around his neck, cautiously approaches the train. I inspect the wheels and the coal tender before scaling the ladder to the engineer's compartment. The camera pans to other children frolicking on the big iron engine. Not me. The end of the film shows my expression of absolute seriousness as I sit in the engineer's seat turning levers, checking pressure dials, and peering over the instrument panel to make sure no oncoming trains approach. It's clear that I do not think I am playing.

Not long after that day my father took me on my first real train trip. Although I was no more than seven or eight years old, the moment when the gleaming silver passenger coaches and sleeper cars of the Zephyr eased into the small station in Fremont is etched in my memory. Porters pulled out little metal step stools so we could climb aboard. I remember the steam hissing from underneath the carriages, the conductor's shout of "all aboard," the faint smell of diesel, and the gentle lurch as the train began its journey.

The Zephyr's ultimate destination was Chicago, but our trip lasted only about two hours. We disembarked in Stockton, and then caught the westbound train home. I spent every minute of the journey with my nose pressed against the window of the dome car. I had ridden this way before, across the dry windblown hill country, in the family station wagon. I was a nervous passenger, and passed those trips either car sick or locked in silent terror, watching vehicles jockeying for passing position on the narrow two-lane road, my imagination fast-forwarding ahead to the fiery head-on collision that seemed inevitable.

But in the steel cocoon of the train, I felt perfectly safe. White-jacketed waiters served food in the elegant dining car. Every carriage had its own bathroom; no need to nag Dad to stop the car or, worse, to wait in quiet agony. I could relax and watch the world unfold at a leisurely pace. The rhythmic beat of the train's steel wheels was comforting, as was the murmured conversation of the passengers. For someone who had never left California, I could only imagine what it would be like to travel all the way to Chicago. Someday, I wanted to be one of those people.

1

The Magic Shoes

wenty-five years later. The old woman pointed to the opposite bunk and motioned for me to sit, then handed over an enormous cabbage as the Trans-Siberian Express eased out of the Novosibirsk Station. Reaching under the bunk, she pulled out a tattered canvas rucksack stuffed with potatoes, leeks, beets, and assorted vegetables. She carefully removed the harvest and spread it onto her bunk. Where she had managed to collect such a horde on the cusp of the Russian winter was beyond me. As the train lurched over a rough patch of track, I held the cabbage close to my chest, as if it were my first-born child.

The woman glared at me with native suspicion. I shifted nervously in my seat, still clutching the cabbage. I felt compelled to say something to allay her apparent fear that I might not return it. With my dark complexion — the product of a Mexican-American, Russian-Jewish heritage — I looked more like someone from Tashkent than Seattle. Using simple Russian phrases that I had memorized, I began to introduce myself when an enormous beetle with a pair of vise grip pinchers emerged from the purplish cabbage leaves and plopped to the floor. With a swift and decisive step, I slammed the heel of my shoe down on the odious bug. The shell crackled. The old woman clapped, and said something that must have meant "Way to go. Nicely done. That's how we deal with vermin in Siberia."

The ice was broken. I finished my pat introduction in Russian while studying my compartment companion, the first *babushka* (grandmother) I had encountered up close on this two-week train trip across Siberia. She was wrapped in layers of clothes topped off by a blue sweater with white flowers embroidered on the sleeves. She wore a frayed wool hat, and protruding from her blue skirt was a pair of log-like legs encased in thick thermal underwear. Her hands were gnarled, as if they had spent a lifetime tilling the soil. I guessed she was in her late sixties, but given the harsh realities of Soviet life, she may have been younger. She seemed the archetype of the old women I had seen throughout the country: withered pensioners with husbands long since dead. Legions of them swept the streets of every Soviet city. I can still hear the scratching of their flimsy brooms on the brick plaza between the Kremlin and onion-domed Saint Basil's Cathedral. The faces of these women, with tired eyes and skin worn by the ages, seemed molded from the clay of the Russian steppe itself. These babushkas carried on their stooped backs the burden of a national history that knew much suffering and little joy. They were the widows of the millions who died during World War II or the grandmothers of those recently killed in Afghanistan. At first glance, the old woman before me seemed no different.

"You speak Russian," she proclaimed once I finished my memorized speech. I feared becoming too fluent with my one line: "I am Bob. I am tourist. I am American. I do not speak Russian." The woman who I began to view as the embodiment of Mother Russia herself issued what seemed like a command, but one that I did not understand. Clueless, I returned the cabbage and, for good measure, said thank you in Russian.

"Yes, you understand," she said, nodding her head in approval.

Mother Russia then launched into a monologue that went far beyond my limited vocabulary. She babbled on for nearly thirty minutes, speaking in earnest tones while I nodded solemnly as if

I understood every word. I fumbled helplessly with my Russian-English phrase book. But it was useless. I sat quietly, nodding occasionally to show that I was listening.

Soon, tears crept down Mother Russia's cheeks. I guessed that she was telling me about her village and her life. I fumbled for my bandanna, and handed it to her. She dabbed her eyes.

When she was finished, Mother Russia looked at me expectantly. In fairness, I felt compelled to say something. But what could I say? How many more times could I introduce myself and say thank you? I looked at the phrase book. With the deliberation of a preacher about to give a sermon from the Bible, I picked up the book. Mother Russia peered at me with an intensity that led me to think she believed I was about to reveal the mysteries of the universe from the small volume with the dog-eared pages. I hoped she was not expecting much.

I randomly turned to a chapter on travel by bicycle and motorcycle. Not quite sure what else to do, I began to slowly recite the phrases, butchering the Russian language as I read my lines.

"...I am fond of cycling...Are your brakes in order?...Yes, but the chain is a bit loose...I must blow my tires..."

At first, Mother Russia stared at me as if I had lost my mind. But as I read, the stony countenance I had observed earlier seemed to soften. I spied a hint of a smile. Small at first, it grew from the corners of her mouth and spread into a grin. This was followed by high-pitched little girl giggles that gurgled up from deep inside her. She pursed her lips and cupped her hand over her mouth, trying to stop the tide of merriment. It seemed as if Mother Russia had not laughed for a long time. Encouraged by her reaction, I continued to recite my lines in a clear, dispassionate tone. I paused at random intervals, inserting inflections of tone at places I thought appropriate. I wanted to hear her continue to laugh. I turned to the chapter on sports.

"Shall we go and watch the game between Leningrad and Moscow? Do you do exercises in the morning? Are you entering for the thousand meters?"

Mother Russia could not contain herself. She erupted. Great peals of laughter gushed from her. Tears of joy welled up in her eyes. She clutched her stomach and lurched back and forth. Thinking she might hurt herself, I paused, but she motioned for me to keep reading. The sermon of the absurd continued.

"Give me the menu and the wine list . . . Fried sturgeon . . . As for poultry, there is turkey, goose, and duck."

As I plowed through the section "In the Restaurant," Mother Russia composed herself enough to proclaim that I must be hungry. She reached under her seat and pulled out a second rucksack. Like a magician pulling rabbits from a hat, she produced several squash, another cabbage, and a bag of potatoes, all of which she stacked neatly on her seat.

"No, no, please, I'm really not hungry," I said in panicky English as the produce piled up. Recalling the empty shelves in the grocery stores, I knew that fresh vegetables were a scarce commodity, likely grown with loving care in Mother Russia's private plot. I did not want to deplete this poor woman's food supply. Mother Russia ignored my protests. She burrowed deeper into her bag.

"Ah ha!" she exclaimed. She held a single egg in her withered hand.

"Please, I cannot eat, you take it," I said, racking my mind for Russian words besides "no, please, and hold the caviar." I flipped through the phrase book, but could only find, "Please, no more sturgeon eggs for me."

Giggling at my latest linguistic miscue, Mother Russia insisted I take the egg. I thanked her profusely. I pulled out my bandanna and spread it on my seat. Then I took the egg and rapped it against my knee. This was a mistake. The shell cracked. It was not hard-boiled. Yoke slimed down my last pair of clean pants. I grabbed the bandanna and tried to clean the mess, knowing that the nearest reputable dry-cleaner was at least 3,000 miles away.

Mother Russia's howl seemed to shake the car. She clutched her stomach and doubled over. She tried to stop, but this only produced little snorts and oinks that caused renewed bouts of laughter. I stood up, helpless before the hysterical woman. The door to the compartment slid open and the conductor, his shirt only half tucked in, peered inside. He glanced at Mother Russia, who was now doubled over on her bunk. He looked at me. I shrugged. Another passenger, a tall thin man with a droopy mustache, peered over the shoulder of the portly conductor.

"What is the commotion? Is there a problem?" I thought I heard the conductor say in Russian.

Mother Russia sat up, tears of gaiety streaming down her face.

"It is okay," she said. "He is a very funny man."

The conductor smiled.

"Is he Mongolian?" asked the conductor.

"Nyet," I replied, understanding this part of the conversation. "Ya Americansky."

Mother Russia, her laugh attack having subsided, spoke to the conductor. She motioned toward me and the remnants of the egg.

"She says that she thinks you are from Byelorussia, where she is from." It was the man in the droopy mustache, speaking in passable English. "There was a man who came to her village and told funny stories and did funny things. He had a magic hat. Then he went away, and no one ever heard of him again. She says you remind her of him."

"What happened to him?" I asked.

The man with the droopy mustache translated for Mother Russia. She shrugged and said something that I understood.

"He was a Jew, and they all went away," she said.

He was a Jew, and they all went away. And suddenly the gears of my mind began to mesh. I mentally searched through a mishmash of memories and recollections about my ancestors' lives in Russia. Could it be? No, it was impossible. But then again . . .

My father once told me he thought his parents were from near Grodno, just a few miles within Byelorussia (now Belarus), east of the Polish border. Most of my relatives, I had been told, immigrated to the United States or Canada between 1903 and 1906. If Mother Russia was in her late sixties, her encounter with the comedian would have occurred in the 1930s, long after the Rubinsteins — my grandmother's maiden name — had left for the New World.

But it was possible that not everyone had left. Perhaps either too poor or stubborn, one of my kin stayed, somehow weathered the czar's anti-Jewish pogroms, survived the Russian Revolution, and managed to retain a sense of humor. Could he have been the same quick-witted man who had entertained Mother Russia some six decades ago?

"Ask her if she knows where he went."

Droopy translated. The last of the gaiety slowly drained from Mother Russia's face.

"She does not know. All she remembers is the terrible times that followed. There was not enough to eat and then war; the Germans invaded. She went to Siberia, to Omsk, and worked in the war factories."

"Did she live near Grodno?" I persisted.

But before the man with the droopy mustache could translate the question, Mother Russia began babbling and pointing excitedly at my feet. At first, I thought the beetle had risen from the dead and was about to counterattack up my pant leg. Horrified at the possibility, I checked the bottom of my shoe. The crushed bug was still there.

"She likes shoes," said Droopy.

Mother Russia pointed at the sixty-five dollar pair of Vasque walking shoes I had purchased specifically for this trip. The shoes represented the largest single investment in footwear I had ever made. The shoe section of the Seattle department store where I bought them was lorded over by an elderly Italian gentleman. "These are the best walking shoes ever made," he told me in a raspy voice that mimicked Marlon Brando in *The Godfather.* "Don't let anyone tell you different." I told him I was off to the Soviet Union in a week. Much walking was planned. "They got nothing like these shoes over there. Those people will go ape shit when they see your shoes."

I reached down and undid the laces, and slid them off my feet.

"Here, go ahead and try them on," I said to the old woman.

Mother Russia did not need the translation. She slipped off her tattered canvas loafers and handed them to me. Clucking like a happy hen, she slipped on my shoes. They fit perfectly. She tied the laces and strutted around the compartment.

"She really likes shoes," said Droopy.

"I can see that."

"She says these are best shoes in all of Russia. She wants them."

"What? They are my only pair of shoes," I said.

Droopy shrugged.

"She's an old woman. She's crazy," he said, rolling his eyes.

Mother Russia prattled on, pointing to the cabbage and beets on her seat. Clearly, she wanted to trade her produce for my shoes.

"Do you like cabbages and beets?" asked Droopy.

"I hate cabbage," I said, testily. Quickly, I dropped my mental speculation about my family's origin and focused on this new crisis that threatened to leave me shoeless in Siberia. I had to get those shoes off Mother Russia before she departed the train. But how was I going to separate the old woman from my shoes without causing an international incident? As I pondered my dilemma, Mother Russia sashayed past me into the corridor. She waltzed to the opposite compartment to show off my sixty-five dollar shoes. Meanwhile, Droopy talked quietly to the conductor. Perhaps they realized the problem and were devising a plan to help me.

Droopy interrupted the fashion show in the next compartment. No doubt about it, my new friend was intervening on my behalf. I listened carefully, but the negotiation did not seem to be going well. There was a heated exchange. Mother Russia poked her head into my compartment and gestured at me. Then she wagged a gnarled finger at Droopy. She seemed to be saying "no way." The conductor smiled.

"What's happening? What did you say to her?"

"I ask her to switch compartments. I have an old woman with me. Better to have old women together. But she says no. She will not give you up."

"That's what you talked about?" I said, exasperated. "What about the shoes?"

"She likes shoes."

"I know! But I've got to get the shoes back."

Droopy shrugged again. This wasn't his problem. I sat stewing in my compartment, as Droopy and the conductor lounged by the door. Mother Russia paced up and down the tiny aisle between the benches, which served as seats during the day and beds at night. I noticed a certain bounce in her step as if the shoes were restoring the vitality that years of hardship had sucked away. While I watched the transformation, a wisp of an idea crossed my mind.

I turned to Droopy. "Tell her they are magic shoes. Only I can wear them. If someone else wears them, it will bring them bad luck."

Droopy looked at me as if I had lost my mind.

"Go ahead," I said. "Tell her."

Reluctantly, he translated. Mother Russia laughed, said something to Droopy, and then bounded out of the compartment.

"Where is she going?"

"She said she wants to show most excellent shoes to friends."

Droopy and the conductor drifted away. The compartment seemed strangely quiet. I stared at the pile of produce, my stocking feet propped up against the opposite bunk. Late afternoon sunlight slanted in from the window and warmed my toes. Outside, vast mounds of hay like piles of shredded wheat dusted with a layer of snow passed by the window. A village of rough-hewed log cabins bisected by a single muddy road followed. Three women, bent and stooped, waited to fetch water from a well.

The minutes ticked by without a sign from my roommate. I lamented the loss of my shoes. I thought of the practical side of the problem. Where could I buy new shoes in Siberia? I wrote in my journal: "Never trust a babushka bearing a cabbage."

Nearly an hour had passed when I heard a commotion coming from the far end of the corridor. I got up and craned my head out the compartment door. Bounding down the aisle, leading what appeared to be a rabble of babushkas and other hangers-on, was Mother Russia, resplendent in my sixty-five dollar shoes. Pointing to me, she proclaimed to the throng, "Look, there he is." I flashed back to the prophecy of the Italian shoe salesman and wondered if this qualified as an "ape shit" moment. I retreated to my compartment and awaited the arrival of the clomping feet.

Seconds later Mother Russia burst in, followed by a coven of old women wrapped in shawls and wearing flower-print dresses. They came in all shapes and sizes; here a big one, there a little one, over there one with an enormous goiter. I cowered in the corner, flummoxed by this turn of events. Mother Russia pointed at the egg stain on my pants. She appeared to be giving a play-by-play account of the now famous raw-egg incident. Everyone chuckled. I smiled weakly. Then Mother Russia, with a grand gesture, pointed at my phrase book.

"You mean you want me to read from this?" I asked motioning to the book.

"Da, da," she said.

Mother Russia ordered the mob to sit. The fat babushka wedged herself in by squishing me against the window. The one with the goiter plopped down on the other side of her. We could barely move. The others helped Mother Russia stash the produce to make room for everyone else. A stern-looking old man, his jacket festooned with medals, wandered in and leaned on his cane near the door. A half-dozen withered faces peered at me curiously as I reached for the book. Silence broken only by the occasional squeal of the train's wheels permeated the compartment.

I flipped through the pages, searching for some choice lines for my guests. I arrived at the dining section, always a crowd-pleaser, and slowly began to read. The room remained silent, the faces impassive.

I read on. Nothing. Feeling panic, I skipped ahead and found the comment about the sturgeon eggs, my best line. I felt a rumble against my side. Something was stirring deep inside the babushka next to me. A giggle came from someone else. I looked up and saw grim, impassive faces slowly breaking into smiles. I read on. There was a snicker and a burble. I kept reading. I heard a trickle of giggles. I turned the page and read with more emphasis, as if I were Orson Wells reciting from *King Lear*. The trickle grew to a torrent, then a cascade of laughter. It could not be stopped.

Above the tumult, Mother Russia shouted something to the effect of "Look, I told you he was funny." I stopped to survey my audience. The two babushkas sharing my bunk were crashing into each other, holding their stomachs. The stern man by the doorway grabbed the compartment door for support with his free hand. His medals jangled and danced wildly. Tears streaked down his face as he clutched his cane, trying to maintain balance in the wobbly train. Read on, beckoned Mother Russia. Other passengers crowded around the door, jamming the corridor. Children slid between the legs of adults to catch a glimpse of the show.

Above the faces clustered in the doorway, I spotted the conductor and Droopy. The conductor was attempting to clear a path through the corridor. The train had stopped, and passengers were trying to get off, but couldn't because of the congestion. Another conductor appeared, shouting at people to clear the way.

Above the din I heard Droopy. "Please stop the show so people can leave train."

"Sorry folks, but we must stop now," I said to the throng in English, dramatically closing the phrase book as my hero Wells would have done. "Maybe we can continue Bad Russian Language Theater after dinner."

As soon as the book closed, the mob burst into conversation. I had no idea what they were saying. Once again I heard Droopy's voice from the hallway.

"She tells them that you own most excellent magic shoes," he said. Mother Russia slid the shoes off her feet. She passed them to the babushka next to her, who then passed them on to the next person. The leather was stroked and pressed for firmness. The soles were examined. I noticed that the dead bug was gone. The shoes circled the compartment, returning to Mother Russia. With reverence, she handed me the shoes as if she were handing me a Fabergé egg. I looked at her, dumbfounded.

She spoke; Droopy translated. "Here are your magic shoes. Wear them in good health for the rest of your life."

Slowly, the crowd thinned. The stern-looking man, now smiling, slapped me on the back like an old friend. He shook my hand, then grabbed his cane and wobbled down the corridor. Far off, from the opposite end of the carriage, I heard the song of the food vendor as she trundled her cart of steaming morsels from compartment to compartment. Outside, the last rays of sunshine gleamed off fields of golden straw that poked through the snow, cheering the sad land. A man hoisting a scythe over his shoulder trudged toward a solitary log cabin. A thin curl of smoke drifted from its chimney. Near the cabin, children played.

Mother Russia spoke. "She says she has not laughed like that since she was a little girl and the Funny Man would come around," she said, through Droopy.

"Ask her if she remembers where he came from. Was he from Grodno?"

Mother Russia listened to the translation. When she replied, she sounded weary. The events of the afternoon had exhausted her.

"It does not matter. I am old woman. My memory is no good. The man, he come from somewhere — maybe Minsk, maybe Vilnius, maybe Grodno. We all come from somewhere. The important thing is that he came back."

"What? He came back?"

Mother Russia lapsed into silence and stared out the window. Dusk had descended, with the cloak of night, quickly darkening the land. Droopy excused himself to go smoke, leaving me alone with the old woman. I pondered this last riddle — *he came back*. What did she mean? And then I knew. I glanced at Mother Russia and wanted to hug her, but she had already transformed herself back into an ageless babushka. She sat like a stone, facing the window that looked into the blackness of Russia itself. She was asleep. Something sinister grazed my ankle. Thinking return of the beetle, I jolted my legs off the floor. But it was only the cabbage rolling around like a forgotten child. I picked it up and tucked it into Mother Russia's rucksack. I stowed my most excellent magic shoes under my seat and curled up on my bunk.

2

The Thin Black Line

". . . I desire you to lay the first stone at Vladivostok for the construction of the Ussuri line, forming part of the Siberian Railway, which is to be carried out at the cost of the State and under direction of the Government. Your participation in the achievement of this work will be testimony to My ardent desire to facilitate the communications between Siberia and the other countries of the Empire and to manifest My extreme anxiety to secure the peaceful prosperity of the Country."

— Order by Czar Alexander III
to construct the Trans-Siberian Railroad

had always dreamed of riding on the Trans-Siberian Express, and perhaps that would have been possible if I had been of traveling age at the turn of the twentieth century when the line first opened. But fate had decreed that my existence begin amid the acrimony of the Cold War. I was a child of the baby boom, born right smack dab in the middle of it: 1955. Not that 1955 was a bad year to enter the world. My fellow boomers and I would witness the dawn of the space age, the birth of the personal computer, and enough social changes to keep most of us in therapy for the rest of our lives. But as far as riding the Trans-Siberian Express was concerned, the metaphorical train had eased up to the station exactly sixty-four years before the day I was born.

On that day, March 17, 1891, Russian Czar Alexander III issued an imperial decree ordering the construction of the world's most ambitious railroad project. A rail line across Siberia was needed to help secure Russia's far eastern territories against Japan and China, as well as to speed the development of the interior and provide an efficient route for settlers. Early plans called for a link to Alaska, connected to Siberia by a tunnel under the Bering Strait.[1] Although that plan fell by the wayside, most of the route across Siberia was completed ten years later. Then, the Russian government did something quite out of character with its past. It welcomed foreigners.

"Any American traveler" with appropriate credentials "and without a mission to reconstruct the government and reform all of its abuses at once" could expect a "hearty welcome" from Russian officials and civilians, reported U.S. Congressman Ebenezer Hill,[2] who took the trip in 1902. Others told of similar experiences, as the czarist government went out of its way to ensure that foreign visitors were pampered.

World War I suspended the golden era of luxury trains rolling across the Siberian steppe. Travel along the line became perilous during the chaotic years after the Russian Revolution. Grim tales of survival by fleeing refugees replaced the accounts by wide-eyed tourists.

"The wide wagons of the Trans-Siberian trains were overfilled with people — soldiers, deserters, women, children. How far a given train might travel was pure chance: derailings and destroyed bridges were common. Rumors of attacks by Reds, by Whites, by Czechs, by Mongolian brigands were constantly in the air, and the consequences of such raids were only too often evident along the way," wrote Michael Shimkin, recalling his harrowing journey across Siberia with his parents in 1918.[3] The Shimkins eventually made it to San Francisco, where Michael grew up to become one of the nation's leading cancer researchers.

When order was restored, the luxury trains were long gone, replaced by the rolling stock of the proletariat. In the ensuing years, few people made the trip unless escorted by Soviet authorities, either as a tourist or a political prisoner. By the time I began dreaming of the trip ninety-six years after the issuance of the imperial decree to construct the line, the door to travelers that had creaked open during the czarist era was still firmly shut. The Cold War was in full frost. The Trans-Siberian was still off-limits to U.S. citizens unless one signed up for an official tour where every stop was carefully choreographed to expose the hapless visitor to a constant stream of propaganda.

Independent travel was technically possible, but securing the appropriate permissions meant navigating a bureaucracy that would have made Kafka proud. You were not going to get on that train without an official government minder, let alone get into the country, unless you were an academic who spoke fluent Russian and had not somehow offended Soviet sensibilities. Even travel writer Paul Theroux, who described his midwinter ride on the Trans-Siberian Express in the final chapters of *The Great Railway Bazaar*, was escorted by a guide from Intourist, the official Soviet tourist agency. Likewise for Eric Newby, the British travel writer, whose trip in 1977 is chronicled in *The Big Red Train Ride*.

So the dream lay dormant. I had no reason to believe that independent train travel in the Soviet Union would ever get any easier in my lifetime.

But in early 1987, a tiny opportunity creaked open when two journalist friends of mine, a husband and wife team, moved to Moscow. Before I could fully comprehend what I was doing, I found myself enmeshed in a bizarre planning process that involved the Soviet Foreign Ministry, an obscure Finnish travel agency, and a hotel night manager obsessed with Russian spies.

Carol Williams had diligently studied Russian while holding down a reporting job in Seattle. Her perseverance paid off when she received a coveted posting to Moscow to report for the

Associated Press. Years earlier Ken Olsen, her husband, and I had become friends while serving reporting stints together at a daily newspaper in Walla Walla, Washington. Our friendship was cemented one bleak wintry day when we convened for a beer after work in the basement bar of the Marcus Whitman Hotel. Ken had just recently been hired, and I could tell from the look on his face that Walla Walla was a more isolated outpost than he had bargained for.

"Look," he told me, "I know I've only known you for a month, but you're the only one around. I've got to tell someone."

"What?"

"I'm getting married."

A couple of months later, Ken clunked away in a decaying used car the size of a tank to join Carol. Eventually, our paths converged again at another small Washington state daily, the *Bellevue Journal-American.* But that was only a temporary way station, as well.

Fed up with a salary that skirted the poverty level, I eventually left journalism for graduate school. Ken followed Carol to the Soviet Union after she landed the Moscow assignment. There he managed to hook up as a stringer for *Time* magazine and CBS radio. They couldn't have timed their move better, arriving in the Soviet capital shortly before Mikhail Gorbachev assumed power.

Although the Soviet Union was bogged down in a hopeless war in Afghanistan, the first warm currents were thawing the Cold War that I had known all my life. Nuclear disarmament was now within reach. After assuming power, Gorbachev initiated a series of economic reforms — *perestroika* — intended to resuscitate the country's moribund economy. An era of openness — *glasnost* — had begun. Ken's letters and our subsequent telephone conversations conveyed a sense of optimism and excitement about the historic transformation that was occurring.

This juncture in history would never come again, I reasoned, though little did I know that the Soviet Union itself would disintegrate four years later. It seemed the perfect time to drop in on my friends. Besides, I was in my last year of graduate school, and I could easily arrange to take a quarter off. That flexibility would end once I graduated and began my new career.

Shortly after Ken and Carol moved to Moscow, I broached the idea of a visit. With an invitation from a foreign resident, I could enter the Soviet Union with a visitor's visa, avoiding the clutches of Intourist. At first I thought I would just bum around with Ken in Moscow and Leningrad, but as I prepared for the trip, I began to fantasize about a more ambitious journey. Why not ride the Trans-Siberian Express? I had always loved trains and rode on them whenever I could, which wasn't often enough. I also knew that the Trans-Siberian was the ultimate train trip, stretching 5,760 miles across the Siberian wilderness.

One night not long after first mentioning the idea, I pulled my *National Geographic Atlas* from the bookcase and flipped to the Soviet Union. The country was immense. It hogged two full pages, spilling over onto a third. A score of Europe-sized countries could fit inside its borders. While staring at the pink-hued expanse of territory, I noticed a network of thin black lines, representing railroads, which emerged like the spokes of a wheel from Moscow. Most of the lines ended in European Russia or diverged to Soviet republics in the north and south. A few lines crossed the Ural Mountains. A solitary line snaked into central Siberia, skirted the southern shore of Lake Baikal, then dipped south and grazed the Chinese border near Manchuria before ending at the Pacific port city of Vladivostok. This was the Trans-Siberian Line. I could not take my eyes off that thin back line, as if closing the book would forever eliminate my chance of riding the famous train. Almost a hundred years earlier, Alexander III had no doubt pondered the same black line, which would forever link the vast, but ungainly, empire.

When I spoke to Ken again, I mentioned the idea of riding the Trans-Siberian, expecting him to tell me that such a trip was impossible.

"Sure, we can arrange that. Just send me your itinerary," he told me, his voice echoing over the phone. "I have a friend in the Foreign Ministry who can help set it up."

When I put down the receiver, I could have done cartwheels. Instead, I jumped up and down and pumped my fists in the air. The grand journey was possible.

That night I pored over guidebooks and mapped out an itinerary starting in Moscow and heading east, with stops at the only three Siberian cities open to foreigners: Novosibirsk in the west, Irkutsk in the middle, and Khabarovsk in the east. I quickly formulated plans to stay two nights in each, continuing the trip aboard successive eastbound trains until I reached the end. Vladivostok, the official end of the line, was off-limits to foreigners because of its military importance as home port of the Soviet Pacific Fleet. That meant I had to leave the train in Khabarovsk, the capital of a vast area that stretched from the Chinese border to the Arctic Circle, and either return to Moscow or fly to Japan. I opted for Japan. The paperwork was formidable. I needed a special visa that authorized travel without an Intourist minder, vouchers for the train and hotels, and plane tickets to get me in and out of the Soviet Union. The Soviets insisted on payment in advance, but they gave no guarantee that the paperwork would be processed on time. Or ever.

3

Quest for the Visa

o, let me get this right. You want to ride a train across Siberia in October and November. What's there to see or do? You know most people would go to a warm place and sun themselves on a beach."

My girlfriend, Ann, was not impressed by the grand journey. We sat on a patch of lawn surrounded by colorful, late-blooming dahlias in the front yard of the house she shared with three other women in Seattle. Ann loved dahlias and never missed an opportunity to tell me so. But I couldn't begin to explain the special love I had for train travel and why a trip on the Trans-Siberian was the ultimate experience for one so inclined.

"Well, yeah," I said lamely.

"Didn't you once say that your father's parents were from Russia?"

"Yes, but I don't know much about the family. There's this one family photo of everyone just after they reassembled in New York City in the early 1900s."

"You should go there to see if anyone remembers your family," she said.

Ann was always telling me what I should do. It drove me nuts even though her comment struck a sensitive chord. I had always been interested in my family's roots. But I knew little about them except that my great-grandparents and their children had lived on a farm near the city of Grodno, tucked inside Byelorussia (now Belarus) near the Polish border. In czarist times, it was part of the Russian Empire. In the intervening years, that region bore witness to two world wars, famine, and the holocaust, not to mention the insanity of the Stalin years. The village probably had been obliterated, and its occupants, if any had survived, scattered. Even if I did want to visit there, the logistics of getting to the Soviet Union and across Siberia would be difficult enough; attempting to add an ill-defined side trip to Belarus was out of the question.

"I just don't think it's possible," I said.

Ann was clearly disappointed with my response. She looked at me like a parent whose child had just failed an important test.

"Well, you should really give it some thought," she huffed.

As departure day moved closer, I discovered that Gorbachev's new openness had not yet filtered down to the bureaucrats responsible for issuing visas or train tickets.

Before I could reserve a place on the train, I needed an index number. Before I could get an index number, I needed a visa. Before I could get a visa, I needed an official letter of invitation from Ken and Carol. And under no circumstances would the Soviet Consulate issue a visa more than two days prior to my departure from the U.S. Thus, all the other paperwork could potentially be delayed until the last minute. I knew I would need help. Following up on a recommendation from a friend, I called Jacque Williams, a local travel agent who specialized in trips to the Soviet Union.

Jacque worked feverishly to secure my visa and train tickets. But with each try, she was rebuffed by the Soviets who seemed to invent new obstacles each time we surmounted a bureaucratic hurdle. One afternoon, a few days before I was to leave for London on the first leg of the trip, I received a frantic call.

"The Russian Consul General is on my other line," said Jacque, breathlessly. "He said he tried to call you at home, but only got your answering machine. Look, I'm going to hang up, and he'll call you back on the same line. Don't go anywhere. My God, this is the first time they've ever called. You must have important friends over there!"

A few seconds later the phone rang again.

"Mr. Goldstein?" A heavily accented voice right out of central casting for the Russian bad guy in a James Bond movie was on the other line. "We have no confirmation from Moscow. I cannot issue visa unless I have confirmation. If I have confirmation, I issue visa in thirty minutes." I imagined him sitting at a desk perfectly clean except for my two-page visa application lying neatly in front of him. I thought he might add, "If I issue visa without confirmation, I will be shot."

I described my previous phone calls to Ken, and a message he had received from the Soviet Foreign Ministry officially approving my trip.

"I'm very sorry," he said, sounding as if he meant it.

I promised to call my friend in Moscow to find out what had happened. I thought I heard the Russian equivalent of "oh shit" on the other end of the line. Then again, maybe it was just "good luck."

The next day, Jacque and I conferred for the last time before I left for London.

"We're out of time. We've got to send your application to Finland. That's the only sure way we can get you on the Trans-Siberian Express."

"Finland," I gulped, trying to form a mental picture of the place, but conjuring up only images of Santa's reindeer. "Are you sure that will work?"

"Yes, we sometimes use a Helsinki travel agency to help with unusual trips. If anyone can get you aboard the Trans-Siberian, it's the Finns," she said confidently. "When you get to London, call Hanna in Helsinki."

I wasn't confident when I boarded London-bound Pan Am flight 122 on a cold gray October day. I didn't have a visa. I didn't have a train ticket. Everyone told me not to worry. I was very worried. I wondered why I had even thought such a journey was possible. Perhaps Ann was right. A beach vacation would have been much more convenient.

4

Waiting in London

In London the rain was relentless. The evening news showed cows swept away by floods or standing forlornly on hillocks surrounded by swirling waters. I holed up in a small hotel, an eighteenth-century row house on Gower Street not far from the British Museum and befriended the night manager, who was intrigued by the possibilities of my trip and its complicated logistics. Harris — I knew him only by his last name — was fascinated by the Soviet Union, an interest fueled by his appetite for cold war spy novels, whose plots delved into the murky world of British and Soviet spies. In particular, he was keen on plots that featured beautiful Russian seductresses. He prattled on about various methods one could succumb to temptation.

Harris, himself, appeared an unlikely target for seduction of any type. He was a small, plump man who bore a striking resemblance to Mr. Potato Head, only larger, with two thin patches of hair clinging to the sides of his otherwise bald head. Even though he was the night manager, he always seemed to linger nearby even during the day. I wondered when he slept.

Throughout my stay, Harris listened sympathetically to my story, adding "oh dear" and "oh my" when appropriate. He patiently explained how the metering system on British pay phones worked, and stocked me with enough pound coins to keep British Telecom operators at bay while I spoke to Jacque in Seattle or Ken in Moscow. I was getting nervous because my departure loomed a few days away, but no progress had been made in prying loose the vital travel documents since my arrival in London.

"It's a damn good plan, if I might say so, sir," Harris told me one night as I climbed the stairs to my room. There were no new developments on my visa problems. "The problem has been with the execution."

Yes, I thought, the execution is killing me. In three days, I was supposed to fly to Moscow, but without the visa I would not be allowed to board the plane. The grand journey had degenerated into a soggy week of high anxiety in the British capital. I yanked open the heavy door to my room, kicked it shut, and undressed for bed. I hoped I would wake up in my apartment back home, relegating my recent experience to nothing more than a long, frustrating dream.

Later that night, the violent pounding of fists upon solid English oak woke me. I burrowed deeper under the quilt.

"Mr. Goldstein. Harris here."

I swam to the surface of consciousness.

"Sorry to wake you, sir. An urgent phone call."

I staggered down the stairs and grabbed the phone.

"They got it!" exclaimed a jubilant Jacque.

"Got what? Who got what?"

"They issued your visa!"

I turned to Harris and gave him the thumbs up.

"Bully for you, sir!"

"Are you sure?" I asked Jacque.

"Yes, the consul general himself called to confirm it. He seemed relieved to send it on its way. Can you believe they've called me twice now? There's one slight problem, though. Please don't panic. The consul said the visa was sent to your apartment in Seattle."

"Seattle! But I'm in London!"

"Indeed you are, sir," chimed in Harris, listening nearby.

"I'm leaving for Moscow in two days. How can they be so stupid? They are a stupid country with stupid rules. How can they possibly be a world power? Answer that!"

"Please calm down," said Jacque. "We have a plan."

Jacque had already arranged to get the visa from my apartment with the help of a friend of mine who had a spare key. A courier had delivered the document to SeaTac Airport. It was now aboard a Pan Am flight bound for London, scheduled to arrive the next afternoon.

"The visa is on its way," I said to Harris, as I hung up. "But there's a problem."

Harris looked concerned.

"Don't worry, they have a plan," I said, wearily explaining a few of the details as I trudged back up the stairs.

"I think it is a damn good plan, if I may say so, sir."

Harris was waiting for me when I returned from Heathrow with my coveted visa.

He handed me a package.

"She called, that woman Hanna from Helsinki, and said a package would arrive for you. I've been on the lookout for it."

The return address was from Helsinki, Finland. I ripped it open. Inside were three pink train voucher booklets, each stamped in Cyrillic and English: *USSR Company for Foreign Travel to the Soviet Union.* One voucher was issued for each leg of the journey, starting with the Moscow to Novosibirsk link.

"I'm really going!" I exclaimed to Harris.

"Indeed you are, sir," replied Harris. He paused, then added in a serious tone: "Be careful, sir. Those Reds are tricky. I wouldn't trust them, if I were you. Watch your back and beware of beautiful women. They could be spies, you know."

5

Not Now, MosKitty!

The doorbell echoed through the Moscow apartment like the tolling of a church bell. I knew it was Ilka, who had generously agreed to give me a ride to the train station. I started for the door, but was ambushed by MosKitty, the resident cat. The cat had the annoying habit of pouncing from a hiding place and hugging the pant cuffs of unsuspecting passersby.

"Not now, MosKitty!" I yelled. The cat was attached to my pants at ankle height. I felt his claws dig into my skin. I shook my leg, but the cat wouldn't budge. I continued down the hall, dragging the feline with me. As I opened the door, MosKitty shimmied higher and wrapped himself around my calf.

"Ilka, thanks again for taking me to the train station," I said, pretending a cat wasn't wrapped around my leg.

"It is not a problem. Moscow can be a very difficult place to get around, particularly for foreigners," he said in perfect English.

Ilka was a correspondent for the *Finnish Press Agency.* He lived with his wife and children downstairs. Ken had told me that if I needed assistance, I could count on Ilka. It seemed odd that another Finn was about to rescue me again. I had fretted all morning about how to get my two backpacks and myself to the correct train station. Moscow had nine. Furthermore, for the past two weeks I had lived under the protective wing of my hosts, who both spoke reasonably good Russian. Their apartment was a welcome sanctuary from my daily forays exploring Moscow. But they had left the previous day for Paris on a much-needed vacation.

I was now on my own. What if I was stopped by a militiaman or, worse yet, the secret police? It was possible.

My dark complexion, the product of a Russian-Jewish-Mexican heritage, has always aroused interest. Once during dinner with friends in a Seattle restaurant, a woman approached from a nearby table and proclaimed that I was the most exotic-looking person she had ever seen. Clearly, she had had too much to drink that night, but I had grown used to these sorts of incidents. During a visit to Israel, I was interrogated by the police, who thought I resembled an Arab terrorist. When traveling in the West Bank, the Palestinians thought I was an Israeli. At various other times and places, I had been mistaken for a Greek, Turk, Palestinian, Iranian, Nepalese, Armenian, and an Indian, the kind from India. Only at the forlorn outpost of Milton-Freewater, Oregon, a tiny town near Walla Walla, did someone actually get it right. After I introduced myself to the secretary to the superintendent of the local school district, she looked up and said "Yes, Mr. Goldstein, you looked exactly as I thought you would." I was gratified by her response.

All this was floating through my mind as I speculated what I might do if I was stopped in the street. I spoke only the few phrases of Russian that I had quickly learned from a little phrase book Ken had lent me. What would I say? No one would believe that I had permission to ride the Trans-Siberian as an independent traveler, even though I had all the right papers. I had visions of being snatched off the street by plainclothes KGB thugs and dragged to the Lubyanka, Moscow's infamous prison, for interrogation. "You must be a spy! Your story about procuring your visa and train vouchers is ridiculous." Too much could go wrong.

Earlier that morning, I had called Ilka and asked if he could be so kind as to give me a lift to the train station. Without hesitation, he agreed.

"Excuse me Bob, but a cat is hanging from your pants," said Ilka, a note of concern in his voice.

"I am aware of that," I said calmly. I invited Ilka inside as I went to collect my packs.

MosKitty would not dislodge himself; the more I shook my leg, the firmer the grip and the louder the playful snarls. I lugged the cat with me as I shoved my bags out the front door.

"MosKitty, not now. I'm leaving. I'm going to Siberia. It's really cold there. You wouldn't like it."

MosKitty wouldn't let go.

"Can we take the cat with us? I can try to pry him off in the car."

Ilka smiled at the suggestion. He knelt, stroked MosKitty behind the ear, and whispered something in Finnish. MosKitty relented.

"Let's go," he said. I grabbed my bags and slammed the door behind us.

A half-hour later I stood in the cavernous Yaroslavsky Station among hundreds of Soviet travelers. Men in imitation leather jackets, heads covered with the ubiquitous fur hats, stood in clusters talking quietly while puffing away at cigarettes. Women in thick woolen sweaters pulled over print dresses sat in small groups or shushed children. They all seemed to clutch worn suitcases, string bags, and parcels wrapped in old newspapers. Some people appeared as if they had been at the station for days, dozing on the cement floor. Despite the crowd, the atmosphere seemed strangely subdued. It was the same hushed tone that I noticed when riding the Moscow subway, even during rush hour when the trains and stations were packed with commuters. Pale men and women rode in silence. Those who dared to converse did so quietly, as if the very words were precious and couldn't be trusted in the ears of strangers. A universal repression seemed to grip the Muscovite masses as they rode their clean and efficient subway. No one smiled. I heard no laughter. At Yaroslavsky Station, this tomb-like quality was broken only by the occasional blare of the loudspeaker announcing the arrival or departure of a train.

Ken and Carol had insisted I pack provisions, as there was no guarantee that the dining car would have enough food. Among my stores were a tinned ham, breadsticks, raisins, mineral water, one can of beer, and a sack of animal crackers. Other valuable articles were the phrase book, a journal, Fodor's tour book, a camera, warm clothes, and a copy of *The Big Red Train Ride*. The night before, I had read with some amusement that author Eric Newby and his party had carted along eighteen pieces of luggage and boxes filled with food and drink. I had only a large backpack and smaller daypack.

I searched for train number eight, which I assumed would be on track eight. But no train was on track eight. As I stared at the empty track, a wave of anxiety welled up from my gut. My hard-won tickets clearly said the train departed at 2:40 p.m., while my Fodor's tour book helpfully tells readers not to miss the departure of the Trans-Siberian Express ("an event rail buffs should see") at 2 p.m. I also knew, from *The Big Red Train Ride*, that the train was red, a unique color among the dull pea green of every Soviet passenger train I had seen so far. There were no red trains at Yaroslavsky Station on that brisk fall afternoon. It was now slightly past 2 p.m. I was worried.

As I mulled over the situation, an old man carrying a plastic sack stopped to ask me a question. I replied in the only Russian that I knew. I told him I did not speak Russian. This did not seem to faze my interrogator, who babbled on. He seemed to want to know where I was from, and asked if I was from usa — slurring the initials of the U.S.A. into a single word. Before I could speak, he asked if I was from *Espaniya* (Spain in Russian). No, I shook my head, but then thinking we might be able to communicate, I explained in my own broken Spanish that I was a tourist from the U.S. My interrogator now seemed satisfied that I was from Mexico.

"Mexico good, U.S.A. bad," he told me, with a smile.

"No, no," I replied, "not Mexico, U.S.," I said.

"Mexico is good," he replied.

Fearing I might miss my train — wherever it was — while debating my place of origin, I agreed that Mexico was a grand place. Then I got down to business. I asked in fractured Spanish where I could find Rossiya, using the Russian nickname for the famous train. He pointed to the platform and then to track number three, gesturing to the departure board. I looked over at track three, where a green train was preparing to leave. The Cyrillic told me that this train was the "Sibirsk." It was bound for Novosibirsk, my first overnight stop. That had to be it. I thanked the old man, then scurried to the track three platform.

As I clambered on board, I showed the ticket to the conductor, who barely glanced at it. Perhaps the Big Red Train had been repainted. Or, was I on the wrong train? Surely, the conductor would have said something.

The Colonel

He was an officer in the Soviet army, a short compact man of middle age, perhaps a colonel or even a general. Two-and-a-half rows of military ribbons with a medal dangling below adorned the front pocket of his olive green uniform coat. Three red stars decorated the shoulder boards. He seemed startled to see me on this train bound for Siberia. My friends had warned me that I would probably endure most of the Trans-Siberian trip alone or in the presence of a KGB informer. They also told me that speaking to soldiers was a good way to get in trouble. Yet, here I was, barely two minutes into the trip, confronting at least a colonel. Why was he here? Wasn't there a war in Afghanistan that needed attending to?

"Dobry den," I blurted, using the phrase I had memorized for "good day." Awkwardly, I continued in my phrase-book Russian. "I am Bob. I am a tourist. I am American. I do not speak Russian."

The colonel stood stiffly at attention and introduced himself, but I did not catch his name in the rush of Russian words. We shook hands, then he sat down. I followed suit and for a few seconds we eyed each other, neither of us sure what to do. I stalled, giving my brain more time to process this unexpected situation, while surveying my new home for the first leg of my trip. The first-class compartment itself seemed comfortable enough, out-fitted with two long, padded benches facing each other. Between the benches was a small table, draped with a pristine lace table-cloth and two tea cups, each with a pyramid of sugar cubes stacked neatly alongside. In contrast to the chill of the Moscow October outside, the compartment felt like a tropical paradise.

I searched for a place to store my bulky backpack, but could find nothing resembling a closet. The colonel, observing my befuddle-ment, showed me that the padded bench served as a seat during the day and a bed at night. It was hinged, revealing ample storage space underneath. After stowing my gear, I rummaged through my day-pack and coat pocket for the phrase book. Once found, I frantically flipped the pages, looking for something useful to say. But there was no section titled "Small talk with the Red Army." Instead, I found phrases of little use for my situation. What good was "For poultry, there is turkey, goose, and duck" or "I must take the tooth out"? If I needed a dentist, though, I now knew what to say.

I showed the colonel the book, smiled and shrugged. We sat in silence, stealing glances at each other. At precisely 2:40 p.m., the exact minute of its scheduled departure, the train began its long journey.

For a moment I forgot about the officer sitting across from me and, for that matter, that I was in a country that President Reagan once referred to as the "Evil Empire." The magic moment had arrived when the train slowly pulled away from the platform, sep-arating the travelers from those who must stay behind. A smatter-ing of people standing on the platform strained to see husbands, wives, and other loved ones through mud-streaked windows. The good-bye waves slowly receded. I pinched myself. I was really aboard the fabled Trans-Siberian Express, following the thin black line that I had traced in the *National Geographic Atlas*. Overshadowing my self-congratulations for getting myself into the Soviet Union and aboard the famous train was the lingering worry that I really wasn't aboard the Trans-Siberian Express. But I was heading for Siberia; for the moment that's all I cared about.

I was not the first train traveler awed by the prospect of crossing the immensity of Siberia. Soon after the opening of the Great Siberian Railway (as it was known when it opened for business in 1900), the first reports from travelers began to filter back to Europe and the United States. Indeed, confusion about which train was which appears to have been a tradition established early in the annals of Trans-Siberian travel. Burton Holmes, one of the first Americans to travel and write about his trip, rushed to the Moscow station in June 1901 only to discover he had missed the "Train de Luxe" — the luxury train. He wound up on the Train d'Etat — the government train — and though he was a bit disgusted with the lack of cleanliness of the dining car and bathroom, one gets the impression from his writing that he was thrilled to be on his way.[1]

In January 1902, Harry De Windt boarded the Trans-Siberian in a blizzard on the second leg of a Paris to New York overland journey. Annoyed that his rifles and pistols had been confiscated at the border by Russian authorities, De Windt's spirits lifted once the Train de Luxe rolled out of Moscow. "This train was truly an ambulant palace of luxury," he wrote in his book *Paris to New York by Land.* "An excellent restaurant, a library, pianos, baths, and, last but not least, a spacious and well-furnished compartment with every comfort, electric and otherwise."[2] De Windt would eventually disembark in Irkutsk, sled across the rest of Siberia, then cross the Bering Strait en route to New York.

Six months later, Congressman Hill completed the journey from Vladivostok to Moscow in thirty-eight days. The ticket cost him, or rather American taxpayers, $157.80.[3] That was a tidy sum in those days, but amazingly my first class tickets had cost only $387. Given the ravages of inflation, I seemed to have stumbled upon the travel bargain of the century. Sure, the piano bar and upholstered furniture were long gone, but I was moving in the right direction and would not have to worry about raids by marauding bandits, frequent derailments, and other calamities that plagued early train travelers.

In 1901 the official schedule claimed the trip could be completed in seventeen and a half days, though the actual time varied considerably depending on derailments and the unpredictable crossing of Lake Baikal aboard a ferry. Another multiday boat ride on the Amur River was required in the Russian Far East, where a rail line had yet to be surveyed. It wasn't until 1905 that the entire continent could be traversed in an unbroken train ride. By the time I had arrived, the journey was down to seven days, but with my planned stops it would take me two weeks to make the crossing.

The train passed drab factories, with smoke belching from tall stacks. Then came row after row of rectangular concrete-block apartments. A depressing sameness characterized the suburban scenery. The landscape lacked color, as if all brightness had been sucked away by a giant vacuum, leaving only shades of grim cement gray.

Railway workers huddled by the tracks, doing nothing in particular. Near a small park, a cluster of red-kerchiefed Young Pioneers — the communist equivalent of the Boy and Girl Scouts — broke ranks and waved as the passengers' carriages slid by.

Ahead of me lay seven time zones' worth of electrified line slicing through some of the most desolate regions of the Soviet Empire.

After the conductor collected our tickets, the colonel stretched out on his bunk and drifted into a fitful sleep, punctuated by an occasional snore. I gazed out the window, watching the apartment blocks thin out as the train gained speed. The last vestiges of the city slipped away, replaced by dozens of brightly painted dachas — the summer homes of Muscovites. Many of these dwellings were no more than sheds surrounded by small garden plots, while a few others were larger and could pass as full-fledged cabins. Though these dwellings were meager by American standards, they were a vast improvement from those seen at the turn of the century. Holmes, who described the trip in his voluminous travelogues, noted the "hopeless aspect of the Russian villages, which look like groups of haystacks or mounds of refuse . . . in these congeries of hovels we touch the very depths of Russian misery."[4] Clearly, there had been improvements in the intervening years.

An hour later, I saw in the distance Zagorsk's Cathedral of the Assumption, its cupolas glinting gold in the late afternoon sun. Not far from the cathedral is the tomb of Boris Godunov, whose rise and fall as czar in the late sixteenth century captures the essence of Russia's turbulent history.

We had traveled only about forty miles. This seemed odd, as I had expected the Trans-Siberian to gain speed once clear of Moscow. But the train continued to grind on at about a forty mile-per-hour clip, another improvement since the turn-of-the-century when speeds averaged between ten and eighteen miles per hour. Nevertheless, it wasn't an impressive pace. It soon became apparent why this alleged express train could not travel faster without lurching off the tracks — because of the unevenness of the track bed, the train was in continual motion, much like a small boat in choppy seas. The swaying and jerking presented some problems when walking between cars. I wondered how well I would sleep as the movement was accompanied by a continuous cacophony of grinding, squealing, and clashing of steel wheels against the rails.

The colonel stirred from his slumber, perhaps awakened by the incessant racket.

"You have girls?" the colonel asked in English, leading me to believe he knew a little more English than I had initially thought. The question seemed natural coming from a soldier. Assuming he referred to a wife or girlfriend, I nodded. He smiled, and held up two fingers.

"I have two boys," he said. He searched for the right words. After a few moments, and with the help of my prompts, I learned that his oldest son attended a military academy in Yaroslavl. The youngest was in school somewhere else.

He looked at me expectantly.

"Oh, I though you meant something else," I replied, not expecting him to understand. "No, I have just one."

In my enthusiasm to communicate, I had unwittingly invented a family for myself. Since our mutual vocabularies were so limited, I decided not to confuse the issue by correcting myself. So I continued with the fiction, inventing my only child as I went. I made a cradling motion, indicating that my daughter was still very young. The colonel looked at me with approval.

A knock at our cabin door interrupted us. Before we could respond, the compartment door slid back and in waddled a rotund babushka, hoisting a huge metal teapot. The tea vendor chatted away as she filled our cups without spilling a drop amid the pitch and roll of the train. Behind her was another portly woman, who was singing and pushing a cart filled with neatly wrapped parcels resembling bulky airline meals. Remembering Ken's warning about food shortages, I nodded yes to whatever it was she sold. The colonel also nodded and motioned to the singing woman. She reached for two of the foil-wrapped boxes, one for each of us. From his billfold, the colonel handed the woman a two-ruble note. It seemed like a reasonable price — about three dollars at the inflated official exchange rate, only sixteen cents at the black market rate. I mimicked the colonel's actions, receiving a pile of kopecks in return. As the woman's song faded down the corridor, I rolled back the foil, revealing four steaming and substantial cutlets and a healthy portion of bulgur. As I waited for the food to cool, the colonel ate as if it were his last meal. He finished before I had begun.

Outside, in the fading light, a dusting of snow covered the ground. The train passed a small village consisting of a dirt road and a few log cabins. Far down the road, bundled in a shawl, walked a solitary figure. Then the village was gone, replaced by vast fields. In the distance, the thin white trunks of leafless birch trees were barely discernible in the fading light. The cupola of a small cathedral was outlined against a blood red sky. Then night descended, and I saw nothing but blackness.

The colonel and I resumed our conversation. The meal seemed to have put him at ease; he was now full of questions. He asked my age and the age of my fictitious daughter. I pulled out the phrase book and for once found an appropriate response. Then I leafed through the book, reading aloud various questions, such as "Do you play football?" "Do you ski?" "Have you heard the weather report?" Even with the phonetic spellings in the phrase book, my pronunciation must have been horrible. The colonel moved to my bunk bench to read the Cyrillic equivalent. Soon, like old school chums, we were thumbing through the book and pointing to weird phrases, laughing and tugging at each other's arms at the absurd translations.

It all seemed so effortless and natural. If it was this easy to make friends and to engage in conversation, I couldn't wait to meet my future compartment mates. The warnings from my friends seemed unnecessary. There was food. It was cheap, too. There was camaraderie. Everything was perfectly fine. What was the fuss all about?

Yaroslavl, the colonel's stop, arrived too quickly. He gathered his bag, and put on his hat and coat with the red stars on the shoulder boards.

I struggled to think of something appropriate to say. I didn't want him to leave. There were other things I wanted to know. I thought of his son at the military academy and the war in Afghanistan. I wanted to know how he felt about the possibility of his son going to war. But I would never know because I didn't know the Russian words. Glasnost was not sufficient to convey a more meaningful conversation. I could only say *do svidaniya* — goodbye — in Russian.

7

Epicurean Paradise

hortly after Rossiya rolled out of Yaroslavl and crossed the Volga, a dour-looking man poked his head around the compartment's door, sniffed the air as if checking for predators, then entered. He carried a worn valise, his only baggage. I assumed he would be on the train for no more than one night. Settling on the edge of the seat by the window, he took no notice of the small man sitting across from him in the dim light. I cleared my throat. Startled, he looked up with a frightened expression.

Buoyed by my communications success with the colonel, I eagerly explained myself in phrase-book Russian, hoping that he could tell me whether I was on the right train. What had been an infrequent, but irritating thought for the first few hours of the trip was becoming a nagging worry. My new companion squinted at me as if a prolonged glance might hurt his eyes. He mumbled something in Russian, then fell silent. I would get no help from him, at least not tonight.

I wrote in my journal, glancing now and then at the other man sitting quietly on his bunk, hands folded on his lap. He stared out the window at the night, occasionally peeking over at me. He seemed threatened, caught off-balance, by my presence. I was certainly not your everyday communist party *apparatchik*. To him, I could have been a dangerous dagger-in-the-belt fanatic from one of the Soviet Union's Moslem republics. To me, in the dim reading light, he seemed like a large rabbit frozen in his tracks by some unknown fear.

The rabbit man and I silently made our beds with the clean sheet and thin blanket left by each bunk. Rabbit man slipped off his shoes and jacket, then burrowed under the sheet without a word. Within minutes, he was snorting horrible little gasps. This discordant symphony was accompanied by a loud banging like some deranged percussionist bashing the underside of the train carriage with a steel baseball bat. To add to my discomfort, the compartment was warming at an alarming rate. I buried my head under the pillow, but the heat and noise were intolerable. I rolled out of the bunk and rummaged through my pack until I found my flashlight. I crawled under the bunk looking for some sort of heat control. A series of hot water pipes ran the length of our compartment, but nothing resembled a modern thermostat. Returning to the bunk, I stripped to my shorts and T-shirt, and wondered how long I could survive without sleep. For a few fitful hours, I dozed. I dreamt I shared a long train journey with an Asian man who never spoke.

In the morning, I picked at my meager provisions; tea and breadsticks wasn't exactly the hearty meal I wanted. But this was the Soviet Union. The feast of the previous night was probably an aberration. I remembered the empty shelves in Moscow stores and the long lines of somber Muscovites waiting for meat and other staples. Even though I vowed to conserve my small stock of food, I offered a precious breadstick to the rabbit man, hoping the gesture would ease the tension between us.

But there was another reason for the offer, one that lingers in the back of every solo traveler's mind. You never knew who the mystery person sitting across from you might be. On the same stretch of track prior to the onset of the Stalinist purges, a young American construction engineer returning from Moscow aboard the Trans-

Siberian offered sardines and other canned food to a plainly dressed Russian woman sitting across from him. A conversion ensued. At some point in the journey the American, perhaps overcome by his engineering urge, snapped a photo of a bridge. The omnipresent secret police appeared from nowhere and seized the camera. The woman promised that she would speak to the police. Much to the engineer's surprise, the camera was returned (minus the film). The mystery woman, as reported in the *The New York Times*,[1] was Yekaterina Ivanovan Kalinina, wife of Soviet President Mikhail Ivanovich Kalinin, one of the few of Stalin's protégés to die a natural death. Unfortunately, Yekaterina's fate was far worse. Years later she was arrested by the secret police, who perhaps remembered her usurpation of their authority aboard the train. She spent her last days in a Siberian forced labor camp.

Rabbit man politely turned down my offer, then reached into his valise as if it were a magic hat and pulled forth a hard-boiled egg, followed by a chunk of greasy sausage and a pastry. It was the same fare he had dined upon last night. With a dramatic snap, he closed the case and smiled at me. Munching on our pathetic breakfasts, we each uttered one word. We established that I was bound for Novosibirsk and he for Perm. End of conversation.

The food routine was depressing, particularly for someone who enjoys eating. I feared my meager diet would leave me lethargic, dulling my senses and diminishing the grand adventure. I needed to do something, to take control. But how? I looked through my pack and found a worn Intourist brochure describing the Trans-Siberian Express. I flipped to the section on cuisine and read:

> "And, of course, you would like to know about how meals are arranged en route. The Rossiya Express has two restaurant cars, which serve smorgasbord as well as inexpensive and varied tables d'hôte."

The solution was right before my eyes! Had lack of sleep dulled my wits to the point where I could no longer comprehend the obvious? The Epicurean paradise lie within my grasp only a few pea green rail cars away. I had been merely distracted the previous night by the colonel and his preference for the portable meal served by singing babushkas. Reinforcing my revelation, not to mention my growing appetite, was a poster on the corridor wall that depicted an elegant dinner scene. I grabbed my breadstick and bolted out the door for a closer look. Though written in Cyrillic, the poster seemed to expound on the wonderful cuisine and cosmopolitan atmosphere that awaited the train's passengers. I stared at the regal couple pictured: a slender dark-haired beauty in an elegant white gown, and a tall handsome man in a dark dinner jacket. They sat at a table set with starched white linen and table napkins folded in tight little hats. A white-jacketed waiter hovered nearby with a bottle of champagne. The handsome man held his flute of bubbly, as if to make a toast. His companion gazed longingly into his eyes.

My mission was to meet these people, unfurl those little napkins, and dine like the last czar.

Slurping down my lukewarm tea, I set off to find the Epicurean paradise, leaving rabbit man nibbling contentedly. Visions of freshly baked loaves of bread, and eggs and potatoes heaped on a plate alongside a steaming cup of thick black coffee streamed through my head. Morning was slipping away, and I desperately wanted to make the breakfast sitting. As the intensity of the imaginary scent grew, I quickened my pace. In full jog, I passed through the relative solitude of the first-class carriages and entered into the train's version of a New York tenement — second class. Men dressed in identical blue jogging suits lounged in clusters at the ends of the carriage, smoking, while others crammed into the four-berth compartments, eating or playing chess. Half-naked children scampered about. Mothers nursed babies in mid-corridor. Most everyone, I noticed, seemed well supplied with food that had been carefully packed beforehand.

I squeezed past the children and sleepy unshaven men, stumbling toward the bathroom. Like drunkards, we staggered from side to side, groping past each other through the wildly swaying corridors. During one violent lurch, I bounced off a wall, nearly ricocheting into a compartment of still-slumbering comrades.

Two carriages later, I shoved open the doors to the dining car. Instead of the pristine elegance promised by the poster, I beheld a scene from the galley of a restaurant about to be raided by the county health department. The table linen was stained a murky brown, no doubt caused from the borscht sloshing over the sides of metal bowls as the train rolled over a particularly bad stretch of track. Only two tables were occupied. One held four morose Russians, grimly eating black bread and cheese. At another sat a solitary man with Asian features (perhaps the fellow from my dream). A babushka waddled down the aisle, hoisting a tray that carried one undersized loaf of coarse black bread. I peered into a side compartment. A troll-like man, wearing a sleeveless under-shirt speckled with a collage of food stains, sliced potatoes that plopped into an enormous kettle. Food scraps littered the floor. A cigarette dangled from his lip. He chatted with two other men, who were also squished into the small space. An encounter with Shakespeare's three witches brooding over their cauldron prophe-sizing the doom of Macbeth would have provided me with a greater measure of comfort than the scene in that kitchen alcove.

"Is there another dining car?" I asked, hopefully. Perhaps this was the snack car, a shadow of the dining grandeur that hid just a few carriages beyond.

The trio looked at me blankly. After a moment the troll seemed to understand my question.

"Here," he grunted.

I thanked them, and slithered past the tables, still hoping this was the second-class diner, and that the real Epicurean paradise was still somewhere ahead. Nearly eighty-six years earlier, Burton Holmes was also unimpressed with the dining room decor, albeit using a different standard than what I expected. "The dining car is a stuffy little affair with a piano at one and a bookcase at the other — but neither music nor literature appeared to appeal to the pas-

sengers, for the ivories remained untouched and the books undis-
turbed," reported Holmes. The food, on the other hand, he
observed, wasn't bad: "Hearty soups . . . sometimes frappes, with a
clinking cake of ice floating on their chilled depths, sometimes
seething hot, with a hunk of steaming beef rising from them like
a volcanic island."[2]

Hope faded as I passed through car after car, then died when I
reached the end of the last carriage. I found neither the clinking
of a cake of ice, nor a beef volcano, but only a tiny open-aired
vestibule, jammed with grim Russian men smoking cigarettes. As
they silently squeezed together to make room for me, I thought it
best not to make inquiries about the obvious. Someone offered me
a cigarette from a carton depicting a husky. I don't smoke, but I
took a few puffs of the dog cigarette anyway and watched the
steppe slide away. When I finished, I thanked my cigarette friend
and carefully made my way back to my compartment, hopping
between the couplings which appeared ready to break apart at
any moment.

After reaching my compartment, I grabbed another breadstick
from my pack and gobbled it down. I eyed the rabbit man's valise,
wondering if it held another sausage and pastry. His fare now
looked appealing. But as I plotted ways to ask him for food, he rose
and gathered his belongings. The train had arrived in Perm. The
rabbit man was not replaced. I took advantage of my privacy and
slipped into my blue sweatpants. At least I would be dressed like
everyone else.

By early afternoon, the train stopped briefly at Kungur, a town
of 60,000 that enjoyed its heyday in the seventeenth century when
it was the tea-trading crossroads of Asia and the budding Russian
Empire. Outside, women wearing thick padded jackets over peas-
ant skirts shoveled sand from a flat car onto the track bed. After
leaving Kungur, the Sibirsk then followed an ice-choked river.
Spindly conifers grew on the far bank. Veering from the river into
a forest of conifers and birch, the train began a gradual ascent. We
were climbing the Ural Mountains, the dividing line between

Europe and Asia. But the Urals are not the grand peaks of the Pacific Northwest or even the gentle hills of the Midwest. In fact, I would not have known we were in the range at all if I had not consulted my guidebook. The book made a big deal about an obelisk marking the division between the continents that was visible from the train. But darkness descended, and I was not sure whether I saw an obelisk or a big white rock.

I drank my lone beer to celebrate crossing into Asia. The prospect of procuring another one seemed bleak, given the latest Soviet crackdown on alcohol. It was illegal to carry it on the train. Violators could get in trouble, though I doubt it meant a sentence to Siberia, an irony that escaped my notice as the train rolled deeper into Gulag territory.

As the gloom of night blacked out the scenery, I resumed my preoccupation with food. I did not want to repeat my lunch fare, a box of raisins. Based on my mid-morning reconnaissance, the dining car was no longer a desirable option. My new strategy was to await the song of the food vendors who supplied the previous night's meal.

An hour later a rotund woman pushing a cart with a large pot and stacks of covered stainless steel bowls shuffled down the corridor. I anxiously waited in my compartment, but the woman and her cart rolled past. I sprang from my bench and dashed into the corridor to stop her, gesturing that I wanted to see what was in the pot. She opened the lid, releasing a billow of steam. Inside sloshed a thick brown soup, with bobbing chunks of meat, carrots, and potatoes. A heavenly aroma found its way to my nose. I motioned that I wanted some soup. "Nyet," she replied, followed by an unintelligible explanation. I felt helpless to make her understand, like a baby who cannot yet talk. My brain kicked into overdrive to think of a way to get at the soup — before it got away. Did I need my own dish and spoon? I darted back to my compartment and returned with my teacup.

"Go ahead, fill it up. I can drink the soup from this," I said, holding the cup, feeling like Oliver Twist. The woman giggled, then trundled off. The hearty aroma of the soup dissipated behind her, leaving me with an empty cup and a ravenous appetite.

I began to think of nothing but food. I played with my leftover raisins, eating the remaining few that stuck to the bottom of the box. I hoarded the animal cookies, thinking greater deprivations may still be ahead. I lapsed into childhood memories of hot dogs and cold Coke on warm September evenings while watching baseball at San Francisco's Candlestick Park. I remembered how easy it was to buy food; just hand money to the man, and you got a hot dog. I promised myself I would never take such convenience for granted again.

A half-hour later, I was jolted out of my fantasy by the distant song of another vendor. I scampered from my compartment and recognized the old woman who sold the cutlets and bulgur to the colonel and me the previous night. When she saw me, she smiled but wagged her finger when I pointed to the horde of foil-wrapped boxes on the lower shelf of the cart.

"You got to give me one!" I demanded. She babbled in Russian, explaining something of great importance. Whatever she said, it was clear I would not get one of the boxes.

"Glasnost. Ya tourist," I continued. She rolled her eyes. With a shrug, she reached under the cart and pulled out two boxes. I wanted only one, but I didn't press the matter; abundance was better than scarcity. I handed her a two-ruble note, which she slipped into her apron pocket. No change was proffered. She trudged off, pushing her cart and muttering to herself. I congratulated myself on my persistence.

Returning to my compartment, I quickly realized that something was wrong. Unlike the previous night when the packets were sold piping hot, these box dinners were as frozen as the landscape outside. I unwrapped one of the boxes and rapped it against the table, chipping off a tiny piece of bulgur. What was I supposed to do with two frozen dinners in the middle of the Ural Mountains? I pulled out the phrase book, hoping that it would provide some guidance. I found the Russian word for heat. Armed with this word and one of the foil boxes, I set off for the dining car. Perhaps there was an oven I could warm it in.

Shortly before I reached my destination, I overtook the old woman who sold me the boxes.

"What am I supposed to do with two frozen dinners?" I blurted in exasperation, forgetting to mention the Russian word for heat. "Where am I supposed to heat this?"

She snapped angrily, then reached into her apron pocket, pulled out a fistful of kopecks, and handed them to me. She stalked off, muttering. Holding the frozen dinner in one hand, I stuffed the pile of change into my front pocket and jangled down the corridor, the weight of the coins threatening to pull down my sweatpants. I marched on, hefting up my pants at critical times.

When I reached the dining car, I glanced into the kitchen alcove. The hairy-armed troll with the stained T-shirt was humming as he stirred the giant cauldron. He gazed up, annoyed by the interruption. For a second, I thought he might plop me into the boiling tempest. I didn't bother to ask about heat because I couldn't remember the word. I stood before him, trembling as I silently watched the big spoon swirl around the vaporous broth. I peeped the Russian equivalent of "good afternoon," then fled, holding up my sagging pants in ignoble retreat.

Back in my compartment, I sat in depressed silence and stared at my little frozen dinner. Hunger gnawed at me. I had searched for the Epicurean paradise, but found the diner from hell instead. I was denied soup for some unfathomable reason. And the two frozen blocks of food I now possessed were inedible unless I sucked on them like Popsicles. I was beginning to hate the Soviet Union, its rules, and the difficulty of carrying out the simplest tasks. How was it possible that this nation could launch a man into space when I couldn't even order dinner on its most famous train?

A flicker of an idea distracted me from my silent rant. I recalled groping about the heating pipes from last night's attempt to cool the sauna-like conditions. With renewed purpose, I crawled under the table, and on my hands and knees looked for the magic heat-giving pipe. The pipe was only warm, but it would do. I placed one of the frozen boxes on top of the pipe casing. In an hour, the meal thawed. I ate the cold slushy mess accompanied by the cacophony of grinding steel wheels and random bashing of metal. As the train lurched, the door to my compartment slid open and shut, revealing glimpses of the poster showing the handsome couple, aboard what was clearly another train, in another time, and quite possibly in another land.

Lost

The train carried me east, peeling away pages of Russian history with each kilometer. I vaguely remembered the stop in Sverdlovsk (now called Yekaterinburg after Catherine the Great) where the last czar, Nicholas II, and his family were herded into a cellar room on July 17, 1918, then brutally executed. Gary Powers, the American U-2 pilot, was shot down near here, an event that further heightened Cold War tensions.

Later we crossed the Tobol and then the Irtysh rivers, said to be haunted by the ghost of Yermak, the Cossack recruited by Czar Ivan IV (later to become known as The Terrible) in 1581 to rid Siberia of the hated Tatars. Ivan was so impressed by Yermak's early victories that he pardoned the Cossacks for past crimes and awarded Yermak a gift of two breastplates. Returning to Siberia to continue the conquest, Yermak's forces, perhaps lulled into complacency by their previous victories, were surprised by the Tatars at the Irtysh River. Yermak dove into the river, but the breastplate, which he apparently was quite fond of, pulled him under.

Nearly a thousand kilometers later, I awoke to see Russians bundled in thick coats and fur caps hurrying along the platform at the station in Omsk, a city that also played a cameo role in the calamitous events following the Russian Revolution. It was a center of anti-Bolshevik activity in the chaotic days following the abdication of Nicholas II and his subsequent execution. Ragtag armies still loyal to the monarchy met here in 1918 in an attempt to unify. The unification effort collapsed and the Whites, as the anti-Bolshevik forces were called, were pushed farther east, along the Trans-Siberian line. By 1920, the Red Army had crushed the last of the counter-revolutionaries. The country plunged into chaos as the Bolsheviks struggled to consolidate power. Famine and purges followed. During the next fifty years, countless political prisoners, crammed into unheated wooden boxcars, rolled through Omsk along these same tracks on their way to slave labor camps in the Soviet Gulag.

I, of course, was thankful I was not a political prisoner, at least not yet. But potentially being on the wrong train was not helping to free my mind to truly enjoy the trip. With each kilometer east, I nursed the growing suspicion that the Sibirsk wasn't going to magically transform into the Trans-Siberian Express. I was rapidly losing faith in my theory that the train was called the Sibirsk only on the segment to Novosibirsk.

My doubts were fed by bits of evidence that had accumulated slowly like the snow flurries that fell outside, whitening the steppe with the first shade of winter. After the initial euphoric day when I had departed from Moscow's Yaroslavsky Station, I had begun to note slight discrepancies between the official schedule and actual stops. As I journeyed farther east, the gaps widened. At first, I thought this was nothing more than a seasonal adjustment, a slight truing of the schedule by the authorities.

My confusion was compounded by the strange way time was kept on the train. Even though we would traverse seven time zones, gaining an hour here and an hour there, the train adhered strictly to Moscow time. A day into the trip, I lost track of the time and wasn't sure whether the schedule reconciled with Moscow time or real time. I couldn't imagine the havoc this would create once we reached the Far East. Would the galley be serving breakfast at 4 p.m.?

The strange time keeping was one thing I couldn't blame on the communists. "The confusion en route is amusing; one never knows when to go to bed or when to eat," reported Michael Myers Shoemaker of his journey in 1902.[1]

Shoemaker's other observations are colored by foreboding, describing the fading light of dusk "like that over the face of the dead" followed by "sobbing and sighing as of lost souls as the wind arises." He was also flummoxed when a conductor approached him with a large vaporizer, then doused the bewildered passenger with perfume. "This is the first day this has occurred, and perhaps it is an Easter greeting," he wrote.

Shoemaker may have reeked with perfume, but at least he was on the right train.

I couldn't stop glancing at the cover of *The Big Red Train Ride*. My train was pea green, the same as all the other trains I had seen in the Soviet Union. I had convinced myself that the Soviets, despite their fondness for the color, had run out of red paint during the intervening decade. Since the authorities seemed to be running out of a lot of other stuff—including food in the dining car—the greenness of the train was not, by itself, alarming. It was, after all, quite big.

The final shred of evidence came at a stop at Barabinsk when another passenger train, heading in the opposite direction, slid to a stop on the next track. I wiped the fog from my window and saw "Moscow-Novosibirsk" on the other train's nameplate. This was clearly our sister train, heading toward Moscow. I scrambled from my seat, sprinted down the corridor and jumped off the train into the Arctic cold. The nameplate, mounted just below my window, still read *Sibirsk*. What could that mean other than Siberian? I already knew I was in Siberia, but where within that vast place was I being taken?

As I rehashed the events that led to my mistake, a conductor, who bore a strange resemblance to a female Jackie Gleason, approached from the opposite end of the corridor. Her girth filled the hall. I rummaged through my mind for any Russian words that would help me, but I knew so very precious few.

"Rossiya?" I blurted, pronouncing the Russian nickname for the Trans-Siberian Express.

A wide grin formed, followed by a jolly cackle.

"Nye Rossiya. Sibirsk."

She squeezed by me, her cackle transforming into a staccato of laughter. This was the funniest thing she had heard in a long time.

I was on the wrong train and didn't think it was funny at all.

Had this been Western Europe or even the Russia that emerged after the Soviet Union collapsed in 1991, the snafu could have easily been corrected with a quick cell phone call or a visit to the information officer on the train. But I was stuck in 1987. The Soviet Union was still the bulwark of the communist world, a place haunted by the leather-jacketed Soviet secret police—the dreaded KGB. There were no cell phones. There was no information officer, nor information office. Indeed, information was not something the Soviets wanted foreigner travelers to possess.

Precious little time remained to reconstruct events. I had more immediate problems. For instance, the Sibirsk would soon arrive and terminate in Novosibirsk, which was nearly twelve hours ahead of the Trans-Siberian, as far as I could estimate. Given my brief encounters with the Soviet bureaucracy, I was not confident that Intourist, which was responsible for meeting me at the train station and taking me to the hotel, could handle an unexpected early arrival. My Russian language skills were a joke. Even if I could find a phone book, I couldn't read it, let alone call the hotel. I was terrified.

Returning to my compartment, I fortified myself with the last of the cold cutlets and bulgur I had squirreled away, then downed my final can of Sourcy, the French mineral water that my friends in Moscow had insisted I pack for an emergency. This was an emergency.

The Sibirsk rattled across a bridge spanning the half-frozen Ob River, then entered the outskirts of Novosibirsk as the grayness of day turned to night. A large thermometer perched atop a building announced it was minus three degrees.

The train shuddered to a stop. Passengers loaded with suitcases and bags poured into the corridor. I pulled on thermal underwear and tore out of its box a fur cap I had purchased in Moscow as a gift for my father. Strapping the smaller daypack to my larger backpack, I hoisted my load and clumsily struggled down the aisle and into the night. An icy wind blasted my face.

The other passengers scurried past, scores of hunched figures wrapped for winter. Soldiers in wool greatcoats, rifles slung over their shoulders, solemnly patrolled the platform. I lingered by the train waiting for someone, anyone, to welcome me to Novosibirsk—New Siberia. Within minutes I was the only person left on the platform. Snow swirled in the wind. My mustache froze. "Lara's Song," the theme from *Dr. Zhivago,* relentlessly played through my mind.

I wandered into the cavernous waiting room, its walls adorned with murals of heroic Soviet workers and soldiers. The terminal was crammed with a motley assortment of morose Russians, Siberians, Asians, Mongolians, and no doubt a few stray Azeris and Armenians. My friends had advised me that if I encountered difficulties, I could seek help at the station's Intourist office. Up a deserted flight of stairs and along a forlorn corridor, I found the office. I did not need to translate the handwritten sign, haphazardly plastered across the door, that read "Closed for the winter." I wandered back down to the main waiting room and slumped into a seat. After willing myself to remain calm, I pulled out my *Fodor's* guidebook and flipped to Novosibirsk. The section was four paragraphs long. The description of my hotel was not encouraging.

> *"(The) Tsentralnaya is terrible — avoid at all costs! When we last stayed there it needed replumbing and general renovations — or demolition!"*[2]

The guide did not bother to list a telephone number. I made a mental note to write to the good people at Fodor's about this oversight—that is, if I ever made it home.

My last hope was to try to reach the hotel by myself. In a normal city, in a normal country, this would have been a simple task. But this was the Soviet Union, where state-induced paranoia about the motives of strangers permeated all levels of society. The trains and stations were still considered military installations, which meant that photographing any of them was a state crime. It was impossible to buy a simple street map of the city because the layout and names of the streets were also considered military secrets—forty-four years after World War II had ended. And there were few taxis to speak of in Siberia.

I holed up in a corner of the station and prepared for my journey. I zipped up my parka, pulled on mittens, and untied the earflaps to the fur cap. These flopped loosely over my ears. I looked like a small version of Sergeant Preston of the Yukon. Bracing myself for the cold, I shoved open the doors leading outside. The force of the wind slammed the door shut and left me standing before a vast, snow-covered parking lot. No vehicles were in sight. I waited a moment for my eyes to adjust to the dim light, and wondered what I should do next.

In the distance, the beams of a car's headlights approached. I frantically waved at what I hoped was a taxi. A Zaporozhets, the bottom line Soviet mini-car that can only muster enough horsepower to match the average U.S. lawn mower, sputtered to a stop. The driver rolled down the passenger window. I launched into my very best Russian.

"Me Bob. Me tourist. I do not speak Russian. Tsentralnaya Hotel."

For good measure I threw in "glasnost" and that I was from America. The driver stared. My earflaps flopped lazily in the wind. Shards of ice hung from my mustache. The driver quickly rolled up the window and stepped on the gas.

"No, don't go!"

My yelp was too late. The vehicle puttered away, slowly gaining momentum against the wind, leaving me standing in the snow and a cloud of exhaust.

Munchkins

I couldn't dislodge "Lara's Theme" from my mind. I remembered the scene in the movie where Yuri, the hero, after escaping from the Red Army, staggers back to the village where he left Lara, his lover. His face and clothes are encrusted with ice as he trudges through a blizzard.

At least Yuri had some vague idea of where to go. I wandered aimlessly down a dark Novosibirsk street as the cold quickly penetrated my clothes. Starting with my nose, then spreading to my jaw, parts of my face began to lose feeling. I knew I had to reach the hotel soon or return to the warmth of the train station or freeze. I was about to retreat when I spied a group of men smoking cigarettes and talking. They leaned against a battered Zhiguli, a Fiat-like car that was a tad classier than the pathetic Zaporozhets. They eyed the approaching apparition with suspicion.

I launched into my spiel. One of the men seemed to understand. He said he spoke some English.

"You American?"

"Yes."

"You know Michael Jackson?"

"Ah no, not really. But I know his music."

He seemed disappointed. Taking a long drag from his cigarette, he relayed this information. His buddies nodded sadly. None of them seemed affected by the bitter cold. My eyes felt on the verge of freezing shut.

"Could I . . . "

"You know Blue Oyster Cult?"

"Look, I don't want to talk about music right now. Could I get a ride to the Tsentralnaya?"

"Okay."

I climbed into the car, while the driver fiddled with a tape player that dangled on exposed wires from the instrument panel. The engine coughed, then sputtered. Puffs of air marked our breath as we waited for the engine to warm. After what seemed like an eternity, the driver slammed a tape into the player, jammed down on the clutch, and shifted into first gear. We puttered through the deserted streets, passing a giant statue of Lenin as "Madness to Method," apparently a Blue Oyster Cult hit in Siberia, blared. A minute later, the Zhiguli pulled up in front of a nondescript multistoried building — the Tsentralnaya Hotel.

My savior wanted to be paid. After showing me ten fingers, I concluded correctly that he wanted ten rubles, about fifteen dollars. It was an exorbitant sum, equal to about a day's pay for the average Soviet worker. But given my options, I had no choice; in fact, it was a bargain.

I staggered up the steps of the Tsentralnaya and opened the large door. A gust of warm air washed over me. The lobby appeared to be full of small Asian men, all wearing green military uniforms. My five-foot, seven-inch frame loomed above the multitude. I blinked to make sure my eyes were not playing tricks on me.

I picked my way through the tiny soldiers, guessing they were Mongolian or from another Soviet republic with a large Asian population. The munchkins, many of them sporting medals and other officer insignia, peered at me curiously as I shed my backpacks and rummaged through various pockets, collecting vouchers, my passport, letters from Finland, and anything else that might prove useful.

At the reception desk, two matronly clerks chatted away, unaware that a hotel guest had just arrived. I cleared my throat, but was ignored. Waving my papers in the air, I finally attracted the attention of one clerk, who snatched my hotel voucher. Muttering, she flipped through it, then thrust it back. She turned and resumed chatting with her companion. I cleared my throat again and said, "excuse me," followed by every word in my limited vocabulary, including "glasnost."

Still, I was ignored. I turned to see if anyone could help and noticed that the munchkins had stopped talking and were nervously observing the exchange. I rolled my eyes at one of the clusters of little men. One of the munchkins smiled sympathetically. A few of them shuffled forward as if they contemplated coming to my rescue. In that instant, the balance of power seemed to shift. I felt a bond among us — the brotherhood of small men. I sensed that they, too, had been beaten down by the system and were now ready to rise up and rebel against the tyranny of the clerks. I was the catalyst that would spark them to action. I was their Dorothy.

I turned back to the clerk, thinking help was on the way. Clearly alarmed by this turn of events, she craned her neck and glared at the munchkins, then let loose an angry volley of words aimed directly at the rank of little men. The munchkin line wavered, then fell back. The clerk continued the verbal offensive. Now in full retreat, the munchkins pulled back to their previous nonthreatening positions, out of earshot. With my allies in disarray, the clerk, eyes smoldering with annoyance, turned to me.

I was doomed. She hissed the words "service bureau" and pointed sternly upstairs. I slithered away, collected my bags, and slowly climbed the stairs into an uncertain exile.

As expected, the service bureau was closed, not to reopen until nine the next morning. Nearby, I found the second floor key clerk and asked about check-in procedures. She looked at me blankly. I wandered farther down the corridor and found a teenage girl, pushing an ancient vacuum cleaner along the carpet. After hearing my clumsy Russian greeting, she smiled shyly — the first genuine smile I had seen in days — then shrugged and continued vacuuming.

Lack of sleep and the enormous effort required to transport myself from the train station to the second floor sitting room had left me exhausted. I plopped into an overstuffed chair that was tucked away in an alcove. It was pleasant enough, warm and comfortable; at least I would not freeze while I collected my thoughts.

I turned to the phrase book, which so far had proved remarkably useless. As expected, no phrase was listed for "how to check into the hotel."

Presumably, tourist visits are all arranged ahead of time; no one simply shows up at a hotel alone to check in, particularly in the middle of Siberia in late October. Such an act was beyond the Soviet experience. I made another mental note to write to the authors of *Basic Russian for English Speakers* and suggest that they test some of their phrases on real Russians before releasing an updated version. The helpful hints in the chapter called "Once at the Hotel" were not, so far, producing the help I needed.

> *After the helpful clerical staff has assigned you to a room, you will find on each floor an attendant, known as the 'dizhurnaya,' who will greet you, then take your key for safekeeping. The dizhurnaya will also gladly assist you with any questions, make cups of tea, call taxis, and show you where you can press your clothes. Do not hesitate to ask her for help.*

I wrote out a few useful phrases about checking in along with their Cyrillic equivalent. Notes in hand, I relocated the vacuum girl, now farther down the hall. I blurted something to the effect of "I need a room." She dropped the vacuum and ran away. I quickly rechecked the phrase to make sure I hadn't said "I want sex, please" or something equally perverse. But no, I had it right. The girl reappeared with the reluctant key clerk in tow. They stood before me expectantly as I again recited from my note, throwing in for good measure that I was from America and knew about glasnost. They looked at me curiously and perhaps with a touch of sympathy. At last, the vacuum girl motioned for me to go back downstairs.

My reappearance at the reception counter prompted one of the clerks to grab the telephone. Perhaps, I thought, she's calling security, the KGB, or the local insane asylum. I recited my message to her comrade, who looked at me blankly, then walked away. The other clerk slammed down the phone, turned away, and also stalked off, leaving me alone at the counter.

I wandered into the lobby looking for help. The munchkins were gone, replaced by smartly dressed men and attractive women resplendent in fur coats and hats. In an adjacent reading lounge, I spotted a man who bore a striking resemblance to Freud. He was reading a book with a dust jacket that was printed in English.

"Excuse me," I said as calmly as possible. "How do you check into a hotel in this country?"

"I cannot help you," he replied, in a thick German accent. "But she can."

He pointed to a woman sitting across the room. "She speaks both Russian and English."

I glanced in the direction he indicated and saw an attractive Russian woman, perhaps in her early thirties, peering intently at me.

I walked over to her and asked for help.

"Where is your group?" she demanded in the sterile voice of the official Soviet Union that I had grown to fear.

"I have no group. I am by myself," I said.

"How can that be? Everyone must be with a group," she snapped. "How did you get here?"

I told her about the train mix-up, the expensive ride to the hotel, and the defeat of the munchkin army. My series of misadventures impressed her. Her tone softened.

"This is an amazing story. You have come a great distance. You have suffered. You have done all of this and you speak terrible Russian."

I nodded.

"I will help you," she declared. "Come with me."

We strode out to the reception desk, where my heroine barked some commands that spurred the clerks, who had returned to their posts, into action. A large key that looked like it once opened the dungeon to the Kremlin materialized. My passport was confiscated. I was assigned a room.

She explained, "Because you were on the wrong train, no one expected you to arrive when you did. If you haven't officially arrived, the clerks will pretend you do not exist. Besides, they were confused. They expected someone from Finland."

"I do not look like a Finn," I said.

"I know, but they don't know that. Your train vouchers were issued in Finland."

"But any idiot can see that I'm not Finnish," I said. "Look at me."

I puffed up my five-foot, seven-inch frame and turned my head to give her a profile of my dark complexion, inherited from my Oaxacan grandfather on my mother's side of the family.

"Don't try to be rational," she said. "You are in the Soviet Union. Your vouchers were issued in Finland. Therefore, you are a Finn."

"Thanks for clearing that up."

My heroine's name was Nina, and I thanked her profusely. I clambered up three flights of stairs, opened the door, and stepped into a room that was no warmer than an igloo. But it was a room, nonetheless, and one that any Finn would have appreciated, given the circumstances. I collapsed, fully clothed, into a bed that was two inches shorter in length than my frame, but just right for a munchkin.

10

The Imperfect Spy

I thought of the sea, then of the sun warming my back in Ann's yard. But mostly I tossed and turned, searching for a sliver of comfort on the thin cotton mattress that rested on a plywood slab in the worst hotel in western Siberia. Hunger finally forced me from the bed.

What time was it? It seemed like an eternity had passed since I arrived at the train station. Checking my watch, I was surprised to discover it was only 8:30 — in the evening. Still time for supper, I thought hopefully. Rifling through my pack, I found a pair of clean trousers and a sports coat, a sad looking herringbone affair that looked as disheveled as I felt. I wandered into the tiny bathroom and reached above the basin for the faucet to wash up. There was none. I discovered yet another shortcoming of Soviet central planning. The tiny bathtub and sink shared a single faucet that swiveled between the two.

Clothed and cleaned, I stood ready to re-enter the world. The triumph over the clerks had infused me with new confidence. Nothing, it seemed, could faze me now. Somehow, I had managed to get to Siberia on my own, on the wrong train, with a Russian vocabulary of twelve words, and reach a hotel, albeit a bad one. I had survived. I wanted to celebrate my triumph over the Red menace and dine in a real Soviet restaurant. Nearly tearing the room door off its hinges, I bounded into the hallway, startling the vacuum girl who was working her way down the hall carpet with her ancient machine.

"Dobry vecher!" I shouted above the din.

She looked up with a warm smile that could have melted all the snow in Siberia. We seemed like old friends greeting each other after a long separation.

I headed downstairs. The restaurant entrance yawned open into a dark cavern. A discordant mix of rock music infused with the thin undertones of a Russian folk melody boomed from the room. Lightning flashes pulsated from somewhere within the deep recesses. I peered through the doorway and could see the dim outline of tables filled with army officers — munchkins and non-munchkins alike — drinking and eating. A band of four musicians clad in leather played in front of an empty dance floor. A revolving glass ball suspended from the ceiling sprayed patterned light around the room like a planetarium show that had gone haywire.

I stood in the doorway in my rumpled sports coat and wrinkled Eddie Bauer wrinkle-free pants and hoped to catch the eye of a waiter. I waited and waited, feeling the meekness that I had thought had been crushed seep back into my being. So this is Siberia, I thought. *This is what Yermak drowned for?*

No one paid any attention to me. Still I waited, too intimidated to just walk in. Smartly dressed Novosibirskans brushed by and disappeared into the darkness. The last of my confidence drained away. I retreated to the lobby and fled up the stairs.

On the fourth floor I found what appeared to be a snack bar. It was empty. As I studied the menu, a thin man with a slightly deranged look emerged from behind a swinging door. I caught a glimpse of smoke and flames before the door settled shut. He wore a dirty white chef's hat and a greasy apron. He clutched a bottle of vodka. The chef wobbled up to the counter, leaned toward me, and blurted "smorfs." At least that is what I thought he said. As usual, I carried my phrase book, though its utility during emergencies was questionable. Pages fell out as I scrambled to find the "eating and drinking" chapter.

The chef, his breath reeking of alcohol, leered at me, then yelled "smorfs" again as he pointed an unsteady finger at the menu board.

"What are smorfs? I don't see smorfs." I stammered in English, pointing to the menu.

"Smorfs!" boomed the wild-eyed chef.

"Sorry, not in the mood for smorfs tonight," I said, backing from the room, as a vision of little furry creatures roasting on a stick popped into my mind. "But thanks for the suggestion."

"Smorfs!"

I scampered down the stairs as the call of "smorfs" receded behind me. Bewildered, I crossed the lobby and found myself once again on the threshold of the dark restaurant, music and stabs of light flashing from its mysterious interior. I steeled myself, eyeing the threshold warily as if it were the Rubicon. Darting inside, I spotted the shadowy form of a nearby table and plopped myself across from a morose munchkin army officer nursing a drink. I smiled. He glanced lethargically in my direction, then returned his stare to the bottom of his shot glass. A waiter appeared and tossed a menu on the table.

As I prepared to settle in for a long session of Cyrillic decoding, I caught a glimpse of an angel entering the room. It was Nina, my savior from a few hours ago. I waved. She glided over to my table, elegant heels tapping across the dance floor. Gone was her business suit, replaced by a long white dress with a slit that showed off the lovely curve of her lower leg, a sight not lost upon me or the other males in the vicinity.

"Are you alone?" I asked.

"Yes."

"Would you like to join me?"

"Of course."

I had thought she was beautiful when I first saw her, but given my overall weariness I had not dwelt upon it. At the time, I was just happy to be alive. Godzilla would have been beautiful if he had uttered the magic words that produced the key to my room. But that was then, and this was now.

Nina slid into the chair opposite me. Her jet-black hair cascaded to her shoulders. A few strands strayed playfully across her face. Her lips were full and red, a perfect match for the porcelain face, with not a blemish anywhere. A strand of pearls hung around her neck. She wore glasses, but these seemed to accent her beauty; besides, I tend to fall for women with glasses.

"Could you help me with this menu? I'm having trouble reading it," I asked.

"Of course, Robert."

She pronounced "Robert" in a seductively accented tone that made my name sound anything but ordinary.

Nina leaned across the table to have a look. I sniffed a whiff of fragrance, like a freshly opened rose that lingered sweetly in the air and then dissipated in the smoky haze. Her posture provided an ample view of her breasts cozily nuzzled against a black brassiere. I tried to look away, but there they were in front of me, pale and sumptuous, as if they were appetizers being offered to a starving man. Nina seemed unaware of the effect that her presence was having on her dinner companion.

Nina translated the menu and pointed out what might be worth ordering. Then a waiter miraculously appeared. Even more miraculous, he seemed eager to serve us, possibly a first in Soviet restaurant history. We ordered salads and tea to start. Later, I had the beef stroganoff. Nina ordered soup. Somewhere between courses, the army officer disappeared. We were alone. In the background, the band played a Russian folk tune. Some of the soldiers, now intoxicated, attempted a *chautski*, the Russian step where the dancer folds his arms in front of his chest and kicks out his legs one at a time from a sitting position.

"They are required to play a traditional song once in awhile," Nina told me. The folk music stirred something deep within me. I was reminded of my Russian-born ancestors. For some unexplainable reason, I had the impression that they lived like the Jews portrayed in *Fiddler on the Roof*, though it was doubtful that they sang and danced as much.

There was, of course, a distinction between being Russian and Jewish, namely the long history of anti-Semitism that plagued Russia throughout its dark history and persisted in the Soviet Union. But the music temporarily transcended that ugliness. My father's record cabinet was full of the Russian classics. I grew up with the haunting folk melodies that permeated the works of Borodin, Tchaikovsky, and Mussorgsky. Something in this music penetrated my soul. Why? Was it because a small part of me came from this culture? For a moment, I felt at home in this Siberian restaurant, as if a fog had briefly lifted from an alien landscape to reveal a glimpse of the familiar. The last strains of the lovely tune had barely faded when the band cut loose with jarring rock music. I snapped back to the present.

Nina told me she had learned English as a student, became a teacher, and then an Intourist guide. Now she was an assistant director of a medical research institute based in Irkutsk, another two-day train journey to the east. She was in Novosibirsk on business. Her husband and young son were back at home in Irkutsk, "a much nicer city than Novosibirsk." I was disappointed to hear she was married, but I kept this to myself as I told her about my life, my career as a journalist, and now my time of carefree travel, while taking time off from my graduate studies.

"I guess it hasn't been all that carefree," I admitted. "A couple more days like today, and I'll be going home with an ulcer."

We talked about Soviet society and the changes brought on by "perestroika" — Gorbachev's economic reforms — and the new openness of "glasnost." She thought these changes were good for the country, but seemed disturbed by certain dark forces that might be unleashed if the reforms moved too quickly. I asked what these might be. Nina paused thoughtfully for more than a few moments, as if her answer would inevitably alter the course of

Soviet history. "I cannot say exactly. It is just a feeling. You know, the Russian people fear chaos more than anything."

She didn't volunteer much more than that. Instead, she wanted to know more about me. I obliged. Minutes drifted into an hour, then another.

As the evening grew late, a thought nagged at me. My American friends in Moscow had repeatedly warned that the KGB — the Soviet secret police — would shadow my every move. After a week in Moscow, I was now convinced that this was more than idle talk. Ken and Carol believed their apartment in Moscow was bugged. Every time we wanted to talk about one of the dissidents or a sensitive article they were writing, we scurried to the bathroom, turned the shower on full blast, then whispered. They told me about an American woman who wanted to take a picture of the infamous Lubyanka prison in Moscow's Dzerzhinsky's Square. The instant the woman snapped the photo, a gaggle of KGB goons materialized, snatched her off the street, and hauled her away for interrogation.

Then there was the story of Nicholas Daniloff, an American reporter, who, after taking a folder of documents from a Soviet source, was promptly arrested. He spent several weeks in prison before an international outcry forced his release. More recently, the press had been full of stories of Marine guards at the U.S. embassy in Moscow who had succumbed to a flock of "sparrows" — the euphemism for female KGB spies who use sex to gain favors. The most damning case involved the seduction of a 25-year-old guard by a tall, slim long-haired blonde named Violetta, who apparently was reported to look quite stunning in a black evening dress. The guard became so infatuated with Violetta that he allegedly helped her and other KGB agents gain access to the embassy. The KGB was not to be trifled with. I had been warned.

But my adventures to date were not exactly ringing endorsements of the omnipotent secret police. For three days, I had traveled through Siberia apparently unsupervised, and now I had unwittingly infiltrated some sort of military high command shindig at the hotel. No one seemed to care. Had I managed to shake my KGB tail? Was I, an American version of Inspector Clouseau, the perfect cover for a spy? What about Nina? Just happened to be in the hotel lobby, watching my desperate pleas for attention while waiting for me to come to her for help? Was she the sparrow who had managed to snare the clever American, disguised as a bumbling graduate student, who had cleverly evaded the Soviet internal security network? Was she now laying the *provokatsiya* — the trap — ordered by Moscow to get me to reveal state secrets?

I gazed into Nina's eyes. If it wasn't love I felt, it was definitely lust. If ever a traveler was ready to be seduced, it was I. At that moment, I would have told her anything if only I could have spent the night with her.

There was only one small, but important, problem with this fantasy. I was not a spy. I had no secrets to reveal. I didn't have the keys to the embassy, didn't even know where it was. I could betray no one. I possessed nothing but a snapshot of my family, a canned ham, and sack of animal crackers.

"Nina, my friends told me that I would be watched by the KGB," I said, sheepishly. "Do you think that's true?"

"KGB this. KGB that. Everyone thinks the KGB is everywhere. Maybe they were watching you in Moscow. But I do not think anyone knows you are here, not even the hotel," she said, smiling.

"You will probably think this is funny, but I thought at first you might be a KGB agent."

She tossed back her head and laughed, exposing the delicate line of her neck. I felt a sensual excitement I didn't think possible after having slept only a few hours during the past three days. Every move she made entranced me, even the seductive way she pronounced her English in that clipped Russian accent, the kind spoken by the beautiful Russian female spies in James Bond movies.

"Oh, Robert, you are so funny."

My imagination — never a tranquil sea — now roiled out of control. For a brief moment, I saw Nina and me living happily in a log cabin in the Siberia wilderness, gaily riding our sleigh to the nearest village. Nina would be dressed in a handsome sable coat with matching hat, while I would be snug in my bearskins, a balalaika slung around my shoulder. "Lara's Theme" swelled to a crescendo in my head. She was speaking . . .

"It is late, and I must go now. But please enjoy your visit here. The hotel administration will take care of you now and plan a program for you."

She pecked me on the cheek. My angel of mercy disappeared out the door. I sat in the darkness, light reflecting off my face from the rotating ball. I felt a bit silly. Maybe she really was the assistant director of a medical research institute. Or, was this evening's encounter part of an elaborate and devious plan to trap me later? I winced at the wild thoughts that popped into my mind. Lingering for a few minutes and listening to the music, I watched a group of men and their wives, girlfriends, or God-knows-what at a nearby table downing shot after shot of vodka. I had come a long way, from nearly freezing to death on a railway platform to sharing dinner with the most beautiful woman I had yet encountered in Siberia, all in the same night. If not the KGB, certainly somebody was looking out for me.

11

Mr. K.'s Most Excellent Program

That night I dreamt of soldiers searching the streets of Novosibirsk, cornering me in the alcove of a massive concrete building. They barked incomprehensible commands. I stood paralyzed in the snow and stared at shadowy figures, unable to speak or move. Behind the soldiers, Nina, elegant in white furs, appeared. She called out: "I will help you."

Too late. There was a bang, followed by another sharp report, a violent pounding that jolted me to the surface of consciousness. I was back in the tiny bed, in the present, in the cold, my feet wrapped in two pairs of socks, dangling off the end.

Someone was knocking at my door. Pound. Pound. Pound. Who the hell could it be at this hour? What hour was it anyway? My arm shot out to an alarm clock that was not there. Then I remembered. I was not home. I was in Siberia. The very thought depressed me. The pounding continued, as if a covey of KGB agents were about to burst in and drag me away. I rolled out of bed and sleepwalked to the door.

Before me stood a smiling man in a rumpled brown suit. A nametag pinned to his lapel identified him in Cyrillic as the hotel administrator. I had learned enough of the alphabet to translate these simple words. I eyed him warily.

"Mr. Goldstein?" he asked, pronouncing the last syllable as "schteen."

"Da."

He stuck out his hand, and introduced himself in Russian. I couldn't understand a word he was saying (my ability to decipher simple words did not extend to speaking or listening), but he seemed earnest in his attempt to communicate. He then pantomimed what I took to be the motion of packing a suitcase followed by marching.

"You want me to march out of my room with my suitcase," I said, repeating the motions.

"Da!" he cried. Then, he made an expansive movement with his arms, pointing to my room number. He then unpacked the invisible suitcase.

I was proficient at charades, and I soon concluded that he wanted me to relocate. I wondered if another helpless fool, perhaps from Norway or Iceland, had arrived during the early morning and demanded an extra cold room. Another victim was needed for the freezer, get the old guy out of there. What the heck, I figured, it couldn't get any worse than this.

"Okay," I said. "I need a few minutes to pack."

Mr. Administrator, a middle-aged man with thinning black hair, stood by as I hastily threw clothes and toiletries into my backpack. I followed him down a corridor into a newer wing. He turned the key to room 308, and I stepped into my new home. I blinked in disbelief. It was not the standard economy-fare hotel room at all, but a palace, at least relative to my experiences so far. I stood in the living room, dominated by a giant television, a sofa, and fresh plastic sunflowers on a coffee table. The other two rooms were bedrooms, each with king-sized beds and enough blankets to keep the entire Mongolian Army warm. The room radiated heat. At last something had gone right. Then it hit me. I grabbed the railroad timetable from my pack and looked up the Trans-Siberian Express. My hunch was confirmed. The visitor from Finland had officially arrived about an hour ago. This was his room.

The guest from Finland was the only person eating breakfast. As if to emphasize this fact, I was seated at a table in the middle of a vast dining room surrounded by at least fifty empty tables. A waitress handed me a plate with five pieces of cheese laid out like a hand of poker, a piece of bread, and a pile of blinis — the Russian equivalent of a pancake. The dry bread soaked the moisture from my throat. I desperately needed coffee. Three waitresses, all young women, probably teenagers, were gabbing around a samovar at the far end of the room. I waved to get their attention. Finally, one of them reluctantly sauntered my way with a coffeepot. She filled the tiny cup. I gulped it down, then I grabbed her by the arm before she could saunter back to her friends.

"More, I got to have more," I croaked. She tilted the pot, but only a thin stream of the precious liquid drooled out, followed by a slurry of grounds, then nothing. Was this the last half-cup of coffee in Novosibirsk? I looked at her. She shrugged, then turned and meandered back to her friends. The gaggle then disappeared into the kitchen. I rationed my little porcelain cup of coffee, sucking up every last drop and even some of the grounds.

When I returned to my suite, I found a note taped to the door. Mr. K. — I could not make out the complete last name — from the service bureau wanted to see me at once. The very name "service bureau" was worrisome. I had already developed enough cynicism about the Soviet bureaucracy to conclude that the sole purpose of the service bureau was to provide as little service as possible. The words "it is not possible" and "it is not convenient" scrolled through my head. These phrases seemed to be the unofficial slogans of the clerks and bureaucrats I had encountered so far. I prepared for battle.

The door was ajar even though a sign hanging from the knob said the office was closed. I pushed it open and walked in, flipping the closed sign to open. A man who was about my height but stockier stood gazing out the window, unaware of my presence. Adorning the office walls were travel posters of a sun-splashed Novosibirsk. One depicted pink-cheeked maidens carrying baskets of flowers, frolicking in a golden poppy field; another, a group of Young Pioneers, looking smart and proper in red kerchiefs, admiring a statue of Lenin in the city center. I stood before a wooden desk, empty save for a notepad and a model of a steam locomotive. Inscribed on the door of the tiny engine was "Rossiya." The man seemed deep in thought.

"Hello."

He whirled around.

"Da," he said, turning to face me, revealing the bushiest eyebrows I had ever seen. A few unruly brow hairs pointed up like they had been charged with static electricity. He squinted and blinked, as if the weight of his eyebrows made it difficult to keep his eyes open. He had the face of Walt Disney with the hairstyle of a giant Chia pet.

He asked in English, "Are you Mr. Goldstein? From Finland?"

"Yes."

His face brightened. His smile, amplified by the crow's feet that radiated from the edge of his eyes, gave him a friendly, grandfatherly look. He bounded from behind the desk, and pumped my hand vigorously as if I were a long lost pal.

"Allow me to introduce myself. I am Mr. K . . . " I still could not discern the last name, but it sounded similar to the famous Soviet-made rifle, the Kalishnikov. Mr. K. returned to the chair behind his desk. He motioned for me to sit in the chair facing the desk.

"We have been looking all over for you. Where have you been? You were not on the train. We were very worried."

I told him my story.

Mr. K. sat transfixed, soaking in every detail. With each added turn of my tale, his face contorted. He winced, when I discovered I had been on the wrong train and was stranded at the station. Relief showed on his face when I told him about my rescue by Nina.

"An excellent story!" said Mr. K., then lowering his voice. "They are idiots in Moscow. Nobody moves unless another gives permission. Life is different in Siberia. We are independent. We use our brains. I can assure you that the rest of your visit in Novosibirsk will be pleasant and cheerful."

"Thank you. I'm feeling much better about things now."

"We want you to go back to Finland and tell your friends about our beautiful city."

It sounded like an order.

"I will do that," I said. I decided not to complicate my life by explaining that I wasn't really from Finland.

Mr. K. leaned forward with a look of anticipation as if he expected me to be more effusive about the wonders of Novosibirsk, which according to Mr. K.'s enthusiasm level should be recognized as the Eighth Wonder of the World.

Mr. K. told me there was much to see and do in the city. "Surely, when you arrived, you must have seen our famous Opera House?"

I nodded indecisively, not sure what I had seen on my way to the hotel. All the buildings looked alike. A look of concern crossed Mr. K.'s face, as if by not actually seeing the opera house, I might insult the greatness of the city. I sensed this and added hastily, "I'm sure all my friends in Finland will be excited to hear about my adventures here."

"Yes, they will!" exclaimed Mr. K., whose level of excitement seemed to be reaching dangerously high levels.

"And now I would like to put together a pogrom for you."

"I hope you mean a program."

"Yes, a program. Forgive me, my English is tired. I do not get a chance to use it in the winter," he said. He continued, "What would you like to see while you are our guest in Novosibirsk? There is so much to do and see. You are here only today and then you must leave tomorrow morning. So little time ... "

Mr. K. was now beside himself with anticipation. Again, he leaned forward from his desk, waiting to hear what I might want to see in this frostbitten city. He dabbed at the dust on the model locomotive as he waited for my response.

"Well," I stammered, scanning my memory for details of the city's highlights.

Frankly, Novosibirsk was the least interesting of the three Soviet cities that were open to visitors. In planning my trip, I had decided to stay in Novosibirsk primarily because it was there and would allow me to stretch my legs and relax — none of which had actually occurred. Pretrip planning had yielded little in the way of interesting things to do. While Irkutsk and Khabarovsk were steeped in the history of Siberia's settlement, Novosibirsk was largely the product of uninspired Soviet central planning. Lenin stopped here in 1897 when the city, then called Novonikolaevsk, was nothing more than a collection of log cabins. The future father of the Republic was not impressed by the scenery en route: "The landscape along the road through western Siberia, which I have just traveled from end to end . . . are (sic) extraordinarily featureless: a bare and empty steppe, snow and sky . . . " I could have told them that. Lenin had nothing to say about the town itself. A 1978 guide to the Soviet Union I had purchased at a used bookstore in Seattle did not contribute to the allure of the city, noting dryly that it contained "no old buildings of any consequence."

There was one possibility, however, and that was Akademogorodok, located about thirty kilometers to the south. The "Academic City" was founded in 1958 to further Soviet research ranging from nuclear physics to history. It was reputed to be one of the more liberal Soviet institutions thanks to its isolation from the party bureaucrats in Moscow. I wasn't quite sure what I would do there, but I thought it might allow me an opportunity to meet some interesting people. Recently, some scientists based at the city had questioned Soviet conventional wisdom about diverting water from Siberia's great rivers to the arid lands in the southern republics. They warned that such actions could disrupt Siberia's delicate ecosystem, leading to unknown and perhaps disastrous environmental consequences. Less earth shattering, the computer center at the Akademogorodok had been used to decipher ancient Mayan, a fact that I found peculiar. Nuclear physics made sense, but Mayan writing? Why would the Soviets be pouring valuable resources into deciphering Mayan when an equal or greater effort was needed to decipher the country's hotel management and reservation system?

"Yes?" asked Mr. K., smiling. Beads of perspiration had collected on his forehead just above his amazing eyebrows, as he waited for my response.

"I would like to visit the Akademogorodok," I proclaimed at last.

"Excellent idea! I shall arrange the trip at once."

Mr. K. picked up the phone, dialed, and began talking in rapid Russian. I could tell from the tone and pace of the conversation that things were not going well. Mr. K.'s smile faded. The enthusiasm that coursed through his body only seconds before seemed to have spent itself. He looked as if a close friend had just died.

"The Akademogorodok is closed," he whispered.

"Closed? How could they close an entire city?"

"The weather," said Mr. K. listlessly, motioning out the window. "No one wants to drive there today. It is too cold. The roads are icy."

"What do you mean? People must drive on icy roads all the time here. This is Siberia," I said.

I wanted to take that last comment back. My cynicism can sometimes be too sharp, a trait my friends recognize and can dismiss. But to someone like Mr. K., who was trying his best to be helpful, these nuances were not obvious. I didn't want him to think I didn't appreciate his help. But it was too late. Mr. K. looked crestfallen, as if an awful truth had just been revealed. I suddenly had the urge to hug him and tell him that Novosibirsk was the Disneyland of Russia, that I was having a swell time, and that it really wasn't that cold outside. But then Mr. K. brightened up by himself.

"You should come back in the spring. Novosibirsk is so beautiful then. It is warm. There is sun. People come from all the Soviet Socialist Republics to see the flowers, so many flowers. And the birch forests, they are lovely. I take my family, our little Natasha, my wife and her mother, for picnics in the forest," said Mr. K.

I imagined Mr. K. and Mrs. K. with the little Ks romping in a poppy-strewn meadow. On a red-checkered blanket rests a wicker picnic basket and the latest book on the Soviet translation of Mayan hieroglyphics.

He turned to the window, no doubt thinking of spring in Siberia. Outside, hard little snow pellets sprayed the window. A gust of wind rattled the wood casement. Mr. K. returned his attention to me.

"Would you like to go on a city tour?" he asked, perking up to this new idea.

"Sure, why not."

"Excellent choice!" exclaimed Mr. K. "I will add that to your program."

Before I could ask to what program my city tour was being added, Mr. K. had picked up the phone again and had started another animated conversation. Once again, the enthusiasm slowly drained from his face. Sheepishly, he turned to me.

"There are no city tours today," he said.

"That's okay," I said, afraid to ask why. "I think I'll just walk around the city on my own. That's how I like to travel anyway."

"An excellent idea!" proclaimed Mr. K.

"And now," said Mr. K., as if introducing the final act in a circus. "I will arrange for a driver and interpreter to take you to the train station tomorrow."

"That would be great."

Mr. K. looked pleased with himself.

"I can arrange to have a French-speaking interpreter, Mrs. P. (the name was a blur, yet again). And Ivan, the driver, speaks excellent Italian."

"I don't speak French or Italian," I protested. "Do you have someone who can speak English?"

"Yes, of course, English would have been my first choice. Unfortunately, I am the English interpreter and tomorrow is my day off, so it is not convenient; otherwise, I would be honored to do it myself. But I can assure you that Mrs. P. speaks excellent French. You will not have a problem understanding her."

It was useless to argue. I had crossed the Rubicon. I now accepted wholeheartedly the absurdities of the country. Left was right, up was down, and I was from Finland — and nothing I could do would change that. I was getting a ride to the train station; that was good enough.

"Thanks."

Mr. K. and I both rose from our seats.

"I think we have put together an excellent program for you," said Mr. K., his enthusiasm once again on the rise.

"It's truly a great program," I deadpanned.

"I hope you enjoy your visit in Novosibirsk, and perhaps you will come back and visit in the spring."

"I might."

"You must!"

"I shall!"

Mr. K. bounded around the desk, pumped my hand, and then unexpectedly enveloped me in a bear hug.

"Thank you, thank you for visiting Novosibirsk."

I was speechless. Mr. K. appeared almost about to cry. He held me as if he knew I was the last visitor who would ever to come to Novosibirsk and that Mr. K. would never have another opportunity to arrange a program, ever again. I wanted to say, "There, there, it will be all right. Some poor slob will show up in the spring." But I said nothing because Mr. K.'s bear hug was squeezing the life from me.

I cleared my throat.

"It's getting late. I need to get on with my program," I said, while pressed against his shoulder.

"Yes, of course," said Mr. K. snapping back to the present. He released me.

"Excellent idea!"

And with that, Mr. K. escorted me from his office and flipped the "closed" sign back in place. With a deft kick, he flicked the door shut. Then he marched down the hallway and disappeared around the corner.

12

Have You Seen Larissa?

The ancient phone in my suite let loose with a shriek that begged to be silenced. Until that moment, I had been absorbed in meticulous preparation for my morning excursion into the cold. With every shred of clothing that could realistically be worn, I transformed myself from a hapless tourist into the Pillsbury Doughboy. Waddling to the phone, I picked up the receiver, wondering who on earth could be calling me.

Barely discernible above the static, a woman babbled in rapid Russian. Without waiting for a cue, I launched into my "I'm Bob, I don't speak Russian" routine. The woman switched to barely decipherable English. She demanded to know my room number. I told her. She asked a second question that sounded like "Kakaya vasha natsyahlnast?"

"What? I do not understand, speak slowly," I replied.

There was a rush of angry words, then the line went dead. I returned to my task. A few minutes later the phone rang again.

It was the same woman who repeated the same incomprehensible question. Hearing no response, she asked in English: "Do you speak English?"

"Yes," I replied, enunciating the word clearly, then throwing in for good measure: "I speak English."

She asked a question in an accent so thick that I couldn't tell whether it was Russian or English.

"Please, speak very slowly," I said very slowly.

The line went dead a second time. Once more I resumed the dress rehearsal. While I was trying to squeeze into a wool sweater — the last garment in my pack — the phone rang a third time. It was the same voice. She demanded that I stop speaking Finnish and switch to English.

"I am speaking English. I don't speak anything else!"

"You do not speak English!" retorted my antagonist. "Don't they teach you English in Finland?"

"Yes, they do!" I screamed back. "It's you. You don't speak English!"

The woman let loose with a tirade of curses before screaming one last time: "You don't speak English!" She hung up.

I sat on the edge of the bed, holding the phone. The cycle of absurdities was accelerating. I half expected Alice to wander in, followed by the White Rabbit, the Mad Hatter, and the Queen of Hearts, with whom I had no doubt just spoken. "Off with his head," I could hear her ordering her minions after the last call. Getting to Novosibirsk was an adventure in itself, but the events transpiring at the Wacko Hotel were now threatening to short circuit the rational part of my brain. I couldn't take much more.

I gathered the postcards that were spread out on my bed, hoisted my daypack, and departed from the warm confines of my room. My mission: find the post office. I trundled through the lobby — scene of the standoff the day before with the clerks — and pushed open the double doors to the outside world. The blast of cold air felt as if someone had clamped a frozen mask on my face. I trudged down the deserted street, leaning into a stiff breeze that frosted my nose hairs and iced my mustache. My cheeks tingled and then froze. My nose went numb, and I could feel my feet degenerating into blocks of ice, even though they were swaddled in two pairs of socks. I reached the end of the block before I realized I had no idea where I was going. There was a good reason why no one wanted to drive me to the Science City today. Realizing I could not continue in the cold much longer, I turned around and retreated to the lobby.

She was sitting in a chair reading, just as I had found her the previous night.

"Nina!" I yelled. She looked up, startled by the sudden appearance of Nanook of the North. Then she recognized me and smiled.

"Robert, you are much bigger today than last night," she said.

Nina laughed when I told her of my dressing strategy and plan to tour the city on foot.

"You are so brave to go into the city in such cold," she said. "And to think you have come here alone and speak terrible Russian."

I actually felt rather foolish, not brave at all, but I kept this to myself.

I showed her the phrase book that I was relying upon. She began to giggle as she leafed through the pages of the tattered volume.

"Robert, this is so funny, these words and phrases," she said, barely able to contain herself. "No one speaks like this. It is like for you old English, very formal."

Nina motioned for me to sit.

"I will write out in English and Russian some of the phrases that you might need on your trip. You can't use this book. People will think you are odd if you try to speak like this."

"I think I have firmly established my oddness here," I said, wondering what I might have told the clerks last night when I tried to check in. Had I barged into the hotel and announced to the befuddled clerks: "Behold fair maidens, and lo for I am in need of succor"? Or something like that, Russian style? No wonder they thought I was a madman. Nina wrote out phrases and words that I would need. Then, we carefully reviewed the pronunciations.

"Robert, it's lunch time. Do you want to eat before you explore the city?"

We found ourselves seated at the same table in the same restaurant as the previous night. It now seemed like our regular table. After we ordered, I described the weird phone call and the encounter with Mr. K.

"No one visits here in the winter," she explained. "They do not know what to do with you. I do not think that the Science City is closed. No one wanted to take you because you are only one person."

"But I would have paid them."

"You would have paid the hotel, and then maybe the driver and guide would have received a few rubles. This is a problem in our country: no one wants to work because they get paid the same whether they work or not. There is another problem and that is the drinking. Maybe the drivers were all drunk on vodka and didn't want to be bothered."

I envisioned myself as a passenger with a drunk Russian at the helm of a badly tuned Zhiguli, the car careening from side to side on an ice-covered road leading to the famed Science City — I killed this train of thought immediately. Instead, I asked about Gorbachev's initiatives to limit the sale of vodka. Nina said most Russians were now turning to home-brewed concoctions with predictable consequences. The problem defied solution. The conversation soon dwindled into an awkward silence.

Nina, fidgeting, leaned forward across the table as if to tell me a secret.

"Robert. May I ask you something, how do you say it, about your life?"

"Yeah, sure."

"Do you have someone, a girl, in Seattle?"

I wasn't prepared for the question, since it came so quickly after our discussion of the failure of Russian-styled socialism and the horrendous drinking problem. I switched gears, not quite sure how to explain my situation.

"Well, I have this friend. Her name is Anastasia. Everyone calls her Ann, though. We are in sort of a relationship," I said.

"Anastasia, this is a Russian name, yes?"

"She's not Russian, I can assure you of that. I think her parents liked Russian literature. I sometimes call her Queen Ann."

"She is English, yes?"

"No, she's American, like me."

"Why do you call her Queen Ann?"

Answering this question was relatively simple. The problem was, it led to more complex issues. Nina, with her innocuous question, was picking at a scab that was far from healed. The fact was that my relationship with Ann was filled with the same ambiguity that shrouded the Soviet Union. How could I explain to a stranger that this was a woman whom I had been with for nearly two years, and yet she remained an enigma? Prying information from Ann about how she felt about us — or anything, for that matter — was next to impossible. When her stepfather died after a long illness, she chose not to tell me until after the funeral. When she did call, the voice on the telephone was that of a stoic — no quivering, no emotion. Ann had locked up her feelings and thrown away the key. It didn't help that I tended to act the same way in similar situations. In many respects, Ann and I seemed cloned from the same personality. A friend once told me that our behavior toward each other reminded him of Princess Diana and Prince Charles. She seemed uncomfortable holding hands or displaying physical contact in public. As the months grew into years, I became starved for affection, settling for the rationed tidbits of love that Ann bestowed upon me in private. In my journal, I referred to her as Queen Ann, though Queen Victoria may have been a more fitting title.

So why did I stick around? Because Ann was a good person: pure of heart, generous, and kind. She never swore. Lying was unimaginable. I didn't think it was possible for me to meet a better human being. I told Nina this, as I picked away at the bratwurst that she had recommended I try.

"Do you miss her?"

Since leaving Moscow, the events that had befallen me had pushed Ann from my mind. I was too focused on survival. Until now.

"I'm not sure," I replied. "This has been a difficult journey . . . "

"Do you love her?" shot back Nina, seemingly impatient with my hemming and hawing.

"I want to love her," I said, thinking I should stop the conversation. But I couldn't. The words tumbled out. The confession continued. Nina, my interrogator, listened intently, her head resting in her cupped hands.

"I have tried to love her. I have stopped asking her if she loves me because I never get a clear answer. Now I'm too afraid to ask because I fear the answer."

"Is this why you have come to Siberia by yourself?"

"I thought I came here because I wanted to experience the trip of a lifetime, to ride one of the world's greatest trains, and to do something few people will ever do. But now I am not so sure. I've started thinking about my family origins. You know, my great-grandparents are from Russia."

"Did you want her to come?" asked Nina, who ignored my musings about my family roots.

"I didn't ask her to come. She never understood why I wanted to take this trip instead of just hanging out at a resort somewhere, practicing my beach etiquette."

I tried to picture Ann at Moscow's Yaroslavsky Station, prim and proper in sensible shoes, surveying the countless steamer trunks that would have been required for the trip. I couldn't imagine how Ann, who loved fine dining, would have survived the three-day journey to Novosibirsk on a diet of frozen bulgur packets, raisins, and bread sticks. Besides, there was too much dirt in Siberia. Queen Ann hated dirt.

Nina looked at me with supreme interest, as if she expected the confession to continue. But I couldn't go on. It was too much for a man who wanted to forget, even if just temporarily. We sat in silence. Wind-driven ice pellets ricocheted off the restaurant window like bullets fired from a machine gun.

"I am very sorry for you, Robert," she said. "So, you are an exile like the other Siberians."

"Yes, Nina, I guess I am in exile."

The remains of my sausage lay like a decomposing corpse on my plate. Lunch was over. Nina rose to put on her coat, a full-length affair fringed in sable with a matching fur hat. We hugged, then she kissed my cheek and reminded me to use the phone number she had scribbled on a piece of paper if I needed assistance when I got to Irkutsk.

"You will like Irkutsk, it is much more interesting than Novosibirsk," she told me. And then she was out the door. From the window, I watched her step into a waiting Zhiguli; my only friend, gone.

I stood in the lobby until the warmth of her embrace melted away. Then I gathered my pack and scuttled out the door with some vague notion of finding a post office and to see what this drab city had to offer. Opening the door, I braced myself for the stinging cold, but was surprised to find that the wind had calmed. As I walked aimlessly down the street, Nina's words — *you are an exile like the other Siberians* — played through my mind. It awakened other questions of introspection — *who am I* and *where do I belong* — questions that I had long avoided because there were no ready answers. I hurried on without direction, trying to shed the depression that now shrouded me like fog. The bleak urban landscape offered no insight. I looked into the faces of the few pedestrians that hustled past me, but I saw only grim despair and resignation, if I saw anything at all. I came to the crossroads of two wide thoroughfares and was not sure which way to turn. I felt utterly alone.

A patch of blue emerged from the cold sky; a sliver of sunlight touched my face. At a nearby square along Krasny Prospekt — Red Avenue — icicles hung from the giant Darth Vader-like statue of Lenin. A cluster of school children, swaddled against the cold, posed for a picture in front of the founder of the communist state. I wandered down Red Avenue, a wide boulevard flanked by gray concrete block buildings that seemed to stretch on forever. A convoy of military trucks stuffed with raw recruits rumbled down the street. Bundled in army-issued green coats, the soldier boys clutched rifles and looked as if they had just been snatched from the warm bosoms of their mothers. More fodder for the Afghan front. The last truck drove past, and one cherub-faced soldier, no more than a boy, waved and flashed me a peace sign. I waved back, and watched the convoy until the last truck turned a corner. The street was once again silent.

A phalanx of heavy clouds momentarily blotted out the sun; a bitter wind kicked up, and mean little pellets of snow fell. I turned up my collar and continued along the avenue. While the convoy was passing, I had noticed another man farther down the street who had also stopped. Instead of watching the trucks, though, he seemed to be watching me. I turned down a side street. The man followed, pacing me from about fifty yards, but rapidly gaining ground. I stopped, casually turned around and caught a glimpse of him darting into a building alcove just as the sun emerged from behind a cloud. Heart pounding, I walked on, trying to stay calm. In the reflection of a shop window, I clearly saw that he was following me. Could this finally be the KGB awakening to its task? I turned into a bookstore and pretended to browse. My stalker remained outside, thumbing through *Pravda*. The behavior was right out of a John le Carré novel, and I felt simultaneously exhilarated and terrified. I lingered in the store, pretending to browse. After purchasing a birthday card for my father, I left. The stalker followed. A surge of panic welled up inside of me. Without thinking, I turned down a narrower street. This was a mistake. The street was deserted. The footsteps grew louder. I glanced from side to side, but there was no place to run or hide.

A gloved hand touched my shoulder. I nearly jumped out of my skin. Terrified, I spun around and stared at my nemesis.

His haggard face was scarred by the untamed acne of a young man. A mangy mustache clung to his upper lip, and his dark eyes shifted as if he were looking for someone else. He wore a rumpled pea coat that had seen too many winters. A frayed ski cap, not one of the fur caps that most everyone wore to fend off the cold, was pulled cockeyed over his head. His wool gloves were patched. He was the antithesis of the superman KGB agent portrayed in cold war spy novels.

We eyed each other. I stood my ground, ready for anything, but now believing that nothing bad would happen. I was bigger and probably stronger, though certainly far less desperate.

"Where are you from?" he hissed in fractured English.

"The United States."

"Want to trade? Want to change money? I can change dollars and traveler's checks. I give good rate."

I was astounded that I, apparently the only tourist in Novosibirsk — certainly the only one wandering the streets at that particular moment — had been sniffed out by the city's only operating tout. The thought that this man could actually change a traveler's check seemed ridiculous. But that was beside the point. I already had too many rubles, and had no desire to acquire more. Prices in the restaurants were incredibly cheap, and there was no easy way I could convert my rubles back to dollars when I left the country. There was little to buy. Most store shelves were meagerly stocked. The only decent shops were the official state stores that catered to foreigners or high-ranking party officials, and required payment in hard currencies — U.S. dollars, German marks, or English pounds. Spending rubles was a major problem in the Soviet Union.

"Rubles are no good," I replied. "I need dollars. I have too many rubles."

The answer seemed to deflate the man.

"Ah, you understand the problem," he sighed.

We stood awkwardly for a few moments, two strangers in the cold, neither of us sure what to do next. At last, I stuck out my hand and introduced myself. As we walked down the street, he told me his name was Fedor, and that he worked for the local telephone company. When he heard I was from Seattle, he grabbed my arm.

"Seattle! It cannot be true. You are from Seattle!" he said. "Have you seen Larissa?"

"Who?"

"Larissa is my sister." From his back pocket, he fished out a worn billfold. He carefully extracted an identity card that contained a black-and-white photo of an unsmiling young woman. I could make out from the card that she was a history major at the University of Washington and lived somewhere on University Avenue. He withdrew the card after only a few seconds. I wasn't sure if he didn't trust me or was afraid that the fragile paper card would disintegrate in the arctic cold.

"We have not heard from her for many months. She is so far from her family, so alone. We do not know if she is well."

"I am a student at the school, too," I said, catching some of his enthusiasm and feeling a new sense of purpose. "I know the place well. Can I give her a message from you?"

Fedor was about to say something, when he spotted trouble. Two militiamen, ponderous shapes in gray greatcoats, had turned the corner and were swaggering down the street toward us. Fedor froze. He clutched my sleeve, but then let go. His face contorted in desperation, as if he wanted to tell me something of great importance, but could not find the words. He looked deathly pale. I thought he might faint.

"Quickly," I said in a whisper. I grabbed him by the shoulders to prop him up. "Tell me. You got to tell me now!"

"Nyet," he said weakly, then switched back to English. "There is nothing."

He tore himself away and was gone in an instant, a small dark figure disappearing down a narrow alley that I had not even noticed between the nearby concrete buildings. It was as if the city had swallowed him whole. Quickening my pace, I walked straight ahead, minding my own business. I remembered that the hotel was holding both my passport and Soviet visa. Without these documents, I was defenseless against questions the police might ask. The hotel was my sanctuary. I had to get back there. Stay calm, I told myself. Behind me, I heard the shuffle of feet, muffled by the freshly fallen snow. I fought back the panic impulse to sprint the final block.

The footsteps dwindled, leaving the street in silence. When I turned, I saw that the militiamen had disappeared, their faint tracks following the same alley in pursuit of the luckless money-changer. Heart pounding, I scurried back to the hotel and brushed past a clerk — one of my tormentors from the night before — who scowled as I rushed by. What would I have done if I had been caught? My few lines of Russian would not have bailed me out this time. I carried no identification, and I bore a striking resemblance to any member of the Afghani mujahedin. The outcome of this scenario was too horrible to contemplate. As for Fedor, I concluded he was a survivor, who knew these cat and mouse games only too well. Somehow, I knew he would survive.

I embarked on no more adventures that day. Instead, I slid off my Vasque walking shoes, turned on the television, and feel asleep watching a documentary on the siege of Leningrad.

In the morning Mrs. P., the French-speaking guide Mr. K. said would take me to the train station, was waiting. Cheerful beams of yellow sunlight filtered in through the lobby windows. It was a splendid day to leave Novosibirsk.

"Bonjour, Monsieur Goldstein," said Mrs. P.

"Bonjour," I replied, using most of my French vocabulary with that one word.

Mrs. P. looked like a character from a 1950s movie. She wore thick horn-rimmed glasses, and her dark hair was wrapped like a honey bun on top of her head. As I stowed my pack in the waiting car, Mrs. P. rambled in French about the fine weather that had descended upon western Siberia — or at least that's what I thought she said. Ivan, the alleged Italian-speaking driver, assisted with the luggage silently.

I had spent most of the previous evening studying the phrases Nina had written out for me, reciting the Cyrillic alphabet and reviewing my phrase book of archaic Russian. I cleared my throat. In my best Russian I said, "I ride the Trans-Siberian Express. I go to Irkutsk."

Mrs. P. and Ivan looked at each other in surprise. Then Mrs. P. turned to the backseat where I was making myself comfortable.

"You speak Russian," said Mrs. P., in perfectly good English.

"You speak English," I replied, also in perfectly good English.

"They said you could not speak English or Russian," replied Mrs. P. "They said you could only speak a strange dialect of Finnish."

Mrs. P. peered at me closely, as if examining a famous painting, but suspecting it might be a fake. She seemed perplexed.

"Are you from Lapland?" she asked, then added: "People have dark skin there. They race reindeers."

This latest bit of identity confusion flummoxed me. If they wanted me to be Lap reindeer racer, so be it, though I was tempted to say that the whole reindeer-racing thing was blown out of proportion. On the other hand, it was true our dialect of Finnish was incomprehensible — even to us. I nodded haphazardly, and this seemed to satisfy her curiosity. I, however, was still confused about why she wasn't speaking French.

"Mr. K. said he was the only English-speaking interpreter, and that you spoke only French," I said.

"I speak better English than French, but Mr. K. is the official English interpreter, and I'm the only one who can speak French," she replied.

We both pondered the absurdity for a moment. I shrugged. Mrs. P. smiled and resumed her French monologue.

After a five-minute drive, we turned into the sun-bathed parking lot of the Novosibirsk train station. The real Trans-Siberian Express with Rossiya clearly visible on the nameplate of each carriage was pulling into the station. The train was green like all the others, but the nameplates affixed to each carriage clearly identified the train as Rossiya. I turned to Mrs. P.

"Rossiya?" I asked, pointing to the train.

"Da," answered both Mrs. P. and Ivan. That was good enough for me.

Conductors leaned from the carriage doors, ready to set down footstools for embarking passengers. I shouldered my pack as Mrs. P. bade me bon voyage. I thanked her and Ivan for the ride, then hurried to the platform in search of my carriage. Finding it, I climbed aboard, turning to wave to Mrs. P. and Ivan, who were leaning against the car, smoking. Overjoyed to return to the relative sanctity of the train, I secretly hoped my compartment would be unoccupied. I needed time to digest the events of the past few days. If I must have a roommate, I hoped for another Nina.

Pack on my back, I struggled down the corridor, found my compartment, and yanked open the sliding door. Inside, grappling with a giant cabbage, sat Mother Russia herself, the babushka of babushkas.

13

Ghosts of Siberia

wakened from my short slumber by the hearty aroma of food, I focused my eyes in time to see an attendant ladling out something that looked and smelled delectable to Mother Russia, who sat ramrod-straight. I had recently completed my recital of random phrases to a roomful of Russian grandmothers, but after the commotion from my performance died away, Mother Russia had transformed back to an irritable old woman. While clenching a wooden spoon, she berated the food bearer with what sounded like complaints. As he left, I followed, tapping his shoulder, then giving my best "what about me" expression. The attendant, a portly young man whose girth suggested that he had succumbed to culinary embezzlement, shook his head gravely no.

The food cart people had become the bane of my existence. They roamed the train pushing giant stainless steel pots of bubbling mush at precisely the time my stomach enzymes were clamoring for sustenance. Not since the colonel and I broke bread nearly a week ago had I managed to snare one of these portable meals (the cold cutlet and bulgur did not count). Would the secret code ever be revealed?

As I turned back to my compartment, the attendant tugged at my shirt. "Go to the dining car. I will show you," he said in Russian. He parked his cart. I followed this pied piper of food, hopping over couplings that, as before, appeared ready to break apart at any second. As we reached the dining car, he turned to me and puckered his lips like a blowfish. For this small favor did this guy really want a kiss? On the lips! I stared at him dumfounded. The now familiar feeling of panic surged in again for yet another attack on my central nervous system, which had long since ceased to work with any degree of efficiency. I was about ready to tell him I liked women when he puckered a second time, accompanied by an exaggerated breathing in sound, and held two fingers in a "v" close to his mouth. I understood. Vastly relieved that I didn't have to give him a smooch, I indicated that I had left my spare pack of cigarettes in the compartment. Come by after dinner, I indicated.

The dining car was what I expected. What was once starched white linen was now spotted with stains of questionable origin. A pile of dirty dishes rested precariously on one table. I found an empty one and spread out my phrase book and the translation notes Nina had written for me. Attired in the black-and-white uniform of her profession, a waitress, who looked like she could have stepped out of a diner from the American Midwest, handed me a menu. When she saw my phrase book and notes, a smile spread across her face. She said something to the effect of "Wait, I'll be back." I almost expected her to return with a steaming pot of coffee and a blue plate special. Even better, she handed me a menu in three languages, one being English. If anyone deserved a smooch, she did. I confined my gratitude to a simple thank you.

At long last, I was in possession of the culinary version of the Rosetta Stone. The mysteries of Rossiya's cuisine lay open before me. With trembling fingers, I turned the laminated pages. On one page were a variety of meat dishes: roast, stroganoff, and something called beef shinks. On another were flocks of chicken dishes galore. Roast goose in sauce! Turkey with dumplings! On the next page: salads, wonderful beautiful salads. And what was this — alcohol! Beer, wine, and, of course, vodka to top off this cornucopia of delights. Perhaps Gorbachev's no-booze edict had not reached this far east. I pored over the menu, re-reading my choices, assembling a meal fit for a czar.

The waitress reappeared with her order pad in hand, ready to record every sumptuous detail of the feast of feasts. But I had barely said hello when I perceived an ominous presence nearing. Her friendly smile evaporated. The hairs on the nape of my neck pricked up. Her boss, a matron of significant proportions, loomed behind me. A meaty arm reached over my shoulder and snatched the menu from my hands. From the depths of an apron pocket, the matron unholstered a gigantic red ink marker. With sadistic delight she proceeded to write the word "off" across almost everything on the menu. "Nyet," she muttered, striking and slashing through the text. With a single bold X, she purged the entire alcohol section, chortling in loud, understandable Russian that booze was now prohibited on trains. This declaration was overheard by three grizzled men at a nearby table who glared at me as if implementation of the unpopular Soviet law was my fault.

After a few more seconds of frantic deleting, she returned the menu to me. With a click, she recapped the pen, smiled the smile of the victorious bully, then marched away. There was little left to choose from. Amid the bloodshed, I found two survivors in the dinner section: chicken noodle soup and beef stroganoff. The only appetizer was tomato salad. My waitress was sympathetic. No doubt she saw the disappointment in my eyes. As she left with my order, I thought I heard her tell me that she would instruct the cook to put an extra beef shink in my stroganoff.

As I glumly wrote in my journal, two men slid onto the seats facing me.

"May we join you?"

The speaker was the man with the droopy mustache who had helped translate for Mother Russia. The other man I had not seen before.

"My name is Yakov," he said, as we shook hands. "This is Anatoly. He doesn't speak English." In contrast to Yakov, who stood a stocky six-feet and was smartly dressed in blue jeans and a leather jacket, Anatoly was short and scrawny with a narrow suspicious face and matted brown hair. He took off his worn imitation leather jacket, revealing arms covered with tattoos. His eyes shifted nervously from object to object. His nose twitched, and his face was several days from its last shave. He was not a handsome man. We did not shake hands. I turned my attention to Yakov.

"Thank you for helping me with the old woman."

"It was nothing. She is crazy old woman."

Yakov fell silent as the waitress came by and started to hand him and Anatoly menus. But they motioned her away. They already knew what they wanted. There was no need to look at a menu that had nothing to offer.

"She is crazy, but one thing she said made me nervous," said Yakov. "It was the man from her village, the funny man. She said he was a Jew."

I didn't say anything. The primeval fear swelled up and lifted me into a high state of alertness. I was painfully aware of the anti-Semitism that prevailed throughout the Soviet Union, and its deep roots in Russian history. Siberia, I hoped, would be different. Could the miles of wilderness and permafrost absorb and dissipate Russia's latent anti-Semitism? I did not want to risk the wrong answer so throughout the trip I had carefully guarded my ethnicity. It no longer bothered me that I was confused for a number of nationalities. That was normal on most of my travels. It was a game I was willing to play to avoid trouble. Now I wondered if the game was about to end.

I looked into Yakov's clear blue eyes, then glanced at Anatoly, who, through the lens of my paranoia, was transformed into a Hitler youth. The mishmash of tattoos flexing on his arms morphed into swastikas. I feared what next might emerge from Yakov's mouth.

Yakov leaned across the table as if to tell me a secret. I prepared to assume my Finnish alias.

"What is your family name?"

I gulped, and briefly considered using my mother's maiden name of Gonzales — not exactly a common Finnish surname. But there was not enough time to fabricate a passable lie. I was stuck with the truth.

"Goldstein."

It was out now, in plain view. There was no place to hide.

"What is yours?" I retorted.

"Bernstein."

The name seemed to glide through my consciousness before it registered. The tension eased.

He knew. He knew all along. He just wanted to be sure.

"How did you know?" I asked.

"I can tell. You have the look; the look on your face when she said, 'He was a Jew and went away'."

"Did you think she might be anti-Semitic?" I asked.

"You never know. You can never be sure. We must be careful," he said. "That is why I try to switch with old woman. It is better that Jews be together."

"Well, truth be known, I'm actually only half Jewish," I admitted.

Yakov smiled. "So I am. Together, we are one Jew."

I reflected upon this.

"What about him?" I asked, nodding toward Anatoly, who certainly did not look Jewish.

"He is my business partner. He is okay."

Dinner arrived in small stainless steel bowls. The chicken noodle soup reminded me of home. The wilted lettuce and worn out tomatoes reminded me of where I actually was. It was not exactly the feast I had envisioned, but that did not matter now. As I ate, Yakov told me about himself. A thirty-year-old electrical engineer, he lived in a cramped apartment in Novosibirsk with his wife and young son and mother-in-law. He was on his way to Irkutsk to work on a problem at the massive hydroelectric dam on the Angara River. His mother, a teacher, had taught him English as a child.

"Is it hard being Jewish here?" I asked.

"It is better in Siberia than in Russia. I do not have a problem. Some of my friends have left for Israel. But Siberia is my home. Under Gorbachev life is better. I have a plan to open a petrol cooperative with Anatoly. It is possible now. Two years ago, it was not possible. Two years ago, we could not talk like this. It was forbidden to speak to foreigners. Now it is better. I am what you say, assimilated."

I heard this term frequently in Moscow from certain Jewish elites who had carved out comfortable niches for themselves in the Soviet hierarchy. Their internal passports branded them as Jews, but little else distinguished them from the glum masses. Meanwhile, the true believers and the disenfranchised were lining up to emigrate to Israel, the U.S., or any other place that would take them. The keeping of the faith was left to those too old to pose a threat to the state. During my week in Moscow, I had stood across the street from the crumbling synagogue on Moscow's Arikhipova Street and watched frail old men slip anonymously through its sacred doors. I wanted to go inside, to say that I had been there, but couldn't bring myself to move from my distant viewpoint. I wasn't one of them, though my ancestors may have been long ago. The arrival of a dark-complexioned stranger, not dressed in appropriate religious attire, and not understanding Hebrew — let alone Russian — would disrupt the frail institution and its adherents. Or, so I rationalized. So I stood across the street and watched. There seemed barely enough worshippers for a minion. I wondered who would carry on after they died.

"How did your family manage to get to Novosibirsk?"

"My father, he was from Minsk, comes first to Birobidzhan, then to Novosibirsk."

My ears perked up. Did I hear right? Did he say Birobidzhan? Birobidzhan was a place you didn't hear about. Certainly, it was not promoted in any of the tour books I had read. Birobidzhan was the capital of the long-forgotten Jewish Autonomous Region, chosen by Stalin as a place to relocate what he perceived as the troublesome Jewish population still concentrated in the Pale of European Russia. Designated a Jewish homeland in the 1920s by the Soviet government, the new Zion, as it was called by its promoters, enticed Jews by the train loads from the Pale, as well from the U.S., Europe, and South America. By the late 1930s, Birobidzhan was the center of a thriving Jewish community numbering in the tens of thousands. The city had synagogues. There was a Yiddish theater and newspaper. Farms that were whacked out of the swamps were the primary geographical feature of this forlorn land located just north of Manchuria, a convenient buffer against potential Chinese expansionism.

And then the dream died. To some it became the nightmare of arrest and deportation to the camps of the Gulag during Stalin's last demented years. Some intermarried and others drifted to more established Siberian cities or sought refuge abroad — any other place that would take them.

By the time I boarded the train in Moscow to begin my trip, Birobidzhan had been consigned to the scrap heap of Soviet history. My travel books mentioned almost nothing except for one seemingly reluctant sentence in the *Fodor's* guide: " ... Birobidzhan, capital of the so-called Autonomous Jewish Region," is " . . . a bleak and swampy area."[1]

"Do you know about Birobidzhan?"

Yakov looked up from his soup bowl, eyebrows furrowed.

"Yes," he whispered.

He did not volunteer any other information.

"Have you been there? Can you tell me about it?" I whispered back.

"There is nothing there. It is finished. They are gone," he said, still whispering, his tone reflecting that he wasn't enthusiastic about discussing this topic.

"Who's gone?"

"They left. Went away, some went to Israel. Those that are still there will leave. It is nothing but old people waiting to turn to ash and dust. Why do you ask?"

"I thought you would know because of your father," I said. "I think it is possible that some of my distant relatives may have come this way to live in Birobidzhan."

The last statement was pure speculation. I was fishing for information.

"My father died when I was a child."

He uttered the last sentence with grim finality. He did not volunteer any other information. My imagination flared to the worst: A knock at the door late at night. The internal security police, desperate to fill their quota of arrests, snatch the elder Bernstein as little Yakov looks on. Arrested for counter-revolutionary activity, he was probably herded into a freight car packed with other prisoners for one last trip along the Trans-Siberian line to the labor camps.

The train rumbled on through the moonless night, boring deeper into the heart of the Gulag. I could accept Birobidzhan as a forgotten memory. The Gulag, on the other hand, remained a living nightmare. Throughout the trip, I tried to reconcile the thought of its existence with the forlorn beauty of the land that unfolded daily beyond my window. The uninformed and naïve could ride the rails in blissful ignorance. But I did not have this luxury. I knew too much.

Diligent to a fault, I had prepared myself. Prior to leaving for the Soviet Union, I had devoured three massive volumes of Aleksandr Solzhenitsyn's *The Gulag Archipelago*. I memorized the maps showing the approximate location of the camps. In Moscow, I quizzed Ken and Carol, but they could shed little new light on the vast prison system. Yes, the flow of prisoners seemed to be ebbing, but no one knew for sure. During the journey, I strained my eyes against mud-streaked windows to glimpse what I thought might be the transit camps that served as holding pens for the prisoners before they were stuffed into boxcars and hauled away. Sometimes I thought I saw cement barracks surrounded by razor wire. But I could not be sure. Always, the train moved on, concealing the land's secrets as quickly as they were revealed.

While I spun possibilities, Yakov seemed lost in his own thoughts. Anatoly greedily wolfed down his stroganoff. At the end of the dining car, two men were locked in grim concentration over a game of chess. I looked out the window, but saw nothing but my own reflection.

In all probability, almost every passenger on the train knew of someone — a father, uncle, aunt, cousin, friend, or neighbor — who had disappeared into the Gulag. Solzhenitsyn said sixty million. Others claimed twenty million. What difference did it make? Out there in the frosty Siberian night wandered the tortured souls of millions of Mother Russia's children, while the living dwelt in a conspiracy of silence being broken each day with revelations spurred by the glasnost.

The last of the soup sloshed in the bowls to the rhythm of Rossiya's unsyncopated beat. A freight train thundered past on the opposite tracks. Yakov glanced out the window and seemed to ponder the passing blur. I wondered what cargo was hidden beyond the barred doors. The rumble shook Yakov from his pensive trance.

"You know," he said, as if he had been following my thoughts. "My father died of tuberculosis after he moved to Novosibirsk."

"You mean he didn't die in the Gulag?"

"No. Novosibirsk," said Yakov, slowly rising from the table. He seemed weary, as if the conversation had sucked away all of his energy. "I am tired. Perhaps I will see you in the morning." He walked out of the dining car. Anatoly followed.

I had been too hasty in my conclusion. The police had never come to drag Yakov's father away. He had left on his own, and died a natural death. Glancing out the window, past my reflection to the darkness of night, I saw the vague outline of trees whizzing by. In the distance, I glimpsed a faint glow, perhaps a lantern burning in a cabin. The light flickered, then was gone.

14

Baby Lenin

The frigid night air hissed through the crevices of poorly insulated windows and the open coupling that separated the last car of the Trans-Siberian Express from the wilderness. A rank of glowing embers and the occasional flare of a freshly struck match revealed the faces of the rough-hewed men huddled in the tiny vestibule. As if in a trance, they silently watched the track recede into the converging forest.

Someone offered me a cigarette from the now-familiar pack adorned with the head of a Siberian Husky. I gratefully accepted even though I didn't smoke. I needed something to keep warm; if not my body, why not my lungs. I also wanted to fit in. Melding into my surroundings was one of my standard operating procedures for travel.

The vile fumes that filled my virgin lungs triggered a coughing fit. "You shouldn't smoke so much," Yakov chided me. He, like the other men, belched smoke like the exhaust from a badly tuned car engine.

"I'm trying to cut back," I said, then whispered to no one in particular, "to about two packs a lifetime."

The somber tone of our earlier conversation had been replaced by an escalating discourse on the economic realities of Soviet life. It began in the dining car. Now it continued here at the end of the train.

"Bob, tell me, do you live in an apartment?"

"Yes."

"How much does it cost?"

I answered questions about food, utilities, and other everyday items. In return, Yakov told me he earned about two hundred rubles a month. That was about three hundred and fifty dollars at the official, though artificially inflated, Soviet exchange rate. The black market rate, a more realistic measure of the ruble's value, ranged between six and eight rubles to the dollar. That placed Yakov's salary at between twenty-five and thirty-three dollars a month. His wife's earnings of one hundred and fifty dollars a month supplemented their household income.

The numbers were pathetic. On the other hand, the monthly rent on Yakov's subsidized apartment was only twenty-eight rubles, while food cost another two hundred rubles. In the rough scheme of things, the socialized state seemed to be taking care of Yakov's basic needs. But once those needs were met, there wasn't much to look forward to. That was clear from the depressed mood that seemed to afflict the country's citizens. At times it seemed as though some omnipotent parent had grounded the entire population — no television, rock music, radio, CDs, or stylish clothes, just food and shelter. No wonder the Soviets cast an envious eye to the West, with its free-roaming citizens and its never-ending supply of pleasure-supplying gizmos.

"Bob, you are a student, yes? How do you manage to take such a big trip, all the way to Siberia?"

I tried to explain, but the more I delved into the intricacies of grants, fellowships, and savings from seven years of labor at a daily newspaper, the more I probably confused the issue. After all, this was a country with no banking system to speak of, at least not in the western sense with checkbooks, credit, and debit cards. Wealth was toted around in liter bottles of vodka or tattered rolls of rubles that were virtually worthless anywhere else in the world. From the look in Yakov's eyes, I could tell that the only thing that registered with him and Anatoly was that I had access to a lot of very good stuff.

The conversation turned to cars.

"I paid 5,000 rubles for a Zhiguli last year," he said. "But Soviet cars are junk. You know what car I would really like?"

"No, I don't."

"A Chevy."

"You got to be kidding."

"No Bob, the American Chevy is my favorite car. I want a Chevy with fins and a cassette player to play "California Girls." You know Beach Boys, Bob?"

A blast of cold air snuffed out my cigarette. Outside it began to snow. The small flakes swirled into the vestibule, dusting the grim men with delicate white specks. Someone flicked open a lighter and lit my stub. I didn't have the heart to tell Yakov that cassette players had not yet been invented when his favorite car was gliding around California's highways.

"Bob, when you lived in California, did you know the Beach Boys?" Earlier in our conversation I had mentioned growing up in California.

"No, I didn't get out much," I quipped.

With a gloved finger on the thin sheen of ice that had frosted the inside of the vestibule's side window, Yakov traced the outline of a Chevy with enormous tail fins.

"How much does such a car cost, Bob?"

"I'm really not an expert on cars, but I would guess $2,000," I said, deliberately low-balling the figure. At that moment, as I watched Yakov and the other Russians sucking on their cheap dog-brand cigarettes, the gulf between our worlds seemed a chasm that was growing wider as the conversation progressed. By valuing a classic Chevrolet with tail fins cheaper than the rattletrap Zhiguli — a hideous manifestation of Soviet central planning — I thought I could at least create the illusion that we were more alike than different. But scarcely after the words left my mouth, I knew I had made a mistake.

Yakov's face lit up like a pinball machine.

"Bob, do you think when you go back to Europe that you can buy a Chevy in Germany and drive across Poland to Lithuania? My brother-in-law can meet you in Vilnius to pick it up."

He must be kidding, I thought. But the look in Yakov's eyes, dimly reflected in the vestibule light, told me he was not. I imagined myself behind the wheel of a classic Chevy convertible with tail fins and white-walled tires. Beach Boys music blares from the radio, a surfboard juts from the back, accompanied by a pair of bikini-clad California girls perched deliciously on the vehicle's rear seat. Pale-faced Polish border guards gawk in absolute amazement as we drive up to the border. Nothing like this had ever crossed the frontier before. Ever.

"Yakov, that is the funniest thing I've heard all night," I said, slapping him on the back. He smiled weakly.

We finished our cigarettes and returned to the warmth of the train's corridor. Yakov invited Anatoly and me to his compartment, which, like my compartment in the next carriage, contained two cushioned benches facing each other. He opened a battered attaché case and pulled out a chocolate bar. With a decisive snap, he broke the bar and handed me a third. Anatoly, reaching with tattooed fingers, grabbed the other third.

We sat in awkward silence for a few moments. I welcomed the respite and hoped it would provide an opportunity to distract Yakov from his preoccupation with Western-made goods. As for me, I wanted to know what Yakov thought about Gorbachev's reforms, particularly their effects on the economy. Would the ruble be allowed to float on the world market? With Yakov heading off to repair some hydroelectronic doodad, surely he could offer an opinion on the potential adverse effects of the dam on Lake Baikal's fragile ecosystem. Should I dare mention the war in Afghanistan, what with the mounting evidence that the fighting was going badly, despite official propaganda that reported victory was at hand? And what about the consequences of glasnost, the talk of the West?

Yakov broke the silence.

"Bob, do you know Mick Jagger and the Rolling Stones?"

"What?"

"How about Michael Jackson?"

I answered as best I could. He seemed disappointed with my replies. It was as if I had let him down. In one respect, I was a pathetic representative of the popular image of the West. I had never met the Beach Boys. Mick Jagger was not my neighbor, and I could not count Michael Jackson as a friend. I did not own the latest electronic gear, and I drove a beat-up old pickup truck that would have fit in nicely in one of the many Siberian villages we passed each day. We lapsed into another awkward silence. The connection I had perceived with him earlier now seemed lost in the static of consumeristic babble and the naming of rock stars. Yakov rambled on about the videotape recorder he purchased during a trip to Japan. But I wanted to know how and why he had been allowed to travel there in the first place.

"Things are better now," he said, dismissing my inquiries with a wave of the hand. "But Bob, this VCR has a hi-fi component that is most excellent." And so it went, until at last we hit upon the one item that had reached icon status among savvy Soviet citizens. Anyone who was anyone owned a pair of blue jeans, including Yakov, who wore his proudly.

"Blue jeans cost between two hundred and two hundred and fifty rubles," he said, speaking of the latest fashion craze in the Soviet Union. "Two years ago, it was three hundred rubles."

Forking over more than an entire month's salary for a pair of pants seemed ludicrous.

"Bob, if you have blue jeans, I can buy them from you for a good price."

"Sorry, I really never cared for blue jeans," I said apathetically.

"You mean you are from America and you do not own blue jeans?"

"Actually, I have a pair at home, but I didn't bring them. I find them too stiff and tight. I'd rather wear other kinds of pants."

"You mean, Bob, that you are not presently using your blue jeans?"

"Yes, that's what I mean," I answered wearily.

Yakov had that look again, the same one he had when he described his scheme to procure a Chevy. His mind's wheels spun into action.

"Bob, when you get home, please send me your blue jeans. I will give you top price."

I laughed again. Yakov looked at me earnestly. I swallowed the last of my gift chocolate. Anatoly eyed me as if I was Levi Strauss himself.

"Okay," I said, pulling out the pen and small notebook I kept in my coat pocket. "Give me your address."

Yakov smiled.

"Bob, when you send the blue jeans, can you also send, for my son, a book on the karate. He loves the karate. Can you do that for me, Bob?"

I was growing annoyed with these requests. On the other hand, I felt I owed Yakov something for helping me with Mother Russia. Sending off a pair of blue jeans that I never wore and a kid's book on karate seemed a small price to pay for fostering Siberian-U.S. relations. I wrote in my notebook: "Buy book on karate." Yakov beamed.

A knock interrupted our little trading session. The door slid open to reveal the conductor, a brute of a man whose rumpled uniform looked like he had slept in it, and the portly kitchen attendant still sporting a food-stained shirt. A sprig of lettuce clung to the side of his head. Yakov waved the duo in. The conductor flashed me a mischievous smile that revealed a missing front tooth. He spoke to Yakov. When the conversation finished, Yakov turned to me.

"Sergei wants to know if you have beers?"

"Why would he think I have beers?"

Yakov relayed this question to Sergei, the conductor.

"He says he thought he saw you drink one earlier in the day."

Sergei mistook a can of mineral water I had purchased in Novosibirsk for beer. The cans looked similar. I explained this to Yakov, who translated. Sergei asked another question.

"He wants to know if you have Schnapps?"

"Why would I have Schnapps?" I said, shrugging.

Sergei looked disappointed. This worried me. A gut instinct alerted me that I needed to produce a gift, and soon. The conductor controlled access to the train, who got on and who got off. He was all-powerful and shouldn't be trifled with. Offending him carried potentially serious consequences. I racked my brain about what to do, then remembered the Camel cigarettes I had stashed in the back of my pocket after dinner. The problem was I only had one pack left, and I had promised it — sort of — to the kitchen attendant.

I reached into my back pocket and pulled out the cigarettes. The conductor and kitchen attendant gaped at the pack as if it were the Hope diamond. I handed it to the conductor, hoping the gift would ensure trouble-free passage to Irkutsk. The train was scheduled to arrive there early the next evening. The kitchen attendant shot me a murderous glance.

"Tell him he must share them with the kitchen attendant and Anatoly," I said.

Yakov translated. The three men nodded happily.

For a few awkward moments we sat in silence.

"Yakov," I asked in a forced effort to resuscitate the conversation. "Is there anything in the Soviet Union, in Siberia, that I would want to buy and take home? It seems that all you want are Western-made goods. There has to be something you guys have that is of interest to me."

Yakov translated the question to the other men who were about to get up and leave, no doubt eager to smoke the Camels. Yakov motioned for them to remain sitting on the opposite bunk, then leaned forward to confer with them in hushed tones of rapid Russian. This continued for several minutes. Sergei became agitated and kept on repeating "nyet." Yakov seemed to be trying to convince him of something. At last, Yakov looked up from the huddle.

"There is one thing that you should try to get," said Yakov. His voice had taken on a reverential tone. He leaned forward on the bench, as did the others. Our heads nearly collided in the center of the compartment.

"The baby. You must get baby Lenin."

"Baby who? What are you talking about?"

"Try to get the baby Lenin," said Yakov, his voice tinged with the strain of conveying a message that I was having trouble comprehending.

"You mean Lenin, the guy with the pointy beard? The guy whose statue is in every city, that Lenin?"

"Yes, that is what I try to tell you. But not the big man Lenin. You must get the baby Lenin, that is very rare."

"What are you talking about? Lenin's dead. I saw his body in the Kremlin Mausoleum a couple of weeks ago. He's no baby."

I recalled a grim morning in Moscow. Hundreds of Soviet citizens are lined up in front of the mausoleum, a low-slung bunker-like building on the flank of Red Square. They shuffle silently into the dark chamber. Inside, in a glass box, lies the great revolutionary himself, reposed in a dark suit. Illuminated by the filtered light of the chamber are the telltale goatee, the domed forehead, and the face with deathly pale skin that appeared to have the same texture as a wasps' nest. Lenin is a very small man.

The four men again conferred in hushed whispers. They seemed to be debating the depths of my ignorance. For my part, I wondered if I had stumbled into some strange cult that believed that Lenin had fathered an illegitimate son who lies mummified in an ice cave somewhere in Siberia. Was that what I was looking for? And how the hell would I get it past customs?

"Excuse me, comrade, but what is that sticking out of your bag?"

"It's nothing much, sir. Just the mummified remains of the baby Lenin. My pals on the Trans-Siberian Express thought it might make a nice souvenir."

Yakov nudged Sergei with his elbow. On this cue, the conductor reached inside his coat pocket and pulled out a small square object swaddled in a checkered handkerchief. He carefully unwrapped it, revealing a delicately painted and lacquered box. The three of us nosed in for a closer look. Perhaps it was the shrunken finger of baby Lenin? The conductor flipped open the clasp of the box, uncovering a tiny object wrapped in cloth. Carefully, he pulled off the cover.

Staring back at us, his face a radiant gold on a white background, fringed with the Soviet red star, was the likeness of a curly-haired brat.

"This is baby Lenin pin," said Yakov. "Very rare."

"Da, baby Lenin," echoed Sergei.

It all made sense now. My brain raced back to a conversation I had with Ken, my friend in Moscow. The day I arrived from London, still bleary eyed with jet lag, Ken showed me his collection of pins that celebrated various Soviet accomplishments, lionized the nation's leaders, or displayed the symbols of various organizations. The pins were traded like baseball cards in the U.S. As I surveyed the collection, neatly arrayed on a bulletin board, Ken told me about the baby Lenin pin that had taken on the status and scarcity of a Mickey Mantle baseball card. "If you see a baby Lenin, buy it. Don't ask what it costs, just buy it and I'll buy it back from you." It was the one pin missing from his collection. Shortly thereafter, the legend of the baby Lenin pin passed from my mind. I could not have cared less. Until now.

"How much do you want for it?" I heard myself saying.

Yakov translated. The conductor waved his arms as if warding off an evil spirit. He carefully wrapped up the icon and slipped it back into its case.

"Not for sale," said Yakov. "He saves for an investment."

The brief view of the brat, combined with the ceremony of unveiling it from the sacred box, had triggered something slumbering within the inner recesses of my brain. It was a single-mindedness that threatened to wreak havoc with my normal rational self. I suddenly wanted that pin as much as I had wanted the Willie Mays baseball card when I was a kid, and certainly as much as Yakov wanted a Chevy, the conductor wanted beers, and God only knew what Anatoly wanted. The urge was irrational, a long-dormant childhood impulse that had surfaced during this strange and stressful journey. It was just a pin, a small piece of cheap metal with a few dabs of red and white enamel in the visage of what looked more like Shirley Temple than Vladimir Ilyich Lenin, the mastermind of the Russian Revolution. Get a grip, I told myself.

But I could not get a grip. In the moments after Sergei had flashed his treasure, the baby Lenin had transformed itself into the Maltese Falcon. I had a touch of baby Lenin fever. But there was, I suspected, more to my desire than the urge to become the biggest baby Lenin collector on the planet. Every minute the train rolled deeper into the Siberian wilderness, it was becoming evident to me that the much-feared Soviet Union was nothing more than a gigantic Potemkin village, teetering on the brink of collapse. That conclusion was inescapable to anyone who had ever tried to buy anything in a Soviet store or check in unannounced at a hotel. This was a country that had repelled the Nazi invasion by incredible perseverance born from a national aptitude for suffering, but it could not manufacture a decent toaster, let alone an automobile. Now with computers, color televisions, and video recorders with hi-fi threatening to breach the Iron Curtain, the facade of the country was about to collapse. The Yakovs of the nation were sooner or later going to demand the good stuff, rather than depend on the kindness of strangers or hoard painted tin pins.

If Lenin's legacy was truly receding into history, then I wanted a piece of him before it disappeared forever. I could not think of a better souvenir of the death of the communist state than the rare pin of its founder as a baby. The great circle would be complete.

"Where can I get one?" I asked, trying to sound uninterested.

"Irkutsk. I think there is still a supply there. Look for a kiosk by the Angara River. Ask for The Baby."

I dutifully wrote this down. "Go to Angara River. Ask for The Baby."

"Got it," I said, tucking the trusty notebook back into my pocket.

Rossiya roared into a tunnel. The lights in the compartment flickered off briefly, basking the faces of my four companions in a ghostly glow from the fluorescent light in the corridor. Sergei fidgeted and seemed nervous, feeling his breast pocket to make sure that the precious baby was still tucked safely inside. Eyeing me warily, he rose and backed out of the room. He said something to Yakov, which in my mind was "you shouldn't have told him about the baby." The kitchen attendant puckered his lips at Sergei. I now knew he wanted a Camel, not a kiss. Anatoly continued to stare at me as if I were made of dollar bills. Yakov slouched pensively on the bench, looking as if he had just given away the last of his country's treasures. As he exited, Sergei motioned for the attendant and Anatoly. They followed him out the door.

I stretched my arms and faked a yawn.

"I think it's time for me to go to bed," I announced, rising to leave.

"Bob?" asked Yakov.

"Yes."

"You might find baby Lenin from a man named Valodia selling near the Angara River. He sells fish, sometimes socks, but he also sells pins, too. Please say that Yakov Bernstein sent you."

"No problem," I said. Then I turned and walked briskly down the corridor in the direction of my compartment. Irkutsk was still a day away. It couldn't come fast enough.

15

The Prostitute

backpack was slung over his shoulder, and he wore the haggard look of a traveler who had journeyed too long in a desperate land. He was lanky and young, probably in his early twenties. Stray strands of blond hair flopped across his forehead. His wire-rimmed glasses were slightly askew. And he looked absolutely miserable. I found him standing in the carriage's corridor as I backed out of my compartment, loaded down with my own pack. We were still a good thirty minutes from Irkutsk, but we both apparently had the same idea of preparing for escape as quickly as possible.

"Hello," I said in English. "Where are you from?"

"Norway," he replied, stiffly.

"I see we made it to Irkutsk," I continued gamely. "I can't tell you how glad I am to get off this train. I've been badgered all day by traders."

The young man rolled his eyes.

"I know," he continued in flawless English. "They are flies. They swarm around and persist, even if you wave them away or ignore them. After I sold my first pair of blue jeans, and then when I sold my cassette player, they still wouldn't go away. I sold almost everything I brought except the clothes I now wear."

His name was Svein, and he had spent the last few hours barricaded in his compartment at the opposite end of the train. I surmised that's why we had not met earlier.

Svein continued: "It felt like I was under siege. What was it like for you?"

"Yes," I said. "It was just like that."

I flashed back to an incident that morning. I had just finished breakfast and was walking back to my compartment when Anatoly slithered up to me. His beady eyes darted from side to side, checking to make sure no one else was in sight. He pointed to my digital watch. He wanted the watch with the same desperation that a starving man craves food. Before I could respond, he yanked out a wallet thick with rubles. He waved a fistful of notes in my face. I shook my head no. But no was not good enough.

"Vodka," he stammered, his eyes wild. "I give you vodka."

"Nyet," I said firmly.

Anatoly grabbed my wrist. I brushed away his hand and shoved my way past him.

"Vodka, I give vodka," came the croaking voice of desperation receding behind me as I jerked open the vestibule door and hustled to the next carriage.

Svein shook his head. It was the same for him, and it had left him exhausted.

"Anatoly," he muttered. "That's the chap who made off with my cassette player. He couldn't wait to get rid of his rubles."

The train squealed to a halt.

"Irkutsk!" shouted the conductor. Passengers poured from their compartments, struggling with suitcases, bags, and flimsy cases held together with lengths of frayed twine. The aisle clogged with humanity. Svein and I were mashed together, and carried along by the mob toward the open door. As we popped off the train onto the platform, I felt the cold invigorating slap of fresh air. I stood, enjoying the moment, dazzled by the brilliant array of stars and the emerging sliver of the moon. Svein wandered down the platform looking for our ride. Someone tapped me on the shoulder.

"You must be the gentleman from Finland." The voice, in heavily accented English, came from a neatly attired man wearing a goatee and thick horn-rimmed glasses. I turned and introduced myself. The man, who said his name was Georgi from Intourist, looked puzzled.

"That's curious, you don't look Finnish."

"I'm from Southern Finland. We tend to be a lot darker down there," I said.

"How interesting," he replied, taking my answer seriously. "I don't think I've ever met a Southern Finn before."

In the meantime, Svein wandered back to where I was standing.

"And this is the gentleman from Norway," I said, introducing Svein to Georgi. "We are both staying at the same hotel."

"Yes, of course, please follow me."

We fell in behind our minder. I slowed my pace so Svein and I were soon out of earshot.

"Look," I whispered. "They think I'm from Finland."

"This is impossible; you don't look anything like a Finn," said Svein.

"I know, but just go along with it for now. Things are going smoothly for me since I became a Finn. I'll explain later."

We clambered into a waiting van that lurched away from the train station, then turned onto a main road that bridged the broad expanse of the Angara River. Beyond the bridge, the lights of Irkutsk beckoned in the crisp night. I had a feeling about Irkutsk; that something good would happen here. Whether this was brought on merely by my own relief after finally escaping Yakov and his cronies, or from knowing that Nina lived somewhere within the twinkling lights of the city, I could not tell. Even if I never saw Nina again, Irkutsk, in its own right, was worth a visit.

Unlike Novosibirsk, a creation of uninspired Soviet central planning, Irkutsk's history was chaotic and colorful. Settled by Cossacks in 1661, it became an important Russian trading center and starting point for expeditions into the nether regions of Siberia. The city grew in spurts, and by the nineteenth century it had attracted a swashbuckling collection of exiles, miners, traders, and trappers. Fire destroyed most of the city in 1879, though it was quickly rebuilt thanks to the new wealth generated when gold was discovered along the Lena River, several hundred miles to the east. Freshly minted millionaires threw lavish parties in their newly constructed stone and brick mansions. The less rich caroused and gambled in numerous drinking dens. Crime was rampant, with the garrote being the tool of choice among criminals who snared unsuspecting travelers caught alone in dark alleys. Not surprisingly, Irkutsk was the last major Russian city to succumb to the Bolsheviks, forever curtailing its carefree days as the Paris of Siberia.

We met for dinner in the hotel that night.

Svein looked up from the chicken carcass. A thin stream of grease had collected in the cleft of his chin. I sucked the last strings of meat from a wishbone.

"Bob, are you still hungry?"

I grunted in the affirmative.

"Let me pay for both meals or even another if we are still hungry."

"I got money, I can certainly pay for my share," I said.

"It's these rubles. I got to get rid of them."

Reaching into his back pocket, Svein pulled out a wad of currency an inch thick. He yanked out another bunch of loose bank notes from an inner jacket pocket. The rubles in various denominations lay scattered on the table.

"Like I told you, the traders were everywhere, very persistent."

On the advice of friends in Norway, he had changed only ten dollars at the Soviet Bank in Moscow. But in his zeal to trade, and perhaps bedazzled by the immense profits accumulating, he had forgotten one important rule: travelers were not supposed to end their trip with more rubles than when they started. That would arouse suspicion of black market trading. It was also illegal to take rubles out of the country. Like a parent explaining some incontrovertible fact of life to his child, I relayed this news to Svein.

"What am I going to do?" he said, holding his face in his hands, the quiet satisfaction of gorging on chicken now replaced by the possibility of a fifteen-year term in a Siberian labor camp.

"How long will you be in Irkutsk?" I asked. "Maybe you could load up on fur caps and warm clothes."

"I'm leaving for Beijing tomorrow on the Trans-Mongolian Express," he replied. "I will not have time to buy anything."

He was probably right. We were not far from the Mongolian border. Once he was on the train, there would be no opportunity to shop. He was stuck with the worthless currency.

"I guess I'll let you pay for dinner and beer," I said, helpfully. "Beyond that, I'm not sure how fast one can spend a pile of rubles in the next twenty-four hours."

We ordered another round of chickens. The waitress did not blink an eye. She had seen this before: travelers desperately dumping rubles, looking to buy anything edible. And in a Soviet restaurant, that was a challenge. I checked the menu. If my math was correct, we could eat two chicken dinners each for breakfast, lunch, and dinner for an entire month and still have money left over. That extrapolation, of course, assumed there were enough chickens to go around.

After dinner number two, we waddled over to the hotel lounge, hoping to off-load more rubles. A balding, gnome-like man who bore a resemblance to Yoda hunched over a beer and muttered to images flickering on a black-and-white television suspended over the bar. A couple of businessmen in rumpled suits lingered at a nearby table. A few sinister-looking leather-jacketed figures lurked in the far reaches of the room. The bartender, wearing a white shirt and vest, nonchalantly toweled shot glasses that appeared to be already dry.

Svein and I ordered a couple of Heinekens. When Svein pulled out a ten-ruble note, the bartender raised both hands as if being robbed.

"Sorry, mate," said Yoda with a distinctly Australian accent. "The ruble's not worth kangaroo shit. They'll only take hard currency."

Svein groaned. He stalked off to find a table. I paid for the beers with some British pounds I had been hoarding for an emergency. As far as I was concerned, this qualified. As I fished out the coins, I glanced at the television, curious to see what was so interesting. Fire trucks were parked in front of an apartment block. Smoke poured from the windows. A couple of harried ambulance attendants came bustling out the door. The camera caught a glimpse of an old man, comatose on a stretcher.

"Bloody shame," muttered the Australian. "Been happening all over Moscow."

"What?" I asked.

"Damn televisions. The Soviets can't make a decent TV. The picture tubes have been blowing up. Leading cause of fires in Moscow this year. Bloody TVs are exploding all over the city. Just think, some poor old bloke who fought his heart out during the Great Patriotic War is sitting on his couch watching the Vremya (The World News), when suddenly there goes the bloody tube. Next thing he knows, he's a friggin' Molotov cocktail."

I wasn't quite sure what to make of this news. I slowly backed away from the television.

"It's true, mate. Stay away from those Soviet TVs. It's KABOOM time!" he yelled, as I back-pedaled to the table Svein had secured.

Svein drank like a fish. I had barely sipped my first Heineken when he had polished off his initial round. He bought a second and a third in quick succession. Beer loosened him up a bit, the Scandinavian reserve dissolving with each swig. I fought off drowsiness while Svein fidgeted. I could tell something was bothering him.

"What is it?" I asked. "You look like you are about to explode."

"Bob, you're the first person in a week I've found that I can really talk to. I must tell you something. I must know your opinion." He chugged his beer, then in short clipped sentences he told me the story of how he came to be sitting in this bar.

He had fallen in love during his final year at the University of London. Her name was Sophie. She was two years his senior, originally from Sweden, but had spent most of her life in Britain. Svein pulled out a picture of a woman with honey-gold locks cascading down her shoulders. An Ingrid Bergman look-alike, she was dressed in a traditional Scandinavian costume — long dress, red apron, and black petticoat.

"We met at this festival in a mountain village," he explained. Her flawless face smiled warmly into the camera. Svein stood shyly at her side. She looked angelic, he bashful and awkward. They fell in love and followed each other to graduate school at Oxford. They moved in together. That's when the trouble started. Squabbles, mostly over petty issues, erupted without warning. "She would never put the cap back on the toothpaste," he said. "I couldn't stand it. She would mush it down and squeeze the tube in the middle."

But there was more to it than that. She wanted to travel and study in China. She planned to go for a year. She wanted him to go with her. But what would he do in Beijing for a year? "She always does things in a big way, never in a small way. Why not go for a few months and see what it's like? Is this not reasonable?"

I tried my best to listen. But I was dreadfully tired, and while the beer had unlocked the heart of my Norwegian companion, it only increased my drowsiness and disorientation. My mind wandered in random directions. I pondered my clean underwear supply, a logistically complex issue because I couldn't remember the last time I had actually changed my clothes. Did I have one pair or two pairs left? I had the sudden urge to dash up to my room and check.

The picture of the bright handsome couple led me to speculate about my own appearance. I hadn't shaved or trimmed my mustache in more than a week. I wondered if my nose hairs, left unchecked, were dangerously overgrown and emerging from my nostrils at that very moment. A hideous image flashed through my mind. I saw myself as a hairy simian-like creature wreaking havoc through the dark city, lovely maidens fleeing from my path while pitchfork-totting peasants hunted me down like a wild beast. "There he is. Get him. Watch out for those nose hairs! Kill the monster!"

Svein had stopped babbling. Had he asked me a question?

"Ah," I stammered, surfacing to the present. "Makes sense to me."

"Yes!" exclaimed Svein, slamming down his beer on the table. "You do understand. Why couldn't she be like you?"

No, no, I thought, you don't want Sophie to be like me. Don't you realize you are sitting in a Siberian bar with a man who is preoccupied with his nose hairs?!

Apparently he did not. The story continued. There were exams, problems with money, and a big argument over something — he couldn't remember what. Then Sophie was gone to distant, exotic, Beijing. "If you love me, you will come in the fall. If not, then we will go our separate ways." That's what she told him. Svein rotted in his flat in the cold damp of the English autumn. He missed her terribly. Unable to study, he returned to Oslo. A letter came. In it she hinted she might have met someone else. She spoke of an American. They visited the Great Wall together. They were friends; at least, that's what the letter said.

"Friends," he said sarcastically. "You know what that means?"

But I had drifted off yet again. Svein's head had transformed into a giant cinnamon roll, the kind that comes out of a can. I really liked that kind, but never had the patience to bake them the full fourteen to eighteen minutes as specified. Anticipating the moment when those sweet morsels would dissolve in my mouth was too much to bear. I would tear open the oven door, grab the soft unbaked rolls, and in a gluttonous orgy stuff them into my mouth. I couldn't stop until I was satiated. I knew it was wrong and that gastronomical consequences would follow. But I ate them anyway. I was younger then and didn't have much self-control.

"Bob . . . Hello."

"Oh right, ah. Let's see, yeah . . . I really hate it when they want to be friends. They do that in Norway, too?"

Svein seemed perplexed by my response. I fought to pay attention.

He said he called her. Over the crackle and pop of long-distance phone lines, he told her he would come. She said that if he came soon, everything would be as it was before. But there were obstacles. Airfares were outrageously high. Friends suggested the train, starting in Helsinki, then on to Leningrad. In Moscow he could hook up with the Trans-Siberian, riding it as far as Irkutsk, then connect with the Trans-Mongolian to Beijing. He just needed to pack extra blue jeans and other concealable consumer knick-knacks that the Soviet masses were so desperate to buy. That would finance the trip.

"Hell of a plan," I said, my mind now plotting for the right moment to politely excuse myself and head off to bed.

"So, now I am here, talking to my friend from Finland. In two days, I will be in Beijing. I will be with Sophie," he said, his demeanor brightening.

I thought that in two days I would be back on that wretched train, searching for spirits of the past that probably didn't exist. And even if they did, there would be nothing waiting for me at the station in Khabarovsk, the end of the line, except the cold embrace of the Siberian wind.

"To Sophie," I said, raising my beer half-heartedly. Our bottles clinked together.

I was about ready to begin my "it's been a nice evening, but I'm really tired and have a nice trip to Mongolia" line, when we were both momentarily distracted. Across the room, lit by a shaft of light that marked her entrance, I noticed first her long shapely legs that tapered into dangerous-looking spiked heels. Her skirt barely concealed her thighs. A tight-fitting black blouse amplified her breasts. She glided across the room like a bird of prey — a condor — surveying the scenery. Alighting on a nearby barstool, she gave her head a sassy shake, freeing tangles in a waist-length mane that was frosty white. She snapped open a shiny black purse and pulled out a silver cigarette lighter. Then she scanned the room while blowing perfect smoke rings that dissipated like ghosts into the gloom.

The pickings were slim.

Condor squinted through the blue haze in our direction. The woman had distracted both of us. Self-consciously, we turned toward each other, then grabbed for our beer bottles. As I pretended to drink from an empty bottle, I had the unmistakable feeling that she was staring at us. But when I snatched a glance in her direction, she was still puffing smoke rings and staring indifferently into space.

I decided to hang around for a while longer.

"Bob, can you tell me about this woman?" asked Svein. "I thought prostitution was outlawed in the Soviet Union."

I had heard the same thing. Apparently, perestroika was loosening up more than just the economy.

"Well, she's certainly not a Young Pioneer," I quipped.

We both stole glances at the woman.

Svein took a long swig of beer, nearly draining the bottle. God, could that guy drink. A bemused smile crossed his face.

"She reminds me of a movie I once saw when I visited a friend in Sweden. It was called the *Super Vixen Women from Outer Space* or something like that. It was about this planet inhabited by beautiful women. They were crazy for sex because all the men on their planet were extinct. These women would climb into spaceships and fly to Earth, where they hung out in bars just like this. They would lure lonely men up to their spaceship, have sex with them, and then kill them. I think they were trying to create a new race of men who would do whatever they wanted. But for some reason the plan just wasn't working."

I wasn't quite sure why I became agitated over the premise of this ridiculous movie, but I couldn't help myself.

"It wasn't working out because they were killing the men. Did they think of that?" I growled. "Wouldn't it have been better if they had returned the men to the bars and zapped their memories instead? I see no need for killing here."

Svein stared at me.

"I think they needed their organs," he said.

"Which organs?"

"Kidneys, livers, those kinds of organs. Look, Bob, don't get so upset; it was a stupid movie. Okay?"

"Sorry, I guess I'm just tired."

He drained his beer. I offered to buy him another, but only if he promised it would be his last. From my pocket, I fished out my last couple of pound coins and sauntered to the bar.

When I returned, Svein had spread his ruble hoard on the table.

"What am I going to do with these?" he chortled. "So rich, yet so poor."

"Svein put that money away!" I snapped, like a father scolding a child. I couldn't stick around to make sure he did; nature was making a call. I got up and headed for the bathroom, thinking I would escort my friend to his room when I returned.

I did my business, washed my hands, and as I rinsed I looked into the cracked mirror above the sink. The face staring back at me was gaunt, overgrown with an untamed beard, and the hair matted with a gaggle of unruly curls. My red parka was pockmarked with food stains. But it was the bloodshot eyes, pupils blacker than coal that startled me. I stared numbly at the reflection and wondered who the hell I had become. And for a moment I actually thought I was the man I had invented, a possible relative, left behind, heading east to save himself.

I made my way back to the lounge.

"Hey, mate, someone's taken your place." It was Yoda.

I strained to see through the dim light. What I saw was not good. Condor was perched in my chair, now moved dangerously close to Svein. One arm was wrapped seductively around his shoulder, while her other hand wandered below the table. She cooed into his ear. Svein, what are you doing, I thought; not now, not after you've come all this way.

I should have left then, minded my own business, returned to my room, shaved, and prepared for tomorrow. That would have been the smart move under the circumstances. But the hardened stranger that I saw reflected in the bathroom mirror was now in charge. My legs, with slow deliberate steps, carried the rest of my unwilling body to the table. My gaze, like radar, locked onto the woman. Sensing trouble, she turned and glared at me. And for a moment, the briefest of moments, I remembered what it was like — the caress of a woman — and how long it had been.

"Sophie," I overheard Svein whisper to her.

My God, he thinks she's Sophie. I looked at the long hair, not quite the right color but close enough, and the outline of her figure. Perhaps there was a similarity. It didn't matter; in his drunken haze, Svein could have thought this was his girlfriend or at least a reasonable proxy. The rubles were still spread on the table like the pot in a friendly poker game. The last of four beer bottles stood empty. The woman tamped her cigarette into one of them.

I now stood before them. Condor turned and blew smoke in my face.

I cleared my throat as if preparing to deliver a speech. I spoke in measured tones my mother would have been proud of.

"Svein, I think we should leave now."

He looked at me passively, as if in dream. Condor stroked his hair. Her breast nuzzled the side of his face. Her other talon was still under the table.

"Svein!" I said more emphatically. "This is not Sophie. Nyet Sophie." I waved my arms like a football referee signaling an incomplete pass.

Condor turned toward me with viciousness that could kill. She hissed something in Russian that could have only been "Get lost!"

That seemed like an excellent idea, but the stranger who had taken over my body wouldn't budge.

"Svein, please! This is not Sophie. You will see Sophie in two days; just hang on, buddy, for another two days."

I wondered why I was pleading with Svein when he seemed so lost. This really was none of my business. If Svein wanted an evening of pleasure, why not let him have it. He certainly could afford it, unless the hookers didn't take rubles, either. Then I remembered how he talked about Sophie and how envious I was of

him for having such an opportunity. I could feel the vague stir-
rings of anger upwelling from deep inside of me. If he hadn't told
me the story about Sophie or shown me the picture, I would not
have cared. But now I cared. My own relationship with Ann was in
shambles. Each day as the train moved farther east, the gap
between us widened. For me, there was no going back. But Svein
had made the decision to save his relationship. He was almost
there, only another day or two on the Trans-Mongolian Express
and he would be back in Sophie's arms. If Svein was anything like
me, he would never be able to live with himself, nor fool Sophie if
he succumbed to the condor. Sophie would know. She would know
the minute he stepped off the train. It would be over for him; he'd
be lost in the middle of China, sent packing back across the
Mongolian wastes, back to Siberia.

"Svein," I said, touching him gently on the shoulder. "This is not
Sophie." Then, I remembered something that might be helpful.

"For crying out loud, Svein, she's a super vixen woman from
outer space!"

A quirky smile crossed his face. Like a zombie, Svein rose slowly from the chair, disengaging himself from condor woman,
whose poisonous glare could have felled a giant. I swept up the
rubles and stuffed them into his coat pocket, but held back a ten-
ruble note from the stash.

"Here," I said to the condor, as I tossed the note on the table. "For
lost business." She snatched the note, wadded it up, and fired a fast-
ball that bounced off my chest.

I put my arm around Svein's shoulder and half escorted, half
pushed him toward the door, our retreat accompanied by a barrage of
curses. I glanced back before we exited to make sure Condor wasn't
about to plunge a knife in my back. But she was already gliding back
to the barstool, retrieving the ruble note and tucking it into her
blouse. She primed herself for easier prey.

"That's how to handle 'em, mate," yelled the Australian.

We left the hotel and stumbled across the street to a promenade
bordered by a low stone wall that protected the walk from the

black, swirling waters of the Angara River. In the moonlight, I could see chunks of ice flowing swiftly downstream. Soon the river would freeze solid. An icy breeze stung my face. A couple embraced a few hundred feet downstream from us, their silhouette prominent upon the walkway. Svein leaned over the stone wall as if he was about to be sick. For a long time, the only sound was the river and crunching of the ice flows. The bracing air seemed to slap Svein back to reality.

"Bob," he said, his voice still slowed by alcohol. "I lost my mind in there. I really did think she was Sophie, but only for a moment."

Svein turned to face me, his back leaning against the wall.

"I have a friend who likes to tell my fortune. She said someone from Finland would help me on my trip."

"You know," I said emphatically, "I am *not* from Finland. I don't drink enough to be a Finn."

We started walking back to the hotel. Svein stiffened.

"Wait!" he shouted. He turned and raced back to the embankment. For a horrible moment, I thought he was going to hurl himself into the icy river. I ran after him, but slipped on the ice and belly flopped on the sidewalk, skidding on my stomach across the surface like a penguin. By the time I reached Svein, the last of the liberated rubles fluttered lazily, like fat snowflakes, sinking from sight into the channel. A few stray notes blew back to the promenade, but Svein gathered these and gleefully hurled them back into the abyss. Some day they would reach the Arctic Ocean.

"I hope you saved a few," I said, wearily.

"Yes, that's exactly what a Finn would say," he said, laughing, as we walked back to the hotel.

16

An Authentic Village

he van blasted down a lonely ribbon of frosted pavement that disappeared into a thick fog. Through the sheen of ice that formed on the inside of the window, I could just barely see the skeletal outline of trees. This was the road to Lake Baikal. At precisely that moment, though, I feared it was really taking me directly to the frozen version of hell.

Sharing this delightful journey with me were four other travelers. All of us had signed up that morning for the day trip. For me, that meant prying myself out of bed after my bizarre evening with Svein. The excursion to Baikal would at least put some distance between the condor woman and me, in case she came hunting for the rest of her fee.

Just before we started, Alexei, our guide, warned us that the van's heater was broken. He suggested that we might want to return to our rooms and put on every piece of clothing we possessed. We followed these wise instructions, returning to the van one by one, clad in a colorful array of parkas, down vests, and mufflers.

"How cold will it get?" demanded a woman with a Spanish accent. Her dark hair was balled into two giant buns that, from a distance, resembled Mouseketeer ears. I quickly learned that her name was Carmen. She and her husband, Jorge, were from Peru.

"I think maybe zero degrees now. Once we start, with the wind, I think perhaps minus two," said Alexei, helpfully.

This news did not please her. She relayed the information to Jorge, who stood shivering nearby, then added an editorial comment in Spanish that roughly translated into "Nothing fucking works in this country. This is a very stupid country. Why did you bring me here?" Poor Jorge shrugged and continued shivering in silent misery, while I watched small ice crystals form on his mustache and eyebrows.

Alexei, an officious and enthusiastic young man with short-cropped dark hair and serious eyes, appeared immune to the cold as he checked our names off the list on his clipboard. Besides the Peruvians, there was Andrew, a white-haired gentleman from Cornwall who wore a deerstalker with fur-lined earflaps. He and I had talked briefly in the lobby. He told me he was looking forward to what he called "his pilgrimage." His grandfather had been sent here in the 1890s to help reassemble a steamship, which had been built in Scotland, then disassembled and shipped to Lake Baikal. The ship was used to ferry the Trans-Siberian Express across the lake because the civil engineers at the time thought it too difficult and expensive to build tracks around its mountainous shores. "I wanted to see the famous lake that grandfather talked about before I was too old to take this kind of trip," he told me.

Rounding out the crew was a shy and fragile-looking girl who introduced herself in a whisper as Moon from Auckland.

After roll call, we squeezed into the van. Alexei and the Peruvians sat in the row behind Boris, the driver. I sat in the back, sandwiched between Moon and Andrew. Boris turned the key. The engine cranked, but did not start. He pumped the gas pedal, but the motor continued to labor. The five of us sat in silent anticipation, as if we were astronauts ready to blast off to the moon, but not sure whether the rocket would really get us there. Finally, the engine fired. Boris slammed down on the accelerator. The van lurched onto the main road, which was cloaked with freezing fog. I wondered if we would make our destination or wind up as filler in the back section of *The New York Times* — "Tourists Turned to Popsicles in Siberian Van."

Once under way, Alexei proceeded to give us the chamber of commerce pep talk about the wonders of Irkutsk, followed by a recitation of numerous production figures. He was particularly proud of the city's fur exchange, which required the slaughter of enormous numbers of rodents to fuel the world's demand for fur hats and coats.

"Those poor animals. It's so cruel," whispered Moon. No one seemed to hear this comment but me.

"Many visitors do not realize the large size of Lake Baikal," continued Alexei, reaching the formal part of his spiel, the part where we would collectively remember why we had chosen on our own free will to sit in this icebox on wheels. "Does anyone want to guess?"

I had read the guidebook. I knew the answer. But I kept my mouth shut because I didn't want to become the group pariah ten minutes into the trip. I imagined Carmen remarking under her breath how Americans always thought they knew everything. She was that kind of woman. I kept silent.

Alexei answered his own question. "If you drained the lake, then with magic power directed all of the world's rivers here, how long would it take to fill? I will tell you how long. More than one year!"

There was deathly silence from the tourists, who were no doubt trying hard to picture unfrozen rivers of any kind flowing into a lake we had yet to see. Perhaps my comrades had already frozen to death. I checked around. Little snorts of fog still issued from the nostrils of my fellow travelers.

"Wow," I said, a bit too late to sound authentic. "That's amazing."

Encouraged, Alexei continued.

"It holds more water than five of your seven Great Lakes in America," he said, enthusiastically. I thought about asking him to name the five, but decided not to play the role of wiseass.

Alexei continued: "There are many unique species found only in Lake Baikal. This is the only freshwater lake in the world with seals. They are called nerpas, and if we are lucky we will see one. That would be a very good omen."

"Are they cute?" asked Moon.

The question perplexed Alexei. He conferred with Boris. The word apparently threw him off.

"This word cute ... "

"Handsome, good-looking creatures with kind faces and friendly eyes," answered Andrew patiently. "Like the Misha Bear symbol your country adopted for the Olympics. That kind of cute."

"I understand now," said Alexei. "Yes, I believe they are what you call cute."

Alexei continued his recital of Baikal's flora and fauna, including a description of an unusually hapless fish called the Big-Eyed Golomyanka. "This fish has only two big eyes, a backbone, and a lot of fat ... " Apparently, Golomyanka occasionally got trapped in unpredictable upwellings. Because of the rapid change in pressure, the fish exploded when it surfaced, leaving great globs of fat to wash up on Baikal's beaches.

"This fish with the big eyes reminds me of your fat brother, Carlos," whispered Carmen to her husband. "Except this fish doesn't drink beer and watch football all day." Jorge grimaced, but said nothing.

"I suppose if we see a goo slick on the beach, that is a bad omen," said Andrew in jest.

"It is not an omen, it is just a pool of fat. There is no significance to it," replied Alexei, seriously. The digression seemed to throw him off. He had been building to a climax. After a pause — his mind seemed to be searching for a passage in a well-read book — he continued.

"The lake is also full of omul, the special fish like salmon that is found only in Siberia. For lunch, you will eat omul!"

I'm not sure whether we were supposed to "ooh and ah" or break into wild applause at the privilege of picking morsels of meat

from the skeleton of an omul, a fish known for its bountiful supply of small needle-like bones.

The van rumbled on. The passengers sat in silent indifference. I
waited for Carmen to make another wisecrack about which relative of Jorge's resembled an omul. But she said nothing.

"That sounds very good," I said, in an attempt to rescue the
beleaguered guide from the oppressive silence.

"I've heard that the lake has become dreadfully polluted over
the last couple of years," declared Andrew. "Can you tell us anything about that?"

Good question, I thought. I wondered whether Alexei would
deny it, skillfully shifting to the argument that whatever little
pollution wound up in Lake Baikal was nothing compared to the
massive dumping of toxic wastes the U.S. and its capitalist lackeys
were foisting on hapless Third World countries.

Alexei was silent. He pondered the question. The young man
was obviously thinking of a clever retort. He turned to face us.
The officious look faded, replaced by a pained expression. In a
hushed voice, he spoke with a passion that was absent from his
earlier tone.

"The pollution is terrible, very terrible. Every year the pulp
mills dump more waste into the water. The omul stock declines.
The nerpa colonies are threatened. We've tried to stop it. We've
pleaded with Moscow."

I couldn't believe what I was hearing. I had expected Soviet tour
guides to stick to the party line that all was wonderful in the
workers' paradise. To do otherwise posed significant personal risks,
at least that was the impression I had packed away in my mind.

"Is there an environmental movement here?" I asked.

"Oh yes. It's small, but growing. We are making ourselves heard,
but the country has so many problems besides pollution that it is
difficult to get anyone's attention."

Alexei described a system of enticements meant to lure workers
to Siberia from the relative comforts of the European end of the
Soviet Union. The labor was needed to build cities in the wilderness,

which, in turn, fed the mines, factories and sawmills that turned the land's bountiful supply of natural resources into useful products. But now those incentives were being withdrawn, and with it the lure needed to keep workers in the frozen hinterlands. Factories were abandoned and those that continued to operate could not be maintained. Existing plants sought shortcuts to make their production quotas, inevitably contributing more waste by-products, albeit from a system that already produced more pollution than the fragile ecosystem could absorb.

"I cannot believe you are telling us this," I blurted out.

"Things have changed in the last year under Gorbachev. I am not afraid to speak my mind anymore. Besides, we are a long way from Moscow."

As Alexei spoke, the road climbed onto a high plateau interspersed with frozen marshes and stands of pine and larch. The fog lifted, revealing trees and shrubs coated in a fine layer of ice. Sunlight reflected off the branches in a stunning display of prismatic light. I stared in awe at the crystal forest, half expecting fairies with magic wands to float among the trees. Even Alexei halted his lament to watch.

"Look," said Moon. "You can see where the elves have made their campfires."

She pointed to the wisps of white clouds floating among the trees. She had been so quiet and unobtrusive that at times I almost forgot she was there. A waif of a girl, with a splatter of freckles on her pallid skin, she appeared to be no older than a teenager, but was probably in her early twenties. She wore a knee-length dress adorned with tiny yellow smiling moons. Over this was a thick down vest. A gigantic muffler was wrapped around her neck. For most of the first thirty minutes of the journey, Moon gazed out of the window, humming quietly to herself. Occasionally, she would crinkle her nose, as if sniffing the air for a mysterious scent.

While Andrew and Alexei resumed their intense discussion on the environment, I turned to Moon, hoping to draw her into a conversation.

"What brings you to Siberia?" I asked.

"My spirit guides," she said. Her voice was a soft whisper, barely audible over the drone of the van's engine.

"What are spirit guides?"

"They are your own personal guides. They make things happen for you, and give you ideas. Some spirit guides are good; others are mischievous. But they always try to keep you from harm's way."

"Do I have a spirit guide?"

"Oh yes. Everyone has spirit guides."

"I see," I said. In another place and time, I would have cynically dismissed Moon's spirit guides as sheer nonsense. But now I wasn't sure. Too much had happened in the past week for me to dismiss her comments about the spirit world. My rescue by the beautiful Nina in Novosibirsk, the day of the magic shoes, and my witness of Svein's redemption were events that almost seemed more predetermined than fortuitous.

I felt a nudge in the ribs from Andrew.

"She's a bit daft," he whispered.

I ignored this and returned my attention to Moon. I told her I had recently begun to believe that a long-lost relative might have come this way many years ago. I had no evidence that such a person existed, other than the speculation that germinated after Mother Russia had described the funny man. It was ridiculous, I knew. But what did she make of this?

"May I see your palm?"

She gently took my hand in her long slender fingers, carefully unfolding them as they had been wrapped in a tight fist for warmth.

"Oh, dear me," she gasped.

"What is it?" I asked, alarmed.

"I'm not sure. This is a very unusual pattern."

She studied my hand, tracing with her finger the creases that crisscrossed my palm like rift zones. I noticed a dab of glitter painted on her fingernail. Her touch felt slightly erotic.

"When is your birthday?"

I told her. She gently put my hand down, reached into her day-pack, and pulled out a rectangular object wrapped in a purple silk cloth. "We really shouldn't do this in the van, but I sense an urgent energy coming from you. I'll do the best I can."

"Do what?"

"I'll do a tarot reading for you," she said. "I can feel your anxi-ety. It's coursing through your hand. The tarot may give you some guidance, at least for the moment. You're a Pisces, too, and depending on the alignment with the other planets . . . well that could be significant."

Before I could ask about my aligned planets, she handed me a pack of brightly printed cards, then motioned for me to shuffle. With cold stiff fingers and the random movement of the van, shuffling was difficult. On the second try, I fumbled the cards. They scattered on my lap, with two cards accidentally flipping up. Staring at me was a wickedly smiling human skeleton with a scythe slung over his shoulder, standing before what could only be the River Styx. The other card appeared to show a clown traips-ing unconcerned along a precipitous path. I quickly turned the cards over.

"Hey, I'm not sure I want to do this . . . to know the future," I said, returning the cards to her. "It seems kind of dangerous."

"Oh my," she said, concerned. "It's very unusual to see two cards from the major arcana. That's very significant. But don't worry about the skeleton. He's kind of a cheeky fellow anyway. It really doesn't mean death, not in the usual way. It just means something very fundamental in you will change; something will end, and something else will begin. The other card was the fool."

"That figures."

"No, it's not like that at all. It could mean that your mind is open to new experiences that are denied to others."

"Okay, that sounds good."

"It could also mean that you are on the verge of insanity."

"Great."

"Don't worry, that was just an accidental flip. We should actually do several readings so the cards can get a sense of you. It's dreadfully cold. We should probably put our mittens on, warm our hands for a few minutes."

"Well . . . "

I did not finish my sentence. The van suddenly veered off the road, accompanied by a spray of ice, then the squeal of brakes and crunching of gravel. My body pressed against Moon's, though I tried mightily to counterbalance. I feared I would crush this delicate girl with the porcelain thin body. The van screeched to a halt at the side of the road.

"Sorry, we almost missed the turn," said Alexei. "I wanted to show you something."

Carmen, eyes smoldering, glared at Alexei.

Boris steered the van onto a side road, then halted the vehicle in a small clearing on a high plateau, surrounded by leafless birch trees. Before us stretched a panorama of low-lying hills and forests bisected by the Angara River. Tied to nearby tree limbs were dozens of colorful ribbons. Broken vodka and champagne bottles littered the ground. Alexei led us to the festooned trees.

"The indigenous people, who we call the Buryats, come here to make offerings to their spirits," explained Alexei. "This is a sacred place for them. In the old days, they came here to perform their pagan rituals. The Buryats are now Buddhists and write prayer messages to Lord Buddha."

He held one of the ribbons and pointed to the script that appeared to be written in Sanskrit.

Alexei lingered by the spot. He seemed eager to tell us more about the people who came here. But everyone except for Moon stood shivering in indifference, hands stuffed inside parka pockets, heads buried in mufflers and hats. Moon stood apart, weaving a delicate pattern with her hands as if casting a magic spell upon the land. A whiff of a breeze swirled up from the valley, dusting us with fine particles of snow. Behind us a giant icicle broke off from a tree limb and silently pierced the snow.

"So, Alexei, are there many Buryat people left?" I asked.

Alexei brightened at the question. Carmen glared at me for prolonging the stop. She whispered something to her miserable husband, who had totally withdrawn into a giant hooded parka, his face obscured by the fur fringes. He looked like the invisible man.

"Many, and they are the largest ethnic group. The others live further north, the Evenk, Goldi, Entsy, Ket, and Dolgan peoples. Before the Russians came, they lived and hunted throughout Siberia," said Alexei, looking out at the plain, as if he could see the hunters stalking their game. "To the north, there were great herds of reindeer. Here there were mostly moose and bears, and one also had to be careful of tigers."

"But the exploitation, wasn't that during czarist times?" I asked, not quite believing that I had assumed the role of Soviet apologist. Someone had to do it.

"It was worse during Stalin and after," snapped Alexei. "The new cities, mines, and factories polluted the land and tore families apart. Vodka, that's what changed everything; vodka by the boatloads, enough vodka to poison everyone. No one hunts the reindeer anymore because everyone is too drunk and because the big reindeer herds have vanished. The people die from accidents, from fights, or they just go to sleep in the snow — drunk — and freeze to death."

Alexei kicked one of the broken bottles. He abruptly turned and headed to the van. Like lemmings we followed, gingerly stepping over glass shards.

Twenty minutes later, after passing through the village of Listvyanka, we again scuttled from the van. Before us lay the grim expanse of Lake Baikal, bordered on the west and south by formidable snow-capped mountains. To the north lay open water, as the lake horizon stretched to gray infinity. Except for Andrew, there was a noticeable lack of excitement among the group upon arriving at the world's deepest freshwater lake.

"I made it," declared Andrew. I wanted to hear more about his grandfather's exploits, but Alexei was trying to get everyone's attention.

"After lunch, you will have an opportunity to walk around and explore, perhaps see a nerpa. But now you must eat," announced Alexei, returning to his officious other self. He motioned to the massive Hotel Baikal on a hill near the road. "Boris and I will meet you here in one hour."

With that, he climbed into the van. It sped away, leaving us standing on the road.

"Let's eat," I said, waving for everyone to follow me into the hotel. Inside, the five of us were escorted through an expansive dining room to a window table. Waiting for us, garnished in lettuce and beet slices, we saw the expressionless eyes and gaping mouth of a very large omul. We gathered around the table, standing awkwardly, as if at a wake, staring at the body of a relative none of us knew very well. No one moved. No one spoke. The seconds ticked by.

"It is disgusting," said Carmen, breaking the silence. She glared at the fish. The fish glared at Carmen. The hatred was mutual.

"I think we help ourselves," I said, worried that a perfectly good fish might go uneaten. I sat, picked up a fork, twisted a flake of meat from the flank, swished it around my mouth to check for bones, then swallowed. It did taste like salmon.

"Well done!" exclaimed Andrew. He thrust his fork into the fish and tore out a chunk. Jorge followed suit. Carmen nibbled at her salad. Moon stared out the window.

"Moon, you should eat something," I said. "But watch for bones, they're tricky."

"I'm a vegetarian."

She opened up her pack and pulled out a granola bar and a sack of dried figs. I wondered how the hell she had made it all the way across Siberia on such meager rations. But then I remembered the spirit guides. There was no other explanation.

I turned my attention to Carmen and Jorge, who sat across the table from me.

"What part of Peru are you from?"

"Lima," answered Carmen. Jorge confirmed this with a nod.

"Why Siberia?"

"My husband was on a trade mission to Moscow. He thought it would be an adventure to ride on this train. We saw the brochures. We saw the elegant dining car and the beautiful scenery. I thought it would be like the luxury trains in Europe. But it was a lie, all lies, like everything here. I thought we would starve. They had nothing to eat in the dining car, and it was so filthy," she said.

Jorge nodded sadly. At last, he spoke.

"I love to ride on trains, and this is the world's greatest train trip. But the journey has been difficult for my Carmencita. It was a mistake coming in the late fall."

I had the feeling that Jorge would suffer a long time for his mistake.

"I would love to visit Peru sometime," I said.

"Yes, you must come," said Carmen enthusiastically. "Peru is beautiful."

In fact, four years earlier I had planned a trip to Bolivia, Peru, and Ecuador. But my girlfriend at the time was more interested in keeping me at home. Rachel wanted to get married and have a baby. That wasn't going to happen with me traipsing around South America. "What about the terrorists?" she would ask. "Did you hear NPR this morning? Those Shining Path nuts blew up another trainload of journalists. They really like to kill journalists (I was a journalist at the time). And you want to go to this place?" She asked this in a tone that made it sound like anyone who even considered a trip to Peru was a certified lunatic. When the Shining Path was particularly productive, Rachel would place newspaper clips describing in graphic detail the latest atrocities next to my morning bagel and coffee. For weeks, I was inundated with horrible news from Peru — journalists hacked to death, buses blown to smithereens, trains derailed, and power stations dynamited. This was not the way I liked to start my day. Frankly, Rachel's campaign annoyed the hell out of me, but in the end it succeeded. I dropped the entire South America trip and instead went to Nepal, where anti-government activity wasn't as widely reported. "You should give our relationship some serious thought while you're wandering around in the Himalayas," scolded Rachel, as she saw me off at the airport. I did. We were history.

I told an abbreviated version of this story to those at the table, emphasizing my reasons for wanting to see Peru and omitting my lack of enthusiasm for procreation. I guessed that Carmen was a fervent Catholic.

"El Sindero Luminoso!" Carmen snarled, pounding her fist on the table at my mention of the terrorist group. The silverware jumped, the water in the glasses sloshed, even the omul, at least the uneaten head, seemed alarmed. Carmen's eyes burned. "That Guzman, he is pure evil," she said, invoking the name of the leader of the Maoist revolutionaries who were making everyone's life in Peru miserable.

She picked up a laminated menu from the next table and began waving it as she ranted.

"The Shining Path is destroying our country. It is keeping tourists and business away. They must be stopped." Her eyes scanned the room. She was looking for a fly or any other small vermin-like creature to pulverize. But this was November in Siberia. The last fly had frozen to death months ago. For a second, I thought she was going to brain Andrew, who sat in rapt concentration across from her, extracting the bones from his share of omul. With a loud thwack she swatted the table, obliterating a sprig of dried parsley that had fallen from the omul tray.

"They must be crushed," she said, flicking away the remaining parsley bits from the table with her fingers.

"Like parsley," I added.

"Yes," she said, a flicker of a smile appearing across her face. "Like parsley."

When we returned to the van, Alexei announced he had a surprise for us. Perhaps, I thought, they had managed to fix the heater while we were off dissecting omul and pulverizing parsley.

"I am sorry to say that we cannot visit the Limnological Institute today because it is closed."

This news didn't much surprise us. The Limnological Institute, a research museum devoted to the study of the lake, had been billed as one of the highlights of the trip. But Andrew and the Peruvians looked relieved that they would not spend the afternoon in a cramped hall, observing mud samples from Baikal's depths and preserved fat globs from the Big-Eyed Golomyanka.

"Is that the surprise?" deadpanned Andrew.

"No," replied Alexei. "I think I have arranged something better. You have been granted permission to visit an authentic Siberian village!"

No one said anything.

"Can we walk around?" I asked.

"Oh, yes. You will have two hours to walk around and inspect the authentic village."

"Are there authentic people living in the authentic village?" quipped Andrew.

"Yes, it is a fishing village just like any other," replied Alexei.

Andrew and I looked at each other.

"What do you make of this?" I asked.

"Maybe this is the part where they show us the model of communism. You know the routine, happy workers, hero mothers, and all that rubbish. I would say it's about time, too. They've been frightfully lax on the propaganda."

"That's got to be it."

Twenty minutes later, the van stopped in front of a motley assortment of log cabins and wood-framed houses. On the other side of the road lay a few battered fishing boats and the lake itself.

"We have arrived at the authentic village," declared Alexei, who remained in the van. "Please look around. I'll be back at 4 p.m. to pick you up." We reluctantly struggled out of the van. I was the last to clamber out. As I slammed the door, Boris gunned the engine. Like castaways, we watched the van disappear around a bend.

"My good man, did you catch the name of the authentic village?" asked Andrew.

"No, he forgot to tell us. I guess it's just Authentic Village," I said, shrugging.

"It really doesn't matter. What's in a name? Doesn't seem to be any model workers around to put on a show. Maybe they're going to surprise us. In the meantime, I think I'll take a wander by the lake. That's where I want to get a sense of things, anyway."

He strolled off in that direction. The others drifted away. Moon, as if in a trance, crossed the road and made her way past beached fishing boats to the lakeshore. Carmen and Jorge stood in the middle of the road and bickered in Spanish. I turned and walked into the village.

Other than the paved main street, the village appeared to be like dozens of others I had seen from the train window. The wood houses were painted dull green or blue. A few were rustic log cabins. But all the dwellings sported bright white shutters, and in the middle of the windowsill, more often than not, was a bright red rose, plastic no doubt.

I ambled over a rickety wood bridge that crossed an ice-encrusted stream, startling an old woman who was using a stick to enlarge a hole in the ice. Beyond, on a gentle slope, three children played among some cows that nuzzled the snow in search of fodder. The children took turns riding a rusty bicycle down the snow slope, weaving among the cows in a crude version of a slalom ride.

I walked past the last houses, some with neat wood fences and frozen laundry hanging in the yard, while others were landscaped with bits of rusting machinery, old fishing nets, and the other detritus of a society that had a substantial maintenance problem on its hands. Near the last house, partially hidden by the encroaching forest, stood a small octagon-shaped church. An onion dome graced the roof, and from this sprouted the Russian orthodox cross. Pushing open the door, I walked through the church toward the altar, where dark icons of a saint unknown to me and the Mother and Child hung on the iconostasis. In the corner was a woodcarving of a snarling double-headed eagle — the symbol of the Romanov dynasty and its last czar.

Stepping outside, I walked to the back yard of the church and found what looked like a temporary shrine to the dead. The deceased stared from sterile black-and-white photos tacked to a board, festooned with wreaths and withered flowers. It appeared that most had died young. Many of the accompanying inscriptions indicated ages in the thirties and forties. Death was probably from alcohol, I surmised, though I wondered how much of Alexei's despair over the decline of the native population had affected my thinking. As I examined the photographs, I thought that this was not exactly the prototype model village Soviet communism would want to display. Was this a real authentic village?

My eyes rested on the picture of a handsome young man in a soldier's uniform and peaked cap. We were both born in the same year, 1955. The coincidence triggered an onslaught of confusing thoughts, then questions. Where was the Soviet Union that I had grown up with, the super-strong, evil state that stood ready to crush democracies everywhere and enslave us all? Where was the propaganda? Where was the secret police, the ubiquitous minders who trailed every western visitor? Where are you guys? But the soldier's grave revealed no insight to my questions.

A childhood memory surfaced. I was with my parents in the family station wagon. The radio droned. President Kennedy was talking about missiles in Cuba and the possibility of nuclear war with the Soviet Union. "Dad, is there going to be a war?" I had asked, very much afraid that there would be. The memory of that night was still vivid; the serious talk between my mother and father, the huddled conversations with neighbors. "Yeah, I think they will bomb Lockheed and Ames Laboratory first," a neighbor told my father, referring to potential targets not far from where we lived. I was only six, but I knew enough to be very scared. At school, we practiced hiding under our desks as air raid sirens wailed. For years, I shuddered every time a jet flew overhead, wondering if a Russian MIG had somehow escaped detection and was about to bomb me into oblivion.

Now, twenty-six years later, I stood within the heart of the beast. I wanted solid evidence to validate my anxiety-ridden childhood spent staring at jets in the sky wondering if this was the one. I wanted reassurance that the CIA, the President, the Army, the Navy, the Air Force, and even Walter Cronkite did not conspire to scare the hell out of me and everyone else in my generation for the wrong reasons. But at that moment I saw nothing but a memorial to the dead, a few wooden houses, and an endless gray sky.

A wave of disillusionment washed over me. I wanted to see a model village with refrigerators that actually worked, and televisions that didn't explode. I wanted a brainwashed tour guide. I wanted missile trucks and flag-waving Slavic supermen saluting proudly on the turrets of tanks. I wanted gigantic posters of Lenin amid a sea of red banners. I wanted the ghost of Khrushchev to explode from the permafrost and shake his fist in my face and shout: "We will bury you!"

The face of the soldier who would have been my age stared back impassively. Had he spent his childhood gazing at the sky, wondering if the Americans were ready to bomb him into oblivion?

"They lied to us," I whispered to the grave. "It was all a big lie."

In the next yard, the door to the outhouse creaked open. An old man, still yanking on his zipper, stumbled out. A cow mooed; its bell clanged lethargically. The old woman, now joined by two others, was still bashing away at the river ice with her stick. The children played on, their lilting laughter wafted across the village like a lost memory.

17

Spirit Train of Baikal

remained at the cemetery until the vision of the Soviet super state had withered away. The shouts of children playing snapped me back to the present. Time was slipping away. I still wanted to explore the shoreline before the van returned. With a renewed sense of urgency, I retraced my steps through the village, crossed the main road, and headed toward Lake Baikal. As I hiked to the water, a ripple of warm air, like a remnant of summer, brushed against my face. I took off my gloves and fur cap, and stuffed them in my pack.

After picking my way through the remains of decrepit fishing boats, I came upon Moon, half hidden behind the skeleton of one of the vessels. Her back was to me so she did not see or hear my approach. With a large stick, perhaps the broken oar of one of the derelicts, Moon traced runic-like symbols in the sand. She had removed her wool cap, revealing a thick braid of auburn hair that swung like a pendulum at her waist. Singing quietly to herself, she gently laid down the stick and fetched a pebble that she reverently placed by one of the symbols. I noticed other pebbles in odd patterns among the runes. She continued this ritual for several minutes, unaware that I was observing her.

How did this delicate New Zealander manage to transport herself to the middle of Siberia? She reminded me of the barefooted sprites in flowing dresses who danced freeform at Grateful Dead concerts. These free spirits dabbled in pagan ritual, celebrated the solstice, and lived in studio apartments infused with incense and lit by beeswax candles. They did not concern themselves with visa applications, train timetables, or any of the other minutiae of travel. Moon's very obliviousness to the conditions, politics, and depression that permeated this country seemed to protect her from the travel-related worries that frequently rampaged through my mind like a herd of spooked buffalo. Most of us mortals battled upstream against the current, while Moon and her ilk seemed to float downstream, washing up on distant shores.

As I observed her, I recalled some of the things she had said to me in the van. When I started the journey, I eagerly looked forward to the adventure of the trip itself and the thrill of riding a route seldom traveled by westerners. I had no inkling of a deeper purpose. But now, as I made my way along the line, I felt tugged — by Moon, as well the others I had encountered — in another direction. The trip was evolving into an inward journey, a hunt for ghosts of the past. With each passing day, I found myself wondering again and again about my Russian-born great-grandparents and whether any of my kin had been left behind or had even come this way. I was baffled, yet intrigued by the uncanny way Finland kept cropping up, either mistakenly as my place of origin or just in happenstance. Finally, I was beginning to believe that the land itself was trying to reveal something of great importance to me, but until now I had been too preoccupied with my various crises to notice.

I stared beyond Moon to the lake, but Baikal, with the veil of a storm brewing in the distance, was not in the mood for revelation. I would search elsewhere.

Leaving Moon to her mysterious meditation, I continued my walk. Water lapped up on the thin beach, nudging bits of newly formed ice toward shore where it collected in slushy pools. In the distance, I saw the solitary figure of a man wearing a deerstalker and staring at a spot in the water. I jogged in his direction, thinking Andrew had spotted a nerpa.

"Can you see one?" I asked, as I stumbled up beside him.

"Aye, I can see it. In my mind's eye, I see it clearly."

I followed his gaze to the open water and scanned the horizon, while Andrew took out a pipe and tobacco pouch from his coat pocket. He lit the pipe and then took a thoughtful puff. He looked like a man at peace with the world.

"I'm afraid I can't see them," I said.

"You can't see it because it is at the bottom. Only the ghosts of those present remain."

Andrew had been speaking in riddles for most of the day, dropping broad hints that this journey to Baikal held special significance to him.

"I'm not quite following what you're saying."

"Alas, I'm afraid the nerpa and its omen of good fortune still eludes us," he said, taking another puff on his pipe. "See that spot of water over there, near the western shore?"

He pointed to a spot amid the gray swells.

"I'm not exactly sure of the location, but I think that's where the disaster happened eighty-three years ago. The accident must have occurred a mile or two off shore from Port Baikal, that's the town next to Listvyanka, where we ate lunch."

I followed his outstretched arm to a point offshore from Listvyanka and Port Baikal. We stood in silence, staring at the spot of gray.

At last I blurted: "What happened?"

"That's where they tried to build the Trans-Siberian."

"Right in the middle of the lake? You must be kidding."

Andrew took his eyes off the lake, and slowly wandered over to a piece of driftwood that made a convenient bench.

"Have a seat. I'll tell you about it."

We quickly discovered a mutual interest in trains, though Andrew's knowledge extended far deeper into the history of railroads. He was a retired civil engineer so it was only natural that he had taken an interest in the construction of the Trans-Siberian rail line. His grandfather had helped build the first ice-breaking ferry designed to carry the trains across Lake Baikal, before track was laid around the southern shore. For my part, I had studied Russian history and, in particular, had spent time in the university library researching various facets of the Trans-Siberian Express, when I really should have been studying economics. What Andrew told me not only corroborated what I already knew, but added fresh details, colored by the adventures of his grandfather.

The Trans-Siberian was a grand vision intended to spur economic development of the vast region. Only when work began did the realities of building a railroad across thousands of miles of inhospitable wilderness sink in. Construction began in the late nineteenth century, from both the European and Pacific ends of the empire. The lines were to meet somewhere in the middle of Siberia. At least that was the plan. But the railroad builders were stymied by the immensity of Lake Baikal and its rugged coast. Blasting tunnels and platforms in the steep slopes of the Trans-Baikal Mountains was deemed too costly.

To keep project costs down, the builders reduced the amount of ballast for the track beds and used low-grade steel for the rails. The strategy proved shortsighted. Soon after the first segments were open to traffic, engineers discovered that the trains could travel no faster than twelve miles per hour because the substandard steel tracks had warped from the extreme temperatures.

"That just goes to show you what happens when you build on the cheap," chided Andrew. "The damn bureaucrats. There was a committee of them. That's right, they built this thing by committee. Should have just let the engineers do their work."

I was too embarrassed to tell him that I was in graduate school studying to be a government manager — a bureaucrat with a specialty in budgeting. At that moment, my sympathy was with the poor junior finance analyst who must have been assigned the task of estimating the cost of laying rails across 5,000 miles of unsur-veyed wilderness, crisscrossed by some of the largest rivers on earth. Because of Siberia's sparse population, thousands of workers had to be recruited in European Russia and shipped off to Siberia. In some instances, where labor was impossible to recruit, prison-ers, of which there was an abundant supply in Siberia, were draft-ed into work gangs in exchange for shorter sentences. Then to be confronted by the deepest freshwater lake in the world surround-ed by towering mountains on all sides; well, it was easy to see how creative solutions might emerge. Shorting the ballast and using cheap steel, not to mention the idea of loading the trains onto ships, must have seemed like brilliant cost-control measures — at least to the czar's number-cruncher who was cozied up in the Winter Palace in St. Petersburg. Hell, if I had been there at the time, I probably would have dreamed up the same ideas.

"I'm sure the czar's treasury was under a bit of stress at the time," I said diplomatically. "They were probably looking for cre-ative ways to get the job done without bankrupting the country."

"Balderdash!" snapped Andrew. "It's the same everywhere. They're doing it in the U.K. now, cutting back on the rail service. The whole bloody thing is starting to rot. It's that Maggie Thatcher and her damn Tories."

We sat in silence for a few minutes. I really wanted to hear more about Andrew's grandfather and less about the Tories.

Andrew, taking another puff from his pipe, said his grandfather first came to Siberia in the 1890s to reassemble the steamship that was used to ferry the trains across the lake.

Stopped by the lake and the daunting prospect of laying track around its shores, the Russians opted to construct an ice-breaking ferry. The problem was that no one in Russia had ever built such a ship, so the government contracted with Walker Shipyard in Newcastle on the Tyne. That's where Andrew's grandfather worked at the time. It also explained Andrew's slight Scottish brogue.

Large enough to hold an entire train on its lower deck, the ferry was equipped with staterooms, a formal dining room, and a banquet hall. The ship was then disassembled, packed into crates, and shipped across the portion of the railroad completed to Lake Baikal. The logistics conjured a jigsaw puzzle-like image of Russian engineers scratching their heads while searching among thousands of mismatched parts lying in the snow. For three years, pieces of the ferry were scattered throughout Siberia, but eventually all the parts managed to find their way to Baikal.

"The Russians wanted help putting Humpty Dumpty back together again, so grandfather came on his own to lend a hand."

Appropriately christened *Baikal*, the ferry was launched in July of 1899. A second ferry, the *Angara*, was also manufactured at the Walker Shipyards and built in Siberia.

Baikal's fickle weather tested the durability of the ships. Ferocious storms and impenetrable fog banks kept the ferries in port for days. When the lake froze, *Baikal's* captain drove the ship like a battering ram to clear a passage. Sometimes the ice was too thick even for the icebreakers.

The system more or less worked for several years. That changed in 1904 when the Japanese attacked Port Arthur, the Pacific Ocean outpost of the Russian Empire. The czar's army, concentrated in European Russia, needed a fast way to transport troops and supplies to the Pacific Coast, particularly in winter, when bad weather slowed the ferries. Surveying and building track around the lake would take too much time. As the war effort floundered, the czar's military advisors arrived at what they thought was a brilliant alternative. Why not take advantage of the Siberian winter and lay the track over the ice? That's what they did.

When finished, a locomotive was prepared to test the track.

I looked back over to the spot in the water and pictured what it must have been like — the locomotive, billowing steam and smoke, edging its way along the rails, the engineers and soldiers watching. Then, without warning, a sharp report like the crack of thunder, followed by the fatal plunge. A gasp, the Russian equivalent of "Oh, shit!" comes from the on-lookers. Even though the surface of Lake Baikal freezes fast by December, the engineers were probably unaware of the deep, warm currents that sometimes cause the ice to buckle and break apart in the middle of winter. The lake ice is prone to these giant, miles-long fissures that suddenly split the ice without warning.

"Grandfather, rest his soul, was there. He saw the whole thing," said Andrew. "They eventually got trains across. But they weren't real confident about it. The army stripped the engines to lighten them and built fancy bracing systems to support the track in case of another ice break. Most of the troops were ferried over on sledges, but a fair amount of supplies and a bunch of locomotives made it over to the other side."

"Did your grandfather tell you this?"

Andrew was six when his grandfather had died. He heard most of the tale secondhand from his father, though he did remember a few bits from his grandfather.

"When I was a lad, I remember Grandfather telling me about Old Man Baikal swallowing up an entire train. Scared the hell out of me. I thought an old man really did eat the train."

I pictured a little Andrew in a deerstalker, bouncing on his grandfather's lap, with a little plastic bubble pipe jutting from his mouth.

The entire event lay dormant in his mind for years. It wasn't until middle age that Andrew, now a graying sixty-five, began to develop a serious interest in the events that happened here. The story about laying the track over the ice and the disastrous test run stuck in his mind. Slowly, he began to assemble the facts with the help of family members and historic archives. One odd thing he encountered was that his grandmother, who lived to a ripe old age, was circumspect on the subject.

"Grandfather returned to Scotland after the *Angara* (the second ferry) was assembled. But something drew him back a few years later. Grandmother hinted that it wasn't all about the challenge of surveying the railroad around the lake. There was something else. Here, I speculate because Grandmother was quite proper about this and would never say an unkind word about her husband. But she dropped hints, and I concluded from them that there might have been a woman he took up with in Irkutsk."

"He was gone a long time. Those things happen," I said.

"Aye, they do. But I didn't pay much heed until one day when me brother Clive and I were sorting through Grandmother's papers. We found several letters written in Russian, addressed to Grandfather. Clive took them to a friend who could read Russian."

The letters were from a woman who said how much she missed him and asked when he would return to Irkutsk. There was reference to the civil war, and the terrible conditions as the city filled with refugees fleeing the advancing Bolshevik (Red) Army.

After the Bolsheviks assumed power in 1917, Russia plunged into civil war. Alexander V. Kolchak, a former vice admiral in the czar's navy, commanded the largest White Army, which consisted of a motley collection of ex-military officers, Cossacks, bureaucrats, boyars, and riffraff who remained loyal to the crown. The Whites won early battles, but were soon forced to retreat east toward Irkutsk and Lake Baikal. Beset by mass desertions, the ragtag army disintegrated. The remnants fled to China, others fortified themselves in armored trains, terrorizing villages along the Trans-Siberian rail line until the Bolsheviks managed to restore order. Kolchak, himself, was caught trying to flee Irkutsk in a private train. He was executed by firing squad a week later.

"The whole bloody army collapsed right here in Irkutsk," said Andrew.

We sat in silent contemplation, each lost in his thoughts. The grandeur of the setting seemed an unlikely location for the human calamity that had occurred near here. I asked Andrew if his grandfather had been aware of the conditions that existed at that time.

"Aye, he must have known if he had read that last letter or had kept up with the news. It had a desperate tone. The other letters were more or less matter-of-fact, almost heroic in a stoic sort of way. But in the final one, she pleaded with him to come back and help her escape. You see, the Reds and Whites, despite the chaos, agreed to keep the Trans-Siberian rail line open. There was a chance she could have taken a train to Petrograd (later renamed Leningrad, now St. Petersburg), then escaped to Finland. Of course, I don't know what really happened. That's part of the mystery. The pessimist in me fears the worst, that she perished in the chaos or the flu epidemic that consumed Irkutsk shortly before the Bolsheviks finally took over."

"You said the railroad was still open. She could have escaped," I said.

"I doubt it."

We both knew why. When Kolchak's army collapsed, even the railroad, the one lifeline that linked the empire, ceased regular operation. The engineers, coal tenders, and stationmasters went unpaid or were given worthless czarist-era paper currency. Crews abandoned their trains, leaving them idle at stations or in the middle of nowhere. Stranded passengers, not robbed or murdered by roving bands of brigands, fled into the tiger-infested wilderness. Many froze or died of starvation.

"It's sort of hard to explain," continued Andrew, "but I've always felt his spirit whenever I've taken similar adventures. I've been drawn here for years. I wanted to see the lake and the spot where it all happened, before I became too old to travel. I feel his presence, his spirit in the wind and rippling through the waves. I know I may seem a bit daft to you, but that's the honest truth."

In the past week, most everyone I met was searching for spirits. I did not think any of them daft, not anymore. Moon had her spirit guides. Alexei was trying to shake the ghost of the communist past and resurrect the spirits of the native cultures. Now I discovered that Andrew was hot on the trail of his intrepid grandfather's spirit.

I envied Andrew. He had a grandfather who had real adventures. There were letters and a mystery lover. What did I have? Only the fragmented memories told by my father and aunt about a village somewhere near Grodno, and my own speculation about an unknown ancestor who had come this way a long time ago.

A cold blast of air sent shivers down my body. Across the lake, I saw the dark shadow of a squall obliterating the few bright splotches of late afternoon sunlight that had managed to break through the clouds. The wavelets turned to white-topped rollers, and the icy crust that lined the shore rustled in the agitated surf. Clouds now obscured the mountains that had so long ago stymied the builders of the Trans-Siberian railroad. I dug out my wool gloves and pulled them on. Andrew appeared oblivious to the gathering storm and sudden drop in temperature.

An object, a small head-like thing bobbing in the surf about fifty yards off shore, caught my attention. It disappeared under the waves. Probably a log, I thought.

"I know what you mean about the spiritual stuff," I said, returning my attention to Andrew. "I've been feeling the same thing, but I've been struggling to figure out what it all means. My path seems to be one of serendipity, while yours is rooted in a definite purpose. I'm glad you found your spot. I think it's a grand story."

Andrew stood, then walked to a nearby rock, perching on top. I followed.

We both stared at the lake. I half expected the locomotive to breach, like a mighty whale, but spouting steam and smoke instead of hot breath. The day darkened as the clouds plugged the last hole in the sky. The wind stoked angry whitecaps. I heard footsteps. Moon and Alexei emerged from the direction of the road.

"Look!" yelled Moon. "I see them. I see the nerpas!"

Andrew, Alexei, and I instantly turned toward the roiling waters. But it was difficult to see anything in the growing gloom.

"I really did see two heads pop out of the water," insisted Moon. "They must be seals. I've seen them in New Zealand."

The four of us stood on shore, straining to see through the dwindling light. I thought I saw something, but I could not make out details. After a few minutes, Alexei turned to walk back to the waiting van that spat and coughed great clouds of white exhaust. We could not stay any longer.

I walked over to Moon. "I thought I spotted a head in the water a few minutes ago, but I assumed it was just a log."

"You mustn't doubt yourself so much," she said, her soft voice barely discernible over the howl of the wind that had begun to gust. "Anything is possible."

18

The Key

staggered from the bed, found the curtain chord, and yanked. Bright sunlight flooded the room, momentarily blinding me. The gloom of yesterday's fog had melted away, replaced by golden morning light. Warmth filled the room, injecting me with new strength, and with this I felt more in control of my destiny. The day seemed full of promise.

As I headed downstairs, I recalled Nina's prediction that my trip would be better once I reached Irkutsk, her hometown. Nevertheless, I approached the dining room warily, scanning the space to make sure trouble was not lurking in some dark corner.

Everything seemed normal. A few couples and clusters of businessmen chatted over coffee or tea. No strangers sidled up to me with weird tales to tell. The characters that had waltzed into my life during the past thirty-six hours were gone. I recalled the van careening to a stop last night in front of the hotel. Moon, who apparently was staying somewhere else, gave me a quick hug, then whispered in my ear, "Let your spirit guides lead you." Before I could ask her to explain, the willowy sprite had vanished into the foggy night.

Andrew and Svein had departed on the Trans-Mongolian Express bound for Peking. There was no sign of condor woman, who seemed more a creature of the night than of a cheery morning.

And what of the quarrelsome Peruvians? I found them sitting in the hotel lobby on my way to breakfast. We greeted each other with the enthusiasm of friends who had endured a great ordeal together. Armed with tour books and brochures, they wore identical khaki safari outfits over a layer of bright red thermal underwear. Only the pith helmets were missing. If we hadn't been in the middle of Siberia, I would have thought they were ready to embark on a journey up the Congo River to search for Doctor Livingstone. After exchanging "good mornings," I continued on my way. I was looking forward to a solitary breakfast where I didn't have to speak or listen to anyone.

At the breakfast table, I surrounded myself with familiar props: my travel books and the much-maligned phrase book. I pondered what to do. My schedule called for me to catch the evening train. I had the entire day to myself. Moon's last words echoed in my mind: *"Let your spirit guides lead you."*

Okay, I thought, lead on spirit guides.

My random ramble led me along the Angara River to the embankment where Svein had liberated his rubles two nights before. Tufts of fog lingered and danced above the ice and snow that caked much of the river's surface. I turned toward the city center, and came upon a monument to the Russian war dead where teenagers in military uniforms and toting machine guns marched imperfectly. Parents beamed in the background.

I continued on to a large Russian Orthodox church where a withered and blind woman crouched in a pile of rags outside the main door. She was the first beggar I had encountered. I wondered how she had managed to evade the authorities, who were charged with enforcing the edict that poverty did not exist in their class-less society. I placed a ruble in her hand, which she grasped in thanks. She murmured a prayer, perhaps for my lost soul.

Passing through a neighborhood of old wooden houses with brightly painted trim, I spied a group of boys playing ice hockey on a side street. A few of the bigger kids grasped old hockey sticks, while the others held brooms or long wooden planks. No one wore skates. Instead, the players skittered in worn canvas shoes on the icy street, whooping and hollering encouragement to teammates and taunting foes.

As I watched, a memory surfaced of other boys a continent and a generation away, playing on hot summer pavement in the California sunshine of my childhood. The decaying softball was held together with electrical tape pinched from my father's toolbox. Garbage can lids and the flaps of old cardboard boxes imitated bases. When the ball inevitably rolled into the storm drain, we drew lots to select who would be lowered, head first, into the stinking hole to retrieve our only ball.

The puck shot past the outstretched arms of the goaltender, rattling around in a large cardboard box. Half the boys erupted in euphoria, waving their sticks in the air and hugging the teammate who scored the goal.

I continued to the next block. Across the street, a woman struggled with the lock on a door that led to a flat. The street was empty. She shouted toward me. I looked around, but there was no one else present. Oh no, I thought, she thinks I am Russian. This was understandable. I wore the fur cap. My clothes were so bedraggled that I was beginning to fit into the scruffy mélange of everyday Siberian life. Warily, I crossed the street. As usual, I felt compelled to explain my presence. In perfect phrase-book Russian, I announced grandly that I was Bob, a tourist from America, and that I did not speak Russian.

"I don't care if you're Peter the Great, I need help with this lock." At least that's what I thought she said.

I looked at the lock, and then I looked at the woman who had a kindly face that aroused within me the odd sensation that we had known each other somewhere or sometime in the past. She appeared to be in her late fifties, though age was difficult to discern among the Russians. They always turned out to be much younger than they looked. Our eyes met. I felt a vague sense of the familiar as my mind sought to make sense of this connection. Then it hit me. She resembled my Russian-born grandmother.

"Who are you?" I blurted in English. Then I answered my own question. "Bubba?"

"Bubba" was the name my sister Maria and I had called our grandmother, Ethel. I'm not sure of its origin, perhaps coming from the Yiddish word for grandparent. This woman was much younger than the frail Bubba I remembered from my childhood. Although I didn't know what Bubba looked like when she was a young woman, I had seen a picture of her as a little girl. In a yellowed photograph taken shortly after her family arrived in New York City, Bubba stared wistfully at the camera while clutching a book. What was so striking in that picture was that her face appeared not to be that of a five-year-old child, but of an older woman's, superimposed on a child's body.

Bubba had already seemed reconciled to the difficult life that lay ahead. Like most young immigrant women of that time, she was swept along in the struggle of daily life. She married in the early 1920s, but her husband, Samuel Goldstein, a barber, fell ill with tuberculosis, a disease that spread rapidly in the ghetto of New York City's Lower East Side. At first the couple sought refuge as caretakers of a chicken farm in the Catskill Mountains, but then left on a one-way transcontinental railroad trip to Denver, where Sam could better recuperate in the dry Rocky Mountain air. He didn't recover and was buried a few years later in a pauper's grave on a wind-swept hill overlooking the Great Plains. Bubba was left with three young children: Harry, Morey, and Frances. Her health declined. She couldn't care for the children, let alone pay for coal to heat their tiny house. One day a social worker came and took the children away to the National Home for Jewish Children, a Denver orphanage.

More than a decade passed. Harry, liberated from the orphanage by the outbreak of World War II, joined the Marines, was captured at Corregidor, survived the Bataan Death March, then spent the rest of the war as a Japanese prisoner, working in the Tokyo railroad yards. Morey joined the Coast Guard and was sent to the Pacific Theater, managing to avoid the fate of his brother. Meanwhile, Bubba survived her illness. After the war, the family reunited in Los Angeles. Harry and Frances married within the faith, as expected. Morey, the family nonconformist, fell for a dark-eyed Mexican-American girl, Magdalena Gonzales, who was a Catholic. They eloped to Las Vegas, roused the local judge at midnight and were married in the county jail with a drunken inmate serving as witness. I came along four years later — a surprise.

By the time I was old enough to have memories of my own, Bubba lived in a Los Angeles nursing home on Fairfax Avenue, a neighborhood of kosher delicatessens and bakeries. I remembered my parents bundling my sister and me into the family car so we could take Bubba to lunch at the nearby farmer's market on warm Sunday afternoons. Even though she was deaf, Bubba could read our lips. She always knew what we were talking about.

The Russian woman looked at me. There was a tiny flinch, as if my use of the Yiddish word for grandmother had triggered a long-lost memory within her. Was I an apparition from a long time ago? Who was this man who called her Bubba? The sun warmed our faces. The faint trace of a breeze touched the gray hairs that sprouted in unruly curls from her scarf. From the next street over, I heard a shout of joy from the hockey boys. Someone had scored another goal.

As if in a trance, the woman handed me an enormous key. Handy with tools, I dug out my Swiss Army knife, removed my gloves, and fiddled with the ancient lock. My hands were numb from the cold, but I continued to work on it. Within minutes I had loosened the spring. The lock snapped into place. She broke into a wide smile, grabbed my hand, and shook it vigorously.

"Not a problem," I said.

She opened the door and beckoned me inside.

"Oh no, I really can't," I said, waving my arms as if warding off an evil spirit, not quite sure if my English reply would make any sense. "I'm just wandering through your lovely city."

"Nyet, nyet," she replied.

Even though she spoke to me in rapid Russian, little of which I actually understood, I had reached that stage in my travels where I seemed able to intuitively translate the meaning of the words. Whether this came from her facial expressions, hand gestures, or some unexplainable psychic connection, I had no way of knowing. But what I did know was that we seemed to communicate as if we were proficient in each other's language.

"Come in and have tea and cake," she said.

"But you were on your way somewhere? It is really not necessary. I like to fix things."

"No, no. Come in, please. Come in out of the cold."

Before I could protest again, she grabbed my elbow and led me into the apartment.

It was small, but immaculately furnished with czarist-era furniture; I saw an overstuffed couch and dining table with clawed feet grabbing at a Persian carpet, its elaborate floral design fringed in rich carmine. Spotless white doilies draped the arms of an overstuffed chair. An ancient clock, numbers set in Roman numerals, hung on a wall above a lawyer's bookcase crammed with old leather-bound volumes. On one of the shelves were framed photographs: a handsome gray-haired man, a young man in a military uniform, and a smiling girl in the white blouse and red kerchief of a Young Pioneer.

"Your husband and children?" I asked.

"Da."

She motioned to the picture of the gray-haired man. I think she told me that he had died, but I wasn't sure, and in her reply about her children, the word Moscow cropped up. That, combined with hand motions, seemed to tell me that they no longer lived in Irkutsk, but had found new lives in European Russia. She gave me that "what is a mother to do" shrug. We stood in a moment of awkward silence, broken only by the ticking of the clock.

"Ah, the tea," she said.

She motioned for me to sit at the table, then disappeared into a small adjoining kitchen. I heard water being poured into a teakettle. She returned with a plate of cookies and slices of chocolate cake, and motioned for me to take off my hat and coat. I started to explain in mixed Russian and English that I had come on the train and had visited Lake Baikal yesterday. The shrill ring of the phone interrupted my story. She excused herself and disappeared into an adjacent room.

"Natasha!" I overheard, but lost the rest of the conversation. Could this have been the daughter calling?

My eyes darted about the room, and settled on a framed photo, yellowed and cracked with age, that I had not previously noticed. It appeared to be a family portrait, with bearded patriarch and a rotund matriarch surrounded by younger adults and children dressed in the turn-of-the-century style.

The photo again reminded me of my family's Russian-born ancestors. The photo with Bubba was the first picture of the Rubins (shortened from Rubinstein by harried immigration officials) after they arrived in New York City, having fled the pogroms initiated by Russian Czar Nicholas II at the turn of the twentieth century.

In the background of the picture stand my three great-uncles, Harry, Sam, and Max — fresh-faced young men dressed in natty suits and ties — and my great-aunt Mary, a stout, matronly woman. They appear confident, eager to make their fortune in the New World. Standing in front, off to the side, her hair in pigtails, is Bubba, still clutching her book. Her little bother Harry, sporting a mischievous smile, stands on the opposite side.

My great-grandfather, Abraham Joseph, is seated in front, his legs bent awkwardly across a rope that must have been part of the portrait studio. A relic of the Old World, he wears a peaked cap from which his piercing eyes stare suspiciously ahead. His full beard blends seamlessly into his dark clothes. He grips the chair tightly with both hands, giving the impression that it might topple over at any moment.

Next to Abraham, her hair wound neatly on the top of her head, sits my great-grandmother. She wears a long flowing skirt, neatly pleated in front. Unlike the distrustful melancholy evinced by my great-grandfather, she smiles wanly, perhaps relieved to have arrived on a friendly shore after the difficult voyage across the North Atlantic.

When I was a child, staring at the photo, I always felt something was different about her, as if she was not part of the family, but a stranger who joined the group along the way. Indeed, she was an enigma. My father and aunt could name everyone in the photo except her. Her first name had been forgotten, her origin a mystery. In the well-ordered universe of my childhood, I could not yet appreciate the nature of events that would follow the reunion captured in that photo, and how it was possible for a name to be forgotten amid the tumult of history and passage of time.

The teakettle whistled. The woman emerged from the other room, then disappeared into the kitchen, reappearing seconds later with a tray, carrying two cups and the teakettle trailing wisps of steam. After pouring, she motioned for me to drink, then returned to the other room to resume her phone conversation.

I sipped the black tea and pondered the photo on the wall. Something was different about one of the men standing in the background. I walked over and examined it more closely. The man's features were darker, more pronounced than those of the other men. He was also shorter and stockier. He was the only one smiling. I picked up the photo and glanced at the back. I could make out "Irkutsk, 1916," but the rest, presumably the names of the family members, wasn't decipherable without the aid of the alphabet printed in the back of my phrase book. I retreated to the table to retrieve the book from my pack. At that moment I heard "do svidaniya" — good-bye — from the other room and the phone returned to its cradle. My hostess returned.

"My daughter, she does not call often," I thought I heard her tell me.

She saw that I was examining the photo. I pointed to the third man and asked who he was. She explained in Russian, but I did not understand. I discerned the word Finland. I excitedly thought to dig out my train ticket and show that I, too, was from Finland. But then I remembered that despite the efforts of the Soviet bureaucracy to convert me into a Finnish citizen, I really wasn't Finnish at all. In fact, I had never set foot in or even thought much about Finland until I had embarked on this trip. At some point the masquerade would have to end.

The clock chimed one o'clock. A look of panic crossed the woman's eyes. She was late for something. She must have lost track of the time. Grabbing her coat, she wrapped her head in the same shawl she was wearing when I first saw her. She babbled in Russian apologetically, then motioned to me that I could stay.

"I need to go, too," I said. Had I stayed, I wouldn't have been sure when she would return — that part of our communication was not intuitive. What if someone else came, a friend, a neighbor? They certainly would not know why a disheveled, dark-skinned stranger with stained pants, a filthy parka, and a nice pair of Vasque walking shoes was sitting in this fine widow's apartment, gorging on cake and sipping tea. And where is Madam? What, you cannot speak Russian? How did you get here? Where are your papers? You beast, you animal, what have you done with Madam? Police!

Before my paranoia could sentence me to thirty years of hard labor in a Siberian prison, I had slipped on my coat and hat, and shouldered my pack. I stole a final glance at the man in the photograph before I was out the door, the woman close behind me. She snapped the door shut. She shook my hand and thanked me again for fixing the lock. The woman seemed to be telling me something, perhaps where to visit. Then she was off, walking smartly down the street, disappearing around a corner with one last wave.

"Wait," I called out too late. "I didn't even get your name."

The street was empty. A thin breeze rustled the few brown leaves that clung to the branches of the trees. The sun's glare hurt my eyes. I looked away. I stood for a moment and wondered how I could let the reincarnation of Bubba slip away.

Bubba died when I was a teenager, long before serious curiosity about my past took root. When she was alive, she never talked much about herself, at least not around me. I knew she had been born in a small village in Byelorussia (now Belarus) that was frequently raided by marauding bands of Cossacks. But that was all I could remember. I knew nothing of her parents, other than what I had seen in the old family photo. Who were they? What were they like?

After sitting in that comfortable living room and examining the photographs of another family, I had the overwhelming desire to see and hear Bubba again, to have one last chance to ask questions that now were terribly important to me. I remembered I once asked my parents where Bubba came from. "Ask her yourself the next time you see her," they said. That was a long time ago. I couldn't remember whether I had.

I scrunched my brow, closed my eyes and forced myself to think back in time. Nothing came. The well of remembrance was dry. I looked up. The street was still silent, the breeze now gone, not even the hockey boys stirred. I could only remember Bubba's end — a shovel of dirt into her grave as the rabbi recited Kaddish, the Jewish prayer for the dead, on a cold November day.

19

The Craziest Man in the World

I returned to the hotel in the late afternoon. After a nap, I packed, and then hauled my backpacks downstairs. I was early, so I stashed the bags in a storage room and wandered aimlessly in the cavernous lobby. Lost in my thoughts, I was startled by a shout coming from the opposite end of the room. I turned to see a woman, resplendent in a full-length white fur coat and matching hat. Even from my distant vantage point, I saw that she was not like most other Russian woman I had encountered. Even the young women seemed old and bent, wrapped in their frayed coats, faces creased with melancholy. This woman was radiant and beautiful.

She called someone's name. The words echoed throughout the vast hall. She walked quickly, her heels tapping an urgent beat on the tile floor. She called again, but there was no reply. At first, I thought she was intercepting a cluster of Russian businessmen, who stood in a porous semi-circle puffing away at cigarettes, cheap vinyl briefcases at their sides. But the woman burst through the circle, looking momentarily like Snow White among the dwarves, as the men parted to let her pass. As she approached, I detected something familiar. Was it the smile framed by the ruby red lips? The walk? Or, just the revival of the crush I once had on Snow

White when I was seven? Some lucky schlub is going to get a nice greeting, I thought apathetically to myself. I glanced behind me to see who the schlub might be. At my end, the vast lobby was empty. I turned back. The vision of loveliness was rapidly approaching. What was the name she continued to shout? I strained to hear her words between the rhythmic clicks of her high heels.

"Robert, Robert!"

I was the schlub.

The woman in white was in my arms an instant before I figured it out. Nina hugged me as if we were long-lost lovers. She planted a moist kiss on each cheek, then stood back to appraise the bedraggled mess that I had become.

"Robert, you look sensational!"

I was speechless. Never in my travels had I received such a reception. I gaped at the fur and what must have been a pearl necklace draped around her porcelain neck.

"Ah, hello Nina, what a surprise," I stammered.

She took my hands and held them as if I were a puppy.

"Did you like Irkutsk?"

There was only one answer to this question. I replied enthusiastically, telling her in a breath about the trip to Baikal, Andrew's story about the train that fell through the ice, and the old woman and the jammed lock. "This is my favorite city in all of Siberia," I declared.

A look of mock anger crossed her radiant face.

"And Robert, why didn't you call me? You say you have been here two days, but you did not call?"

"I thought you said I should call only if I needed help, if I got into trouble," I said defensively.

She tossed back her head and laughed. "Yes, yes, that is exactly what I said. You are such a magnificent traveler. You have arrived in Irkutsk all by yourself without a group. You speak terrible Russian. Your clothes are close to rags and that hat with the flaps sticking out. No one wears a hat like that. You are the craziest man in the world."

We both laughed because it was absurd, yet true.

"Robert, I would like you to meet someone."

In the excitement I had not noticed the tall gaunt man with a wispy goatee who had trailed Nina and now stood behind her. With pallid skin shrink-wrapped around a thin face, he was a dead-ringer for the keynote speaker at an undertaker's convention. He seemed to be everything Nina wasn't. I wondered if this was her husband.

"This is Otto. He is from Germany and is here to negotiate an agreement with my research institute."

We shook hands. Otto's grip was limp and cold. I wondered if Otto's firm was supplying cadavers to Nina's institute, but I did not dwell long on that thought. My mind focused on Nina and began to concoct romantic possibilities. The Trans-Siberian departed in less than an hour. Maybe I could suggest a rendezvous on the train, or better yet, in Khabarovsk, my last stop. Once there, I envisioned a candlelit dinner in a cozy café, followed by a stroll, arm in arm, on a promenade along the Amur River (assuming there was a café and a promenade). Afterward, we would return to the privacy of my hotel room. An awkward moment would pass as I solved the mystery of the buttons on the back of her dress. I could almost feel her soft skin and see the curve of her breast in the moonlight. In the passionate frenzy that would surely follow, she would call out my name.

"Robert, you crazy man!"

Nina was calling my name, but not as part of my fantasy. I was jolted back to reality and the cavernous lobby of the Intourist Hotel.

"Robert? Are you well?"

She placed the back of her hand on my forehead.

"You are warm. You must get some rest."

"I'm fine. But I was just thinking . . . ."

"No more thinking, Robert," she chided, then pressed her index finger against my lips. "It was so good to see you again. But I must go now. Otto will take care of you."

"What?" I whimpered. "You're leaving so soon?"

I glanced at Otto. The last fragment of my Nina fantasy quickly dissolved into a World War II film clip of German soldiers goosestepping through the Arc De Triumph.

"I've told Otto all about you. You still have time to meet the rest of the German delegation. I didn't think I would see you again, but I'm sure they would like to hear directly from you about your amazing trip."

I was in her arms one last time. The warmth of her body seeped into mine like life-giving tonic. She broke from my embrace and walked swiftly away, pausing dramatically at the door for one last wave. Then she was gone; a flash of white elegance that had appeared from nowhere when I needed help. I wondered what might have happened if she had not run off. Would my romantic vision have come true?

Of course not! What was I thinking? Was I truly out of my mind? Nina was right. I really was the craziest man in the world, and I almost became the most foolish, as well. As I fought to regain control of my emotions, I realized that my intense attraction to her was a symptom of my difficult and lonely trip. I really didn't know Nina any more than I understood Russia itself. Even if she were a KGB agent — a mystery I would probably never solve — she had played the part of friend and companion to perfection. In Novosibirsk, she had prepared me to survive the rest of my trip. In Irkutsk, I was grateful she had merely remembered who I was in a country so vast that it seemed to swallow you up and digest you whole. Nina had called out my name in a nation of cold strangers. That had meant everything to me, and that was why I could have fallen in love with her a few short moments ago. But the spirits evidently had another fate in store for me.

I turned to Otto, who smiled at me with thin lips. We regarded each other warily.

"Please come with me, Herr Robert," he said coldly. "Please join us for a drink."

20

Secret Agent Man

I am not sure what compelled me to nod affirmatively to Herr Otto when my sense of self-preservation should have advised me to flee. An invisible hand seemed to push me along, accompanied by an inner voice that nagged: "What the heck, a drink with a delegation of German undertakers isn't going to kill you."

The elevator stopped at the third floor. We got off and entered a standard room, thick with smoke. Through the haze, I saw two chubby men wearing ill-fitted polyester suits, puffing away on cigarettes. One of them sported a perfectly bald dome — a dead ringer for Uncle Fester of *Addams Family* fame. A third person, a thickset woman who looked like she could play fullback for the Green Bay Packers, sat at a table in the corner, sawing away at a giant sausage. Bottles of vodka and champagne were lined up on the credenza. On top of a dresser, a boom box blared a melody sung in Russian that sounded familiar. When the singers cooed "choo-choo," the tune was unmistakable. It was "Chattanooga Choo-Choo" sung in a high-pitched nasal tone that sounded like a Slavic version of Alvin and the Chipmunks on amphetamines.

Over the yammering of the chipmunks, Otto introduced me to Herr Willy, Herr Boris, and Frau Wolf. Willy, the hairless one, was a part of the mysterious delegation, while Boris was their Russian escort. Otto explained Wolf's role, but I had trouble understanding exactly what he said because of his thick accent. I started across the room to shake her hand, when she suddenly barked in German something that sounded like "Can we eat him?" My German was little better than my Russian, but as a precaution I stopped, ready to bolt at the slightest hint of cannibalistic behavior. Wolf grasped her knife and fork like she meant business. She looked hungry.

"Would you like something to eat?" interpreted Otto.

"No thanks," I said, as Wolf loosened her grip on the cutlery. "But I think I will take you up on the drink."

Willy poured me a slug of vodka. Otto proposed a toast to friendship. We slammed down our shots. Willy refilled the glasses.

"Can you turn the stereo down?" I shouted.

Otto, whose English appeared somewhat limited, seemed confused by the request, but then brightened.

He turned the volume up. The song started over again. "Is very popular American song?" He shouted. "You like?"

"Was popular about fifty years ago," I shouted back.

Willy, his bald noggin shining brightly in the room lights, pumped his arms in time to the music, mimicking the pistons of a steam locomotive. When the chorus came around to "choo-choo," he joined in. Boris threw back another slug of vodka, then took a long satisfying drag on his cigarette, releasing more smoke into the smoggy room. Otto apparently was the only one of the four who spoke passable English.

The smoke, the song, and the vodka nauseated me. I found a place to sit on the edge of the bed and tried to keep track of the time. As a rule, I restrict my drinking when traveling alone in strange places. This definitely was not a good time to get bombed. I didn't want to miss the real choo-choo. But I also wanted to know who these guys were. Recalling that Nina said she had worked for a medical research institute in Irkutsk, I could only speculate that this crew was connected with that enterprise.

"You have been to Germany, yes?" asked Otto.

"No, but I have a friend who lives in Frankfurt," I replied.

"Frankfurt is in the Vest," said Otto.

"Yes," I said, beginning to realize that something was not quite right. "Are you talking about the other Germany?"

What little coloring was in Otto's face drained way. He stared at me, then turned and said something to the others. They were not smiling. Awkward seconds slowly ticked by. What had I done now?

"Ve are from the GDR," he said solemnly.

The names of communist states and their acronyms confused me. I was always getting the official names of the Germanys, Koreas, and Chinas of the world confused. My general rule was that countries with the most mention of "people's republic" and "democratic" in their title were the least republican and democratic of all.

My brain finally figured it out. These guys were from the German Democratic Republic. East Germany. Bad Germany. As in the Germany that made it a national pastime to drug its Olympic athletes. This was also the country whose citizens were so miserable that scores of them risked their lives to scale the Berlin Wall and dash to freedom. Climbers not agile or lucky enough were shot by the efficient border guards or hauled away by the secret police. Wolf, herself, looked as if she could easily torture prisoners while eating a pleasant lunch and enjoying a big stein of beer. The fact was that I hadn't heard a lot of good stuff about East Germany. I was also vaguely aware that the U.S. State Department was not keen on U.S. citizens meeting with East German officials. On the other hand, I wasn't sure what direction the State Department would give to a fellow citizen who blundered into a smoke-filled room with an ill-defined delegation of East Germans, swigging vodka and singing along to "Chattanooga Choo-Choo." At least it was an American song, even if sung by Russian-speaking chipmunks.

I took another sip of vodka. The burning was much less intense this time. My head swam.

"Oh, East Germany, how about that," I said lamely. "I have never met any East Germans before. What city are you from?"

"Ve are from Dresden."

"You wouldn't happen to be real East German officials, would you?" I blurted.

"Ve are official East German delegation," said Otto defensively. "Ve are here to assist Soviet medical research institute."

"Ah, I didn't mean to imply you weren't. I am sure you are great delegates. Tell me again, why are you here?"

The Germans looked at the Russian. The Russian looked at the Germans. More awkward silence ensued. The chipmunks chattered on, the track apparently snagged on endless replay. Wolf continued to glare at me with suspicion. Without diverting her gaze, she raised the knife and stabbed another sausage chunk, then flicked it off with her fork. The meat plopped onto her plate. Otto leaned over and whispered something into Boris's ear. I was beginning to wonder what sort of medical research business these guys were involved with. Or, was that just a cover? Had I really stumbled onto something else, something sensitive, perhaps even sinister — something the State Department would be interested in?

"Ve sell sanitation and medical equipment," said Otto.

I detected a waver of nervousness in his reply. Something wasn't quite right. I could see beads of perspiration forming on Boris's brow as he fidgeted on the bed. Uncle Fester had stopped pumping his arms to the music, though he continued to mouth the lyrics. I kept an eye on Wolf to make sure the knife stayed in the vicinity of the sausage. Nervous seconds passed to the accompaniment of the chipmunks.

Medical equipment — that's what they all said. I felt the urge to press for more information. If the guys back home could only see me now, I thought. *Bob Goldstein: Secret Agent Man.* The phrase had a certain ring, a rhythm and pace all its own ... *secret agent man.* I saw myself pursued by black-suited bad guys, an entire gaggle of Uncle Fester look-alikes sprinting after me through the gray streets of some undemocratic and unrepublican country. I leap between speeding trains, dodge a knife hurled by an evil spy-mistress, and drive my specially equipped secret agent car through a wall of flames before I am cornered. But wait. All is not lost. I pull a cord inside my blazer, and suddenly the thrusters of my jet pack fire into action. I blast off to safety. They can never catch me because I am too fast, too quick, too smart, and too damn handsome. Torture me. Never! I am too tough. Seduce me with beautiful women; well maybe, but not for long, once I remember I am incorruptible because I am Bob Goldstein: Secret Agent Man! The chipmunks dissolve into my own theme song, a sassy tune that anyone would recognize as a rip-off from an old James Bond film.

"What kind of equipment?" I asked casually.

Otto and Willy conferred with Boris in hushed tones. They looked tense and upset, as if a plot had been prematurely revealed. I sat on the bed, nervously jiggling the ice in my vodka glass. With a thud, Wolf lopped off another chunk of sausage. The surge of adrenaline that had fueled my *secret agent man* fantasy began to ebb. Had I really stumbled upon some secret deal between these evil governments? Otto and Willy looked at me again, then to Boris. Boris gave an almost imperceptible nod. My muscles tensed. I needed a jet pack real bad.

Reaching under the bed, Willy pulled out a large white cardboard cylinder. From the canister, he unsheathed a thick roll of blueprints.

They are going to show me the secret plans, I thought. Another round of the theme song played through my head. With a snap of the wrist, Otto unrolled the plans onto the bed. A set of smudged blueprints lay before me. Yes, it looked like a large factory of some sort, with a gigantic water tank and intricate valves. Perhaps it was a cooling tower for a nuclear reactor.

"What is it?" I asked innocently.

"Vis is der vasser closet!" declared Otto triumphantly.

"You mean this is a toilet?"

"Jah," replied Uncle Fester.

Bob Goldstein: Secret Agent Man crashes to earth in a smoking pile of rubble. Bob Goldstein, the traveling schlub with the hyperactive imagination, looked at the not-so-secret blueprints for what appeared to be a giant East German toilet, complete with an easy-to-reach toilet paper dispenser for the infirm and a convenient pull lever at the top of the tank. Willy, who apparently was the engineer of this marvel, beamed.

"Ve think this vasser closet is better for medical institute. Uses little vasser and very clean," said Otto, earnestly. "You like?"

"Very nice."

"Russian vasser closets no good, kaput!" said Otto, giving me a conspiratorial wink out of view of Boris.

More awkward silence followed while Willy, Otto, and Boris beamed at the blueprints. I pretended to study the plans, asking polite questions about valves, pipes, and capacity. Wolf, still seated at the table, grunted as she attacked a surviving hunk of sausage. I downed another slug of vodka, having apparently forgotten my rule about over-imbibing. Then I looked at my watch.

I stood. The delegates stood. Even Wolf stood. We shook hands all around. I mumbled something about what a fine toilet it was, a great idea. Otto tried to give me a sales pitch, something about other special vasser closet technologies their firm was developing under the direction of the brilliant Herr Willy and maybe I could pass on a good word to my American manufacturing friends about these remarkable designs emerging from that citadel of innovation, the GDR. "Is good for business, no?" he asked. *Good things from Bad Germany.* I thought that might make a good advertising pitch, but then again, sales was never one of my strengths.

"You know American-Standard?" asked Otto, sensing he was losing his audience.

"Yes, I've heard of them," I said, puzzled.

American-Standard was the U.S. conglomerate that seemed to have cornered the free world market on ceramic bathroom equipment. I knew this for a fact because every time I peed at a public urinal, I stared into the corporate logo stamped on the drain.

"I mean, I don't know them personally," I added.

"Please speak to American-Standard about der vasser closet," said Otto, earnestly.

"Okay," I said, thinking that was the most expedient reply to speed my departure. It was getting late. "I'll give Mr. Standard a call when I get home, first thing after picking up my mail."

Otto smiled broadly as he interpreted for the others. An impromptu celebration erupted. Willy stood up and performed a weird soft-shoe routine to the rhythm of the music. Wolf cut loose with an "American-Standard, jah!" raising her hands in twin fists as if to signal a Packers touchdown. Boris remained calm, puffing on his cigarette, his eyes glazed from the Russian curse — vodka. I wondered if Otto had told them I was the Russian sales representative for American-Standard and had just ordered a dozen of the contraptions. Willy soft-shoed to the credenza and poured me another drink. But that was not what I had in mind. I edged toward the door.

I shook hands with Otto, then backed out of the room to one final chorus of Russian-accented "Choo-Choo." I slammed the door, and blundered down the hall, my head swaddled in vodka-induced numbness. Not wanting to wait for the elevator, I stumbled down the stairs and into the lobby.

An hour later, I stood on the station platform and tried to make sense of the day. Until recently, I had never given serious consideration to the connection of seemingly random events. If I had given it any thought before, I would not have taken it seriously. I was a practical sort of guy, with feet firmly planted in the earth. If I couldn't see, eat, or smell it — whatever it was — it probably did not exist. But too much weird stuff had happened in the past ten days. I was still thinking about Mother Russia's story about the funny man and whether it was meant to kindle the thought that possibly a distant relative had come this way. It could not have been an accident that I had stumbled upon the woman fumbling with the lock, and that her family photos would trigger vivid memories of my own Bubba. Nina's reappearance was meant to prepare me for the final leg of my journey. I could not make heads or tails out of the encounter with the East German toilet delegation, other than to think my spirit guides had thrown them into the mix for comic relief. The last act notwithstanding, I felt a strong premonition that something big, something significant, would happen before my journey ended. It would have to happen soon; the end was less than three days away.

The glare of the lights had sucked away all color, leaving the platform at the Irkutsk train station populated by distant shadows. Glancing furtively about my surroundings, I half expected phantom Cossacks to spring forth and drag me away. I clapped my hands and stomped my feet to keep warm. Most of all, I wanted to still my rising apprehension that evil lurked around every corner.

The temperature had plummeted. Tiny ice crystals, suspended in the night air like fairy dust, floated in shafts of light beaming down from flood lamps mounted on steel girders. A woman, warped with age and bundled like a vagabond in shawl and heavy wool coat, squatted next to me. Another woman brushed by me, pushing an ancient pram. Two tiny faces, each swaddled in fur, peered tentatively at me through the covers, like a pair of muskrats getting their first glimpse of life. One of the babes pointed a tiny finger at me and shrieked. Farther down, stern-faced militiamen in gray greatcoats, rifles slung over their shoulders, morosely patrolled the platform.

The loudspeaker blared the pending arrival of the eastbound Trans-Siberian Express. On cue, dozens of passengers emerged from the dark recesses of the station. They scuttled into the light, lugging worn suitcases, ancient trunks, and tired boxes tied together with frayed twine.

At first, the sound was faint, like the rumble of distant thunder. The storm approached, followed by the clanking of the bell, then the shriek of the horn. A ray of light pierced the night air, illuminating the tracks ahead. At last the engine rolled into view, the red star prominent on its nose. Conductors waving red signal flags leaned from the narrow step at the end of each carriage. The long line of coaches rolled slowly by, venting plumes of steam from hidden fissures.

The scene was like an old black-and-white film. For a moment, I imagined I was no longer in Irkutsk, but on the platform of Petrograd's Finland Station. It is April 1917, and Lenin is aboard the train that is pulling into the station. He is returning from exile. In the coming months, he would begin to orchestrate the October revolution that would topple the provisional government. Civil war would spread throughout the land, with the last embers of revolt smothered not far from where I stood.

With a final jolt, the Trans-Siberian stopped. I grabbed my backpack and waded into the sea of humanity that surged forward. I found carriage number seven, handed my ticket to an attractive female conductor, a curl of blond hair straying from under her fur-lined cap, then climbed aboard.

Relieved to find my compartment empty, I swung my packs off and stowed them in the rack above the seat. I was hoping for a respite, to make sense of the trip's events, as well as to put myself back together. Physically, I was a mess. East German cigarette smoke, vodka, and the frosty night enhanced the stirring of a cold that was fermenting in my throat and head. Evidence of a runny nose was slowly accumulating on my jacket sleeve. A thin sliver of chicken − the remains of dinner − had managed to wedge itself between my front teeth.

I was preoccupied with dislodging the morsel with my index finger when the door to my compartment slid open; before me stood a powerfully built Adonis who could have graced the cover of any men's health magazine. His face was chiseled from flawless granite, never marred by pimple or blemish. He slid a fur coat off his muscular trunk, and carefully removed an enormous rust-colored fur hat that made it appear as if a marmot had curled up on top of his head. A shock of blond hair cascaded to his shoulders.

I stared dumbfounded at this magnificent specimen of half-man, half-boy. When he had finished stowing his gear, he turned and stared with steely blue eyes at the small man in the parka with mucous-stained sleeves.

The script was not going to allow a respite. There was only one thing to do. I yanked my finger from my mouth, stood up, and extended the same hand in greeting.

"Good evening. I am Bob, the tourist from America. I don't speak Russian," I said in Russian.

I couldn't resist adding one last tagline in English.

"Thor, I presume?"

21

The Hero

Thor stared down at me. A smile spread slowly across his face, revealing a perfect set of teeth that gleamed in the light that was slanting through the compartment window. He gently set down his bag, pulled off a pair of mittens, then extended a powerful paw. His enthusiastic handshake nearly crushed the weary bones in my hand.

With a lurch, the train began its eastward journey. I lost my balance, stumbling into the steel chest of the stranger, only to bounce off like a ping-pong ball. The godlike creature clamped a firm grip on my shoulder. I was steadied.

"Hello Bob, the tourist," he said in slow Russian, as he shook my hand. "I am Andrei, the Siberian. I do not speak English."

He spoke in the same perfect phrase-book Russian I had used. For a moment, I thought he might be mocking me. I was tense, fearing what might happen next. But that quickly passed as I sensed a friendly and curious aura about my new roommate, who appeared to be in his late teens or early twenties.

Andrei sat on the opposite bunk. He spoke slowly as if time was the key to translating the Russian words. I fumbled through my pack and found the phrase book. Andrei could see that my attempt to look up each word was hopeless. He moved to my bunk, and together we began to construct crude sentences. When the phrase book failed us, Andrei sifted through his bag and took out a giant pad of ruled paper, the kind I once practiced penmanship on in elementary school. I half expected Andrei to produce a fat green pencil to complement the big paper. But he had nothing to write with. I found an extra pen in my pack, took the pad, and sketched a picture of the United States, marking Seattle in the far upper left corner. When I was done, he drew a picture of the Soviet Union with a thin line across its girth. "Rossiya," he pointed, as he drew a picture of a little train heading toward the east. In Cyrillic, he wrote out Ulan Ude, which I knew to be the next major stop. That's where he was from.

We talked — if you want to call it that — late into the night. Occasionally, one of us would stop and glance at the window, motioning to the other when a particularly good view flashed by. Even though it was night, the light from the moon reflected off the still waters of Lake Baikal as the train skirted its southern shore. When not passing through tunnels, Rossiya hugged the sides of the steep, snow-covered Trans-Baikal Mountains.

As the evening wore on, I got the nagging feeling that I had seen Andrei before. But where? He looked familiar. Then I remembered the posters.

Throughout the Soviet Union, gigantic posters depicted its powerful fair-haired youth in heroic poses. Muscled arms gripped hammers, wielded sickles, or clutched huge wrenches. They stood proudly on the turrets of tanks, drove mighty combines through fields of golden wheat, or emerged triumphantly from gleaming space capsules. Usually the word "production" or some other slogan exhorting the proletariat to greater feats of sacrifice was inscribed across the top in bright red letters. This was the vision that Soviet leaders once saw for their country: selfless individual sacrifice for the good of the state. Many of these posters were now faded and in otherwise sad repair. The propaganda machine was sputtering, and what was left was decaying as quietly as the state itself. When

I saw these portraits, I wondered where these beautiful muscled youth were hiding. From my narrow vantage point, I had observed a country only populated with short, pasty-faced men and old women, whose collective muscle tissue had withered away long ago. Was I too quick to judge? Here, before me, sat perhaps the last physical embodiment of all that was noble about the utopia that the Soviet state had promised.

If Andrei was aware of his resemblance to the models I remembered, he didn't let on. Instead, he exuded modesty that bordered on innocence. His questions to me were earnest and sincere. He showed no interest in the blue jeans trade that consumed his countrymen. There was no mention of covert deals to ship videotape recorders across borders, or hushed whispers concerning the exchange of foreign currency. I came to perceive Andrei not as the Nordic god that first appeared in my compartment, but as the Siberian version of the Iowa farm boy away from home for the first time. This perception was reinforced when he indicated to me that he had been visiting his grandmother in Irkutsk. He was now returning home. At the mention of his grandmother, I was again reminded of my own recent epiphany about my Russian-born Bubba.

Andrei rummaged through his satchel, withdrawing a jar of jam and a bottle of dark red liquid. I hoped it wasn't beet juice, if there was such a substance.

"For you," he said. "My grandmother makes."

I protested, but to no avail. He insisted.

My grandmother was always giving my sister and me small gifts: a pen, coloring book, candy. I often wondered how she managed to smuggle the stuff into the nursing home. After each gift giving, my parents were quick to remind me to thank Bubba by sending either a thank-you note or a reciprocal gift. Those parental commands, still firmly implanted, were now reactivated. I rummaged through my bag. My gift supply was running dangerously low. One decent felt-tip pen remained. That would make an appropriate gift, I thought.

Andrei accepted the pen graciously. After stowing it, he seemed for a moment uncertain, then his face brightened as if he had just received instructions from an invisible guide on what to do next. With a flourish, he opened his bag and pulled out a pack of cigarettes.

"For you," he said, triumphantly. I protested again, indicating that I did not smoke. He would not take the cigarettes back.

"For Russian friends," he said.

I took the cigarettes, then looked into my pack to see if there was anything left to give him. Other than dirty underwear — not exactly gift material — I was out of stuff. In my mind, I heard the voice of my mother demanding to know if I had reciprocated yet. I smiled weakly at Andrei, while my brain raced through an inventory of my remaining possessions. There had to be something.

The cocktail sausages! That was it. I had purchased a can of cocktail sausages in Novosibirsk, the only edible meat available to supplement my dwindling supply of survival rations. I was nearly finished with the trip. In thirty-six hours, I would be safe and sound in Khabarovsk, the end of the line.

I pulled the shiny can from its plastic bag, presenting the sausages to Andrei like they were the crown jewels. He looked perplexed, raising his palms in the international sign of no thanks. He couldn't accept the gift. I continued to hold the can in front of him. Maybe he wasn't sure what was in the tin. I pantomimed eating and drinking, adding that that they were snacks best consumed with vodka or beer.

"I do not drink," said Andrei.

Great, I thought, I had managed to meet the only young man in Russia who did not drink. "But," I indicated in partial English and partial Russian. "It is for your friends who do drink or for your mother and father."

He accepted the gift.

After stashing the can under his bunk, Andrei seemed more befuddled than ever.

"Aha!" he said. He smiled broadly. I watched in horror as he opened his satchel. Not again, I thought. How much stuff does he have in that bag? He pulled out a sack.

"For you, from my grandmother," he said, handing me an enormous sack that held enough cookies to feed all of Ulan Ude. I added the cookies to the other stuff piling up on my side of the bunk.

I smiled at Andrei. Andrei smiled wanly at me. We were in a gift-giving death spiral, and we both knew it. Other than ripping off my clothes and presenting them as a final offering, I could not think of anything else to do. I shifted self-consciously in my seat. Andrei read the label on the can of his cocktail sausages.

"Andrei, would you like to see a picture of my family?" I said, while pulling out the photo from my bag. Then added as an afterthought, "Not a gift."

Andrei broke into a big smile. The uncertainty left his face. He picked up my fur cap and examined the bald spots where tufts of fur had fallen out.

"Hat no good," he said, shaking his head solemnly. He showed me the large rust-colored hat that I had first admired when he entered the compartment, then he gently placed it on my head. "Not a gift," he said, laughing. The hat was several sizes too big. It threatened to engulf my entire head.

"Aha! Bob, the tourist from America, is now Bob, the Siberian!" He stood aside so I could see myself in the mirror on the compartment wall. A small grizzled face peeked out from the enormous pile of fur resting on my head. As the train rocked and rolled, the hat fell over my eyes, swallowing half my head; several minutes passed before we both stopped laughing. When the gaiety had died down, he explained with the help of my phrase book that his father was a trapper. The hat itself was hand-stitched by his mother from muskrat hides, as were his coat and mittens.

By midnight we had talked and pantomimed ourselves to near exhaustion. Eventually, I had turned to journal writing. Andrei read a newspaper. I was dozing off when I felt a tug at my sleeve. Andrei looked concerned. "Spid," he repeated, a note of intensity in his voice.

"What is it?"

The phrase book was not helpful. He showed me the newspaper and pointed to an article. Before I could puzzle out the Cyrillic, Andrei grabbed his throat and with bugged out eyes, he dropped to the floor and began writhing. It was a splendid performance.

"Shakespeare, William Shakespeare!" I yelled, thinking that perhaps the Russian nickname for the great writer was William Spid. But Andrei shook his head sadly.

"Boris Godonov!" I said, trying a Russian tragic hero.

That wasn't it, either.

He showed me the newspaper and pointed to a word in Cyrillic. I sounded out each letter, and translated to the appropriate sound in English. I then realized that the letter I had thought was a "p" was actually a "d." The anagram was now clear.

"You're asking me about AIDS?" I shouted, as if I were a contestant on the television show *Jeopardy.*

"Da!" he exclaimed.

In 1987 the AIDS epidemic was in its infancy, confined in the U.S., mostly to the gay community and drug users who pricked themselves with needles. I certainly was not an expert on the subject. Attempting to discuss AIDS with a phrase book limited to archaic expressions for ordering in a restaurant and asking directions to the ballet was a problem. I grabbed the *Pravda* from which Andrei found the acronym. Glancing at the article, I could discern only a few additional bits of information. It appeared to indicate that the disease was prevalent among American blacks, but that eventually the entire U.S. population would succumb.

How could I tell him how the disease was transmitted, and who was at risk? I flashed back to a conversation I had in Moscow with my friend Ken and other journalists. "Have you ever seen a Russian condom?" asked one member of the group, a wise guy from Italy. I thought he was telling a joke. "They are like the fingers of rubber garden gloves. Like most things in this country, the majority of them are defective after they leave the factory. No one uses them." The country was ripe for AIDS, though the Soviets blamed African exchange students for causing the few publicly acknowledged cases. It seemed only a matter of time before the plague spread throughout the Soviet Union.

I used sign language and the limited vocabulary available to us, but this was much more difficult than establishing where we lived and the occupations of our parents. How do you convey the sexual act between men when words wouldn't suffice? Sign language combined with modesty would only take me so far. Andrei's face was a study in concentration as I struggled for words. I grabbed the pad and drew pictures, first of intravenous injection, then of two stick figures doing the unmentionable. Was he merely curious about the article that introduced a subject that had not reached Ulan Ude? Or was there something else? Was he gay, perhaps not yet even aware of his own sexual orientation?

I studied the young man — the strong body, the perfect face — and wondered why every young maiden this side of Irkutsk wasn't knocking down the compartment door to get a glimpse of this superman. This thought led to another about whether I should set a boundary, to establish myself as a bona fide heterosexual male. "Hey, you should have seen this chick I met in Irkutsk the other day," I would say, then slap Andrei on his back, like he was one of the guys. But I did none of this. I felt no threat, only impotence for not being able to fully answer his questions and satisfy his inquisitiveness.

Our gaze met for a fraction of a second. I saw steel blue eyes and the hunger for information. Please do not be gay, I thought to myself, because if you are, you have no chance. I saw a vision of Andrei — a gaunt face attached to a thin body, scabbed with sores — a god dying from a disease the state said officially did not exist. The image was too grim. I willed it away. This cannot happen. You're too good. You're the hero youth, the hope of the future. I recalled a poster I had seen in Moscow. In it, the muscular arm of a young man hoists a sickle amid a golden wheat field; the Soviet Star above radiates crimson rays across the land. This is the future I wanted to believe was in store for Andrei, if not for his country.

At some point in the early morning hours, I motioned that I was exhausted and needed to sleep. We retreated to our own bunks.

Seemingly in the next instant, the conductor was knocking on our compartment door, shouting "Ulan Ude!" The train slowed, its wheels screeching in the cold night. The bright lights of the station again slanted into the compartment. Andrei was already dressed, his size exaggerated by the stark light.

Bleary-eyed, I roused myself. He extended his hand. I hugged him, engulfing myself in the fur of his coat.

"Good-bye, my friend," he whispered, in the English I had taught him. Then he was gone.

I gazed out the window. I caught one last glimpse of perfection striding confidently head and shoulders above his hunched and stooped countrymen, shivering in the predawn cold.

22

Phantom Father

Although I had spent only a few hours with Andrei, I felt I could have trusted him with my life. He was the strong and resourceful companion one needed on this kind of trip. Now I was alone in a place that seemed to grow stranger and more foreign by the hour. I watched the lights of the Ulan Ude station recede. It seemed as if Andrei himself sucked away the luminous rays as he made his way down the platform.

As Rossiya plunged back into the Siberian night, I imagined the friendly giant padding up to the doorstep of his own home. There would be hugs all around, and then he would tell the story of the unusual traveler with whom he had shared a compartment. What an adventurous soul! He came all the way from Seattle and was by himself. His Russian was terrible and his hat ridiculous. And yet he had made it all this way. The story would grow over time, embellished, until the mystery traveler had reached legend status worthy of Marco Polo. He was a spy. He was looking for a long-lost relative. He had fled his homeland heartbroken, having been spurned by his lover, and was seeking exile. He was stricken with the dreaded SPID and was looking for a place to die.

But at that moment, the real adventurous soul could only think about how much he wanted to be in his own living room with its cherished view of Lake Washington. The romanticism of solitary travel through a foreign land had long since ebbed. Perhaps other travelers could endure weeks or months of hardship and loneliness. One thing was for sure; I was not like the legendary Marco Polo, but rather an ordinary traveler who found himself on an extraordinary journey.

I was ready to go home, and yet, home seemed impossibly far away. I felt small and insignificant, a mere speck against the endless backdrop of forest, steppe, and mountains that passed before my window. I now understood why exile to Siberia was a horrible sentence, like death. Unless you bought a train ticket, escape was hopeless. The land was too immense; the rivers too wide and ice-choked, the mountains too high, and the steppe too vast. The czars and later the Soviets knew that this place was the best prison of them all. Siberia swallowed you whole, and there you remained. You adapted, you went crazy, or you died.

In the black night that enveloped the train, I now perceived a wicked presence that seemed to follow Rossiya as it groaned and creaked around each bend in the track. Only the thin metal walls protected the passengers from this invisible menace. For nearly two hours, I sat wrapped in a blanket paralyzed with fear. I saw myself dashing through the train shaking dozing passengers, urging them to flee from the unseen terror. "Get out while you can!" I cried. But Rossiya's occupants stared at me with apathetic eyes. They would not budge. Rossiya will protect us, they seemed to say with their eyes. She always has. "But who will protect me?" I asked. The question went unanswered.

At last shaking myself from the trance, I changed into my sweatpants, and burrowed under the thin blankets. Hours later, when I peeked from my cocoon, I saw that night had been replaced by the somber half-light of early morning.

My body ached. My throat was sore. My head was on fire. The dark forces I had perceived earlier had manifested themselves in my body. I stretched out in the bunk as the sickness invaded. Mantra-like, I willed myself not to get sick; not now, not while roaming this land of quiet desperation. I marshaled my troops, but they were no match for the onslaught of illness. The chills and fever spread quickly, sapping my strength and dulling my spirit.

Later that morning, I managed to worm out of the covers and hoist myself to the ice-encrusted window. Sunshine burst through fierce clouds, highlighting a forest of thin Siberian firs. A sawmill yard rolled into view, then a rusting wigwam belching smoke. Thousands of trees stacked like matchsticks in a muddy yard awaited the blade. These trees are too small, too skinny, too young to be cut, I thought. More forests of emaciated firs replaced the sawmill. I had read that the Siberian fir grows slowly in harsh conditions. This was as big as they got, mere toothpicks compared to the towering Douglas firs I lived among in the Pacific Northwest. The forests were being cut far faster than they could grow back. Another clearing came into view, another sawmill. The scene repeated itself throughout the morning until I finally lapsed into a restless sleep. I dreamed of an endless procession of whimpering, malnourished trees feeding a voracious sawmill.

When I awoke, the trees and sawmills had been replaced with barren hills covered with snow. In this stark landscape, miles from any settlement, I saw a solitary man carrying a worn brown rucksack. A single-barreled shotgun was slung over his shoulder. I thought he might be a hunter. His stride was purposeful. He paused to look at the train, then turned his back and headed up a gentle incline, his body framed against a horizon of clouds and cracks of blue that stretched forever.

Who are you? In my growing delirium, I imagine I am that man; alone, searching for my identity on an endless horizon. I hear the crunch of the snow beneath my boots. Despite the solitude, I feel a sense of the familiar. The hills and open spaces call to me. They are the landscapes that resonate within my ancestral soul. I am the wanderer, searching the frozen plain for a familiar face that I sensed once trudged this way. I wonder where these thoughts come from, as I have never thought them before.

The train slowed for a stop. With a groan, I again hoisted myself to the window. The Cyrillic lettering on the station roof announced that we were in Motch (or something that looked like that), a town not on my map. I stared apathetically at the crowd shuffling around on the platform as Rossiya eased into the station. Something was different about this village, but I couldn't immediately figure out what.

People smiled when greeting each other. Bright red streamers hung from the station awning and stretched across the platform. Near the station's entrance, a half-dozen musicians strummed balalaikas. Young women in flowered aprons with bright red ribbons tied in their hair performed a folk dance in a semi-circle around the musicians. The sun shone.

Mesmerized by the festivities, I was momentarily distracted by a man, my father's age, moving rapidly across the platform toward the train. I blinked and rubbed my eyes to make sure they were not tricking me. The man was still in view. The mustache, the lean build, the Omar Sharif face were so familiar. I smacked myself on the side of the head to make sure I wasn't dreaming. Sure enough, the man bore an uncanny resemblance to my father. Magically, he had been re-created here, in the middle of Siberia. I pressed my face against the window and waved.

"Dad, over here! It's me. It's Robert. It's me, here on the train," I whispered hoarsely into the rapidly fogging glass, while allowing my mind to suspend belief. There was so much I wanted to ask him. How did he get to Motch? Did any of our relatives come this way? Is Motch full of people like you and me? The questions bounced randomly in my fevered head. My gaze fixed on the man.

He did not see me. Through the crowd he walked, with the same quick and purposeful strides I knew so well. As a child, I was always trying to keep up with my father. When I was older, I would chide him for walking so fast. "What is the rush?" I would ask. He would say he wanted to beat the traffic. I spent my entire childhood chasing after my father, beating the traffic.

The man was searching for someone. His eyes impatiently scanned the platform, then moved to the carriage windows. Suddenly, he glanced in my direction.

Yes, here I am.

His stare bore through me as if I were a ghost. I waved frantically.

My thoughts raced. Here I am! Don't you see me? I am on this train, and I am alone, so alone. His eyes moved on, searching the next compartment window, then the next, moving down the row of windows in a rapid, logical progression, just the way I knew he would; the way I know I would.

Can't you see me! I screamed, but I had no voice.

I had to get off the train. I scrambled to my feet, searching for my famous shoes.

Piles of clothes, a sack of cookies, and pages from my phrase book lie scattered in the compartment. The shoes were hiding somewhere. I pawed through my ragtag possessions. Time was running out. If nothing else, Rossiya was always on time, never dawdling for more than a few minutes at village stations.

With a lurch, the train began to move. I darted back to the window. The man was shrinking as the platform slowly receded. I waved frantically.

Stop the train. Please stop the train.

But it was too late. Rossiya had resumed its relentless journey, leaving the man whom I thought was my father on the station platform in the middle of Siberia. The band, the dancing girls, and the streamers shimmering in the golden light faded from view. Rossiya rounded a bend. Motch was gone, swallowed up by the wilderness.

In despair, I slumped onto my bunk, consumed by loss even though I had only lost an illusion. Within the part of my brain still functioning properly, I knew the man couldn't possibly have been my father. Yet the image seemed so real and my sense of loneliness was so intense that even the loss of a phantom father was too much to bear. Propping myself against the cold window, I stared listlessly at the opposite bunk, now empty. I felt myself dropping into an abyss. Hours passed. The sky darkened. Afterward, I remembered nothing of that time except the anguish of depression.

Someone was shaking me. I opened my eyes. The kitchen attendant, a look of concern on his face, hovered nearby. He had wheeled a stainless steel cart carrying bowls of chicken soup and other delectable delights into the compartment. Without speaking, he ladled soup into a bowl and handed it to me. The aroma stirred me from my lethargy. I sat up smartly and greedily ate my meal, feeling the life-affirming liquid coursing through my body.

After eating, I slept in fitful starts. I lost track of time. Was it morning or evening? Occasionally, I eased myself up to the window and watched the gray scenery. Villages, interspersed with long stretches of wilderness, rolled by, but none of them were like Motch. I saw no bands, no pretty girls, and no one who even remotely resembled my father.

While the train was stopped in Chita, the door to my compartment slid open. I propped myself up on my bunk and rubbed my eyes in disbelief. A chunky man with a thin brown mustache entered. A surge of adrenaline shot through my veins.

"Mike!" I yelled out, happily. The man looked exactly like a lifelong friend, Mike Bellinghausen, whom I first met when we were undergraduates at Oregon State University. We had been roommates for nearly three years. His presence on the train both delighted and confused me.

"Mike, is that really you? Mike, why are you on this train? Why are you speaking in Russian?" I babbled.

A tired, befuddled expression crossed the man's face. No, he was not Mike. He was Yuri, and he looked about as sick as I was. Without another word, Yuri took off his hat and coat, removed his shoes, and slid under the covers of the opposite bunk. I stared at the now-slumbering Yuri, and waited for him to spring back to life as my buddy Mike.

"Mike, I saw my father back there, and now you. How about that!" That's what I would have said, the enthusiasm of the moment moving my words. But Yuri just snored.

With each snort, this new illusion faded, and I slid back into the abyss. This trip, originally pursued for the simple joy of taking a grand train ride, had transformed into an overland version of *The Odyssey.* Day after day of intense and strange encounters, coupled with the need to be in a constant state of mental alertness, had taken its toll. I feared the stress and sleep deprivation were leading to a rapid deterioration of my mental health. Was this the path to insanity revealed by the accidental flip of Moon's tarot card?

To save myself, I knew I would soon need to touch, feel, or be with someone or something familiar. I recalled my conversation with Moon about spirit guides. *Everyone has spirit guides,* she told me in her clipped New Zealand accent. Mine, it seemed, had abandoned me. I begged them to return, promising to be good forever if only they would guide me out of the abyss. Meanwhile, Rossiya continued on without pause, rattling and jerking along a rail bed built by criminals and political exiles and warped by permafrost.

That night I dreamt of hamburgers, french fries, and golden arches. About to sink my teeth into a juicy quarter-pounder (with cheese), I was jolted back to reality by the loud invitation to breakfast by the kitchen attendant. My first instinct was to throttle him for interrupting what would have been a sumptuous meal. But then I remembered his kindness of the previous day. He indicated with sign language that food was being served in the restaurant car. I thanked him, but was too depressed to get up. I lay in my bunk and listened to Yuri snore, while watching the shadow patterns dance on the ceiling of the compartment.

The morning passed much like the previous day. In the late afternoon, I managed to stagger into the restaurant car. Despite loneliness, I found that I wanted to be alone. I could not face strangers. My wish was granted. The car was empty except for a woman sporting a pageboy haircut, and she was leaving. With my tattered phrase book and notes from Nina, I began to translate the menu. The waitress, clucking like a hen, strutted over to my table. A look of consternation replaced her smile when she saw me hunched over the book. She snatched the menu from my hands and disappeared into the galley. I did not protest or try to stop her. It was useless. A minute later she reappeared with another menu. Wonderful, I thought, this is the menu that has everything crossed out.

I opened the new menu. Nothing was crossed out. The words were in English.

The warmth of the beef broth that was soon delivered to my table filled me with new strength. My troops were counterattacking. I felt the illness retreating. Outside, the scenery seemed to be building to a climax. Deep chasms and rugged mountains replaced the pleasant hills of yesterday. Huge snowflakes fluttered from the sky like confetti, adding to the deep snow already on the ground. I knew we were near the part of the line that came close to the Chinese border. Tension between the two countries was palpable. Somewhere in these canyons and mountains, thousands of Soviet and Chinese troops faced off against each other. Rossiya crossed numerous steel girder bridges, each guarded by armed sentries standing at attention in the middle of nowhere. Elsewhere, railroad workers clad in bright orange vests huddled by fires alongside the track.

For years this section of track, known as the Amur line, had been the Siberian version of the missing link. When Burton Holmes and Congressman Ebenezer Hill traveled the Trans-Siberian, the rails ended at Sretensk, where passengers boarded ferries for the journey via the Amur River to Khabarovsk. From Khabarovsk, they reboarded trains for the final leg to Vladivostok. Deterred by the high cost of building a railroad through the mountains and marshes, the Russians preferred to cut straight across the flat lands of Manchuria that protruded into Siberia like a camel's hump. The Chinese granted the concession, and by 1903 passengers could ride between Moscow and Vladivostok with the only interruption being the troublesome crossing at Lake Baikal. But the ever-changing political climate, particularly the instability in China and the growing power of Japan, convinced the czarist government to build the Amur line, which was safely tucked away in Russian territory. It opened in 1916.

The lonely sentries guarding the tracks also reminded me of one of the more bizarre events during the chaotic years following the Russian Revolution. After the Bolsheviks withdrew Russia from World War I, a corps of 12,000 Czech soldiers, formerly allied with czarist forces against the Central Powers, found themselves stranded in the Ukraine, and their march home blocked by the German army. Granted safe passage to Vladivostok by the newly established Bolshevik government, the Czechs planned to circumnavigate German lines via Siberia and then sail back home. Before the plan could be fully executed, Russia plunged into civil war, leaving Czech forces scattered along the Trans-Siberian railroad.

For a year, the well-armed Czech Legion controlled vast stretches of the railroad, patrolling the tracks in armored cars, refusing to cede it to the Bolsheviks. The plight of the Czechs and their control of the railroad drew the attention of U.S. President Woodrow Wilson, who, along with the other Allied leaders, knew the strategic importance of keeping the line open and repatriating the Czechs.

In 1918, a U.S. expeditionary force landed in Vladivostok to help the Czechs leave and to guard the railroad. The Americans were deployed along the tracks at roughly one-hundred-mile intervals between Ulan Ude and Mysovsk, on the eastern shore of Lake Baikal. Other U.S. troops were garrisoned in Khabarovsk and Vladivostok. Thrust into the middle of a bloody civil war, the Americans found themselves targets of Bolsheviks, Chinese bandits, and roving bands of Cossacks, as well as a large contingent of Japanese soldiers also sent to guard the rails.

"We learned of the crimes and secret murders by the Bolsheviki, of the resulting execution without burial by the Cossacks, and of Americans stepping in with force to prevent this needless expenditure of life," wrote C. G. Fairfax Channing, a U.S. first lieutenant who published a lively firsthand account of the expeditionary force's exploits in *Siberia's Untouched Treasure.* "As a result we were accused of being meddlers, the Cossacks said we were Bolsheviks and the Bolsheviks said we were trying to combine forces with the Cossacks to take over the country."[1]

When World War I ended, the U.S. contingent, having grown to include four hundred Russian women who married American soldiers and one brown bear (presumably unmarried), withdrew after a stay of nineteen months. Soon thereafter, allied ships plucked the Czechs from Vladivostok and returned them home.

"Excuse me, I saw you reading the English menu in the dining car."

The young woman with the pageboy haircut stopped me in the corridor as I returned to my compartment. She spoke in German-accented English. She wore a Western-style Gore-Tex® parka and fine wool pants. Too well dressed to be Russian, I thought.

"You are not Russian, are you?" she asked.

I explained who I was. For once, I did this without relying on my memorized Russian greeting.

Her name was Christine. She and her friend Pierre had boarded the train in Irkutsk when I had. They also had begun their journey in Moscow, though unlike me, they were fortunate enough to catch the correct train to Novosibirsk.

"We haven't seen any other foreigners on the train until we saw you heading to the dining wagon. At first, I thought you were Armenian or from Turkestan because you were wearing a sweat suit like everyone else. I wasn't sure because you were also wearing such exceptional shoes. When I heard you thank the waitress for the English menu, I thought you were either from India or England."

"Saved by my shoes again!" I exclaimed. I saw from the look on her face that she was puzzled by my outburst.

"I'll explain later," I continued, "but the fact is I've been sick and pretty much stayed in bed the last two days. Had I known you guys were aboard, well, it would have helped me a lot."

"Would you like to join us in our compartment? We are tired of being badgered by the Russians. It would be fun to compare stories."

She was an angel. Pierre, sight unseen, was a saint.

Their compartment was several cars away. I followed Christine with giddy, rejuvenated steps. She slid open the door.

"He's an American!" proclaimed Christine to Pierre.

An older man, with a graying beard and friendly, twinkling eyes, stood and shook my hand enthusiastically. The compartment was warm and cozy. Pierre cleared a spot on one of the bunks and motioned for me to sit. I felt as if I were among long-lost friends.

"You vant und beer? asked Pierre.

Before I could respond, Pierre, as if by magic, produced a pristine bottle of Heineken. I watched in fascination as tiny beads of condensation formed on the bottle's surface. Pierre searched for something to pry the lid off. I checked my pockets, but discovered I had left my knife in the mess strewn about my compartment.

"Give me a second. I'll fetch my Swiss Army knife," I said, helpfully.

Pierre motioned for me to remain sitting.

"Ve are Swiss. Ve have this knife."

In another second, he had found the national knife and had popped off the top. A wisp of vapor wafted from the bottle, and for a second I wondered if a genie would appear. I could barely say thank you, so happy was I to be in that compartment. Warmth and strength flowed back into my body even before I took my first sip.

23

Zorro

We talked about the black-market traders. We talked about the moneychangers. We talked about the restaurants with no food, and the long lines of morose Russians standing in the snow waiting for the vodka shops to open. We talked about this country where nothing seemed to work except the fear that was instilled in the population.

"In our hotel room in Irkutsk, we tried to turn off the radio," said Christine, referring to the obnoxious speakers that piped in patriotic music to each room. "But when Pierre turned the knob, it burst into flames."

This didn't surprise me, though it was cathartic to share the experience of a country falling apart at the seams. For hours our conversation ebbed and flowed as the train rattled forward into the dusk. During a moment of pensive silence, I realized that my grand journey would soon end. I glanced out the window as kilometer post 7,519 whizzed by, seven time zones away from Moscow. The last rays of golden daylight touched the tops of snow-capped mountains. Next to the tracks, a stream tumbled over ice-encrusted boulders. The raw, natural beauty of the land was showing itself on my last eve.

When I returned to my compartment, I was struck by the pungent odor of travelers who have journeyed too long without a shower. I was probably among the worst offenders. But there was nothing I could do about it. In another day, I could enjoy a hot bath.

I confined myself to my bunk and wrote in my journal. At around 10 p.m., Yuri rose Lazarus-like from his bunk, stuffed his few possessions into a small suitcase, and groggily wandered from the compartment. I hoped he would not be replaced. Being alone was the only way of ensuring a good night's sleep. I wanted to be fresh when the train arrived in Khabarovsk in the morning.

This hope, however, was soon dashed. Minutes after Yuri departed, two men appeared in the doorway. The first, middle-aged with the girth of an under-exercised gorilla, wore an enormous fur coat. Little slicks of hair stuck to the sides of his otherwise bald head, and the remnant of a scar traced down his right cheek. His young sidekick wore a worn leather coat that hung limply on his thin frame. His gaunt face was pocked from acne. His eyes darted furtively around the compartment, weasel-like. I rose to greet my visitors.

"Ivan," grunted the big man, quickly shaking my hand.

Before I could return the introduction, he and his companion pushed past me into the compartment. They seemed bent on a mission as they surveyed the nooks and crannies, jabbering between themselves with emphatic bursts of Russian, as I found my way back to my bunk. Like a baseball umpire thumbing an out at first base, Ivan rousted me from my seat. Wanting to be cooperative, I obliged. Under my bunk, he found the latch that held the bench down over the storage locker. Ivan lifted the hinged bench. With satisfaction, they examined the large amount of space remaining in the locker.

"Da," muttered Ivan, now smiling as he slapped me on the back like I was one of the guys. I was tired and indicated that I wanted to flip the seat down so I could sit.

"Nyet, nyet," Ivan cried, wagging a hairy finger at me.

In the next moment, the two men were hauling a dozen or so newspaper-wrapped parcels that had been temporarily stored in the corridor. They stowed the packages in my locker.

"Sure, go ahead, take the space, I'm not using it," I said, good-naturedly in English, as the two worked feverishly. "What do you have in there anyway, vodka?"

I made the last comment in jest, knowing that the recent Gorbachev decree had outlawed possession of alcohol on Soviet trains. The ban was not popular, but it seemed to be working. I had noticed little public drinking aboard the train, though what occurred in the privacy of one's compartment was another matter. The big man, alarmed, glared at me.

"Da, vodka, champagne, and beer," he whispered. He raised his index finger across his lips indicating that I should pipe down. My new companions were storing enough booze under my seat to send all of us to a Siberian prison for a long time. My only solace was that I was already in Siberia.

With a thwack, Ivan slammed down the bench and motioned that I could now sit. In fact, he seemed to indicate that I should stay seated for the duration of the trip. Smiling meekly, I returned to my seat.

Ivan issued another command. The weasel scurried to his feet and pawed through a valise that he had stashed on the top rack above Ivan's bunk; he removed three parcels. Ivan snatched them, and stripped off the newspapers from two of the packages, revealing more bottles of champagne and beer. He ripped open the third packet. Out came cold cuts, fruit the likes of which I hadn't seen in a month, caviar, and other delicacies. Ivan shoved a beer toward me. He and the weasel hoisted their bottles, then clinked them together with mine.

"To Perestroika!" shouted Ivan, who then let loose with an evil cackle that was mimicked by the weasel.

"Where are you going with all of this?" I asked, motioning to the loot.

"We go to Nakhodka, then to Singapore," said Ivan, replying in hesitant English. "We are businessmen."

The two men winked at each other, then burst out laughing as if this was the funniest thing they had ever heard. I didn't think it was particularly funny. They didn't look like businessmen, certainly not in the conventional sense. Wouldn't real businessmen ship their wares in sealed boxes with the appropriate paperwork approved by the authorities? Wasn't the blatant transport of alcohol aboard the train a tad on the illegal side? Ivan spoke a smattering of English, but certainly not to the extent that would allow him to conduct business in Singapore. No, I concluded, these guys probably weren't businessmen — unless you stretched the definition of smuggler, which was possible in this country where the distinction between legitimate and illegitimate was, at best, blurred. I eyed them warily.

Once again, I tried to make small talk, attempting to stretch my Russian vocabulary to its outer limits. My pat introduction failed to impress them.

"You cannot be an American. You don't look like American. Americans never come here in the winter. It is not possible," declared Ivan.

I insisted I was from America.

Ivan insisted I was not. He nudged the weasel.

In Russian, he said, "Bob is from Baku. Baku Bob. He must be from Armenia because he speaks bad Russian."

"Wait a minute!" I blurted. "Baku is the capital of Azerbaijan, not Armenia. You guys don't even know the capitals of your own Republics. What kind of businessmen are you?"

"Baku Bob. Baku Bob." They chorused together, breaking into giggles between swigs of beer.

"I am not from Armenia!" I said, exasperated. "Or Azerbaijan!"

"Baku Bob. Baku Bob." They mimicked the words like a pair of schoolyard bullies taunting a victim.

I could feel the anger rising, a thermal of primitive energy that heated my blood and focused my mind. Something deep had been triggered, though for the moment the deeper cause was not apparent. I had no recollection of ever being the victim of schoolyard taunts, at least not any more than normal. Perhaps the explanation was simply that the long journey had eroded my tolerance for acts of childish idiocy that I normally would have ignored. Or, was it uneasiness about my own ethnicity, a polyglot of cultures that had always confused even me. At that moment, I didn't need more confusion in my life. I thought about brandishing my passport to prove to these fools that I was authentic, a real American. Ask Pierre and Christine at the other end of the train? But I did none of this.

My passport stayed hidden in its pouch. If Ivan and the weasel were smugglers, the last thing I wanted to do was show them the coveted document. I tried another tactic. These clowns had probably no idea that the U.S. population was as diverse as Siberia's. Perhaps I could teach them something.

"I am a Mexican-American," I said, hoping that would explain my dark complexion.

Ivan polished off his beer, then stripped off the foil from the neck of a champagne bottle. My remark caught his attention.

"Mexico?" he said, squinting at me to get another look. "Da, Mexico."

He jabbed the weasel, who was staring wistfully at the champagne bottle.

"He is Mexico. He is Zorro."

"Da, Zorro!" yelled the weasel gleefully.

I rolled my eyes. I could not believe that I would have to spend the entire night with these monkeys.

"Zorro!" yelped Ivan, leaping to his feet, clutching the neck of the champagne bottle in his meaty hand. "En garde!" He tossed a rolled up *Pravada* to me, then advanced waving the bottle in my face as if it were a dueling foil.

"En garde, Zorro!"

I grabbed the newspapers, rolled them into what looked more like a bouquet than a paper sword. I crossed Ivan's bottle. The battle began. I parried Ivan's bottle thrusts. The weasel clapped and giggled as the mock sword fight unfolded. Ivan, showing surprising dexterity for a man his size, leaped onto his bunk, then jumped back into the aisle between the bunks yelling "en garde, Zorro" and prodding me with the blunt bottom of the bottle. I was backed into the corner of the compartment. If there had been a chandelier, I'm sure he would have grabbed onto it and swung himself across the room. As I defended myself, I wondered how these two knew about Zorro. Did Soviet central planners decide that old Zorro films were appropriate movie fare for the proletariat? All of Siberia must have thought Mexican men spent their entire lives dashing around in black capes wearing masks, waving swords at each other, and yelling "en garde." Ivan pushed through with a thrust that knocked my paper sword to the ground. He would have skewered me if he had a real foil. As it was, the condensation on the bottle bottom left a wet zero on the chest area of my shirt.

"Touché!" he yelled, returning triumphantly to his seat. He barked a command at the weasel. The weasel took out three champagne flutes. Ivan uncorked the bottle and filled the glasses.

"To Zorro!" yelled Ivan, lifting his glass.

For the next hour, I engaged in the most bizarre conversation of my life. As Ivan and the weasel drank, they became more boisterous. Ivan seemed to forget his rudimentary English. He barked questions at me in Russian, then turned and giggled with the weasel when I could not answer. At first, I tried my best to decipher what he was saying. But concentrating on his words was hopeless, even with the assistance of my tattered phrase book. It seemed they were poking fun at me, hurling insults in Russian, while I sat limply across from them, sipping champagne and smiling. Unlike Andrei, who I would have trusted with my life, I felt the opposite about these two men. What if they were plotting to rob me after sedating me with alcohol? I was too weary to defend myself. Given my fatigue and rundown condition, the last thing I needed was to get drunk or, worse yet, lose consciousness. Mentally, I noted the location of my wallet and passport.

The one-sided conversation continued. More giggles. Enough was enough.

"So Ivan, if the Soviets are so great, why did your ice hockey team lose in the 1980 Winter Olympics?" I blurted, referring to the U.S. team's improbable four-to-three victory over what was considered an invincible Soviet squad. Ironically, that was the semi-final game, but few remembered that the U.S. had to beat Finland in the finals to claim the Gold medal. There it was again, Finland. The reference to that country would not go away.

Ivan looked me blankly.

"Yeah, I bet you remember that. You and the weasel over there, you're repressing that one. You're losers, I say!"

Ivan and the weasel conferred, not quite sure what Zorro was up to now. Ivan then continued his questions, giggling again with the weasel. As they spoke, I recalled out-loud great baseball games I had seen, then I relived my high school basketball season. The compartment filled with incomprehensible babble. They drank. I sipped. We wagged fingers at each other to make our points, then shouted at each other in a babble of Russian and English. The theater of the absurd had returned on this last night aboard Rossiya. None of us understood a word that was spoken to the other.

Within an hour, we had worn each other out. At some point, the weasel could force no more giggles and slunk out of the compartment. Ivan and I, like punch-drunk boxers, glowered at each other in silence over the wreckage of the food spread, empty beer and champagne bottles. He seemed bigger and nastier looking than ever. I got the distinct impression that he wanted to slit my throat.

I wanted desperately to sleep, but dared not close my eyes. I could not take the chance with the personification of Ivan the Terrible glaring at me from the opposite bench. So we sat, minute after silent minute, as Rossiya pushed on to the Pacific.

With a grunt, Ivan lifted his massive frame, reached into his valise, grabbed a few more parcels and another bottle of champagne, and lumbered from the room. I heard him knock at the next compartment. This was the conductor's room, presently occupied by the attractive blond who had checked my ticket when I boarded at Irkutsk. I heard the door slide open, then the grunt of "dobry vecher" (good evening), followed by the woman's greeting of happy surprise. The door slammed shut. Within minutes, I heard muffled laughter. It seemed the "businessman" was taking care of business. At best, he was bribing her; at worst . . . I didn't want to think about it. Good riddance, I thought.

Still, I was nervous about having the contraband so blatantly visible. With each lurch of the train, empty beer and champagne bottles rolled across the floor. I was about ready to stow them under my seat when I remembered that the locker was already stuffed with alcohol. I kicked the empties over to Ivan's side.

Turning my attention to the matter of sleep, I changed out of my sweat pants into long underwear. This would make dressing easier in the morning. All I would need to do was slip on my pants and sweaters. I could be ready to leave in seconds. I assumed Ivan would be back, but judging from the commotion in the next compartment, I suspected that it would be much later. Nevertheless, I didn't want to risk falling asleep.

I lay curled in my bunk, waiting for the big man to return. The longer I waited, the more I feared him. I managed to convince myself that I really was being set up for robbery or worse. I wasn't going to let it happen, not now, not so close to the end. I unpacked my Swiss Army knife, and pried open the main blade, feeling the cold steel between my thumb and index finger. Switching off the light, I lay in the dull glow of the moonlight that bathed the compartment. Hang on, I told myself, for a few more hours.

My mind drifted. I thought of Mr. K. from Novosibirsk and his tuft of Chia pet hair. Suddenly, he appeared on the opposite bunk, transformed into a giant white rabbit. He sat on his haunches, nibbling nervously on a carrot and exclaiming with unbridled enthusiasm. "We have a great program planned for you today!" I was about to ask him about the festivities when a scream pierced the night. Mr. K. bolted from my subconscious.

With a start, I sat up in my bunk, dazed by the commotion and the absurd dream. Another scream ripped through the wall. Every muscle in my body tensed, my senses now fully alert. There was no doubt about it. The scream came from the next compartment, the one that housed the cute conductor, the same compartment that Ivan the Terrible had sweet-talked his way into a few hours earlier with booze and food.

Should I run in and save her, I thought in panic. But then I remembered that running in and saving people wasn't something that I had a lot of experience with, especially when it involved grappling with a drunk Russian twice my size. I slid my fingers under the pillow and felt for the Swiss Army knife. It was gone. Where was it? Where was my only weapon? In the dark, I frantically ran my hands inside my pack, feeling through layers of dirty clothes. I felt under the bunk, but only touched the shape of beer and champagne bottles stowed earlier. I found the paper bouquet sword. But the knife was lost.

What should I do? Was it a tradition to rape the conductor on the last night of the trip? Was the scream one of passion or of distress? Or, was it a product of my imagination, the same subconscious that had temporarily transformed Mr. K. into a giant white rabbit? What did I know? The answer was painfully obvious. After traveling through the heart of the country for nearly two weeks, I knew enough to know that things were never as they seemed.

I listened for more sounds of trouble from next door, but heard only the clacking of Rossiya's progress. I sat for long minutes, not sure how much time had elapsed, when I thought I noticed the train slowing. Or was that the shuffle of feet? Instinctively, I stood, not sure what I would do next. The blood rushed from my head. The room spun as I felt consciousness ebb. I reached for the handle above my bunk, but clutched only air. I could not resist anymore. I sank to the bunk and shut my eyes, thinking to rest for a moment, only a moment. By then it was too late. The overwhelming fatigue that had been building over the course of the trip finally burst through the dam; sleep overcame my exhausted and sick body.

The dream came in fragments; bits and pieces of the trip surfacing in disconnected scenes that began with Ivan bursting into my compartment with armed soldiers.

"Zorro!" roars Ivan, pointing an accusing finger at me, then at the empty champagne and beer bottles that have rolled back to my side of the compartment. The lights flick on. Two faceless Russian soldiers grab me by the armpits, haul me from the bunk, and drag me into the corridor.

"Please let me get my shoes," I plead. The appeal falls on deaf ears. A door slides open, and I am tossed into the night, plopped into a snow bank. Scrambling to my feet, I desperately try to climb back onto the train, but the handrails I clutch at disappear just as I grab for them. The last car rolls by. My grasping hands claw only night air.

I watch the dark form of Rossiya recede, then disappear around a bend as I stand watching from the middle of the track.

In the next instant, I hear what sounds like the distant clap of thunder. Thinking that perhaps another train is coming from the opposite direction, I turn to see three horsemen rapidly approaching. Sabers flash in the white moonlight. Instinctively, I know who they are, but cannot bring myself to move. Mesmerized by the spectacle, I stand frozen in place. The horses are in full gallop; clots of snow spray high in their wake; yellow flame snorts from their nostrils.

A cold wind brushes my face. Musical voices like in a Gregorian chant issue from the Siberian pines that grow alongside the track. They urge: Run and hide! Keep down! Don't tell them! The voice is familiar. I make the connection. It's Bubba's voice, distant and faint, calling from the beyond.

The Cossacks thunder closer, yet I stand and stare, replaying childhood nightmares of unseen monsters creaking through the house toward my bedroom while I lay paralyzed, unable to speak or move. And like in those dreams, just as the moment of oblivion is about to consume me, I am saved.

I blinked my eyes and stared at the dark outlines of the compartment's ceiling. I was safe, back within the comforting womb of

Rossiya. But the end of the dream had triggered a distant memory. I lay in a state of subconscious reflection, as the old memory bubbled to the surface of my mind.

I was a child again, six or seven years old, visiting the nursing home on Fairfax Avenue where Bubba lived during her final years. Her room, infused with the antiseptic smell of a hospital ward, is spartan: a bed, two chairs, and a black-and-white television, which shares the corner of a dresser with a bottle of Milk of Magnesia. I had no idea what Bubba did when we weren't visiting. To me, at that time, it seemed as if she had lived her entire life in that room. Even the Milk of Magnesia seemed eternal. When I grew older, I wondered how she reconciled the events of her life. The King Solomon Nursing Home was a long way from her birthplace on the Russian-Polish border.

My sister and I fidget on the couch, while Mom and Dad make small talk with the deaf family matriarch. She reads our lips with uncanny precision. Bubba is talking about the Cossacks. My mother whispers in my ear that Cossacks are like bandits, only worse.

This is the first time I've heard her talk about life in Russia. Even at this young age, I am fascinated by our family history, mostly because my parents know so little about the Goldstein-Rubin origins. My playmates have grandparents and great-grandparents, all of whom seem to live in large houses, where they host barbecues in yards brimming with cousins and nephews. On the other hand, I am not even aware I had great-grandparents. No one has ever suggested the possibility. I had just assumed that my two living grandmothers had sprung from the earth as elderly women.

I listen carefully, absorbing every word, every detail. Bubba tells of the time that the Cossacks rode into the village, how her mother had grabbed her and her little brother, my great-uncle Harry, and hid them in the cellar.

"'She told us to hide, to get down!' she said. 'Don't tell them who you are. Don't tell them you are a Jew.'"

I form a mental image of the village and the approach of large wild men, with wicked mustaches and unkempt hair, astride black horses that snort hot breath.

"But Bubba, who was the woman who told you to get down?" I ask, fascinated by the fact that another layer of kin existed. Bubba cannot continue. Tears well up in her eyes. Her mouth moves, but nothing comes out. As she sobs, I feel shame because I have made my grandmother cry. I have never seen an adult cry. I did not think it was possible. I am very sorry for asking the question that has upset Bubba.

Nevertheless, a seed is planted. Even though I am very young, I know that if this mystery woman, my great-grandmother, hadn't hidden Bubba and her brother, I would not exist. I lay awake now, in my bunk, pondering the question over and over: Who was she? I had to know the answer.

At some point, I fell asleep again and lapsed into another series of dreams. In one fragment, Nina waves to me from the back of the train. She is exquisite in white furs and hat, a necklace of pearls around her neck glints in the moonlight. Then she is gone.

I am half awake, vaguely aware of my surroundings, but unconcerned, the memory of the scream temporarily locked away in another part of my brain. My subconscious is still lucid, seemingly on an automatic rewind of my childhood. Scenes flash before me of family gatherings and forgotten relatives. Long suppressed memories seem to burst forth with freshness.

"I can tell you who your great-grandmother is!"

The bellowing voice with the thick Lower East Side New York accent comes not from Nina, but from a big, friendly man who vigorously shakes my small hand.

"This is your Uncle Bernie." My father is introducing me to a relative I had not previously met. The family is gathered at my aunt and uncle's house for some event. Uncle Bernie is telling me about the old family photograph, the same old one that I had stared at countless times, wondering who those people were, especially my nameless great-grandmother.

"Are those my great-grandparents?" I ask, pointing to the woman with the wan smile sitting in front, next to the stern-looking bearded patriarch. I detect something strange about him. He seems to have too many fingers on one hand. Before I can point out this oddity, Uncle Bernie clamps a hand on my shoulder, bends to my level, and points to the patriarch.

"You see that guy, Bobby, in the foreground? That is your great-grandfather, Abraham. He had two thumbs on one hand," says Bernie. "Can you imagine that, two thumbs!"

I really can't imagine it, and can only think that an extra thumb would make tasks like tying shoes more difficult. The extra appendage seemed a great inconvenience. Once it became clear to Uncle Bernie that I fully comprehended the wonder of a two-thumbed great-grandfather, he continued.

"Next to him is your great-grandmother."

"Where did she come from?"

"Helsinki."

"Where's that?" I ask, imaging a beautiful city like a fantasy castle sitting on top of a hill, golden spires glinting in the afternoon sun.

"In Finland."

I am now fully awake, but the lucidity fades as if my mind's batteries have drained to a dangerously low level. I am soaked in perspiration, the remnants of the fever. I replayed what had just coursed through my head: Bernie's booming thick Lower East Side accent, and that magic place — Finland. Then a surge of energy shot through my veins, instantly pumping life back into my body. I pounded my fist on the compartment wall, but the ecstatic thumping was absorbed into Rossiya's usual cacophony of thumps and squeals.

I now vividly recalled someone, either my Aunt Frances or Uncle Bernie, telling me that my great-grandmother — the woman who saved Bubba from the Cossacks — was from Finland! It was during a family gathering of some sort that happened a long time ago. That's all I remembered for sure, but it was enough.

The long trip, marked by sleeplessness and the stress of always being alert, combined with clues like breadcrumbs sprinkled along the way, had conspired to clear a path through my memory to this last fragment. The feeling I experienced was akin to visiting a strange place or seeing an object that triggers unexplainable feelings of familiarity. The dream was that object. The fact that the memory was triggered by a dream about Bubba probably had deep significance, but I would have to decipher that later. I laughed out loud. A part of me really was from Finland.

I wondered if there was more to the revelation. I had always accepted the fact that the entire Rubinstein clan had escaped czarist Russia, then headed west to America. But then again, family branches extend in all directions, little known limbs could have broken off and fallen amid the turmoil of Russian history. Perhaps, as Mother Russia had hinted, I was the funny man, the proverbial son who had returned, a reminder of what could have been, instead of what was. I was thankful for the path the Rubinsteins had chosen, now that I had glimpsed the grim possibilities of what might have happened to our family had they boarded the train and headed for Siberia.

I stared out the window at the blackness of the predawn morning, willing Rossiya to speed up its leisurely pace. I wanted the journey to end so I could sprint home and confirm my discovery. But the old train patiently rolled along through the dark morning as it had through the rest of Siberia, all 5,760 miles of it.

24

The Gentleman from Finland

The compartment door banged open, interrupting my
moment of reflection. Before me, his enormous girth filling
the doorway, stood the black silhouette of Ivan the Terrible.
Like a cobra, I coiled at the end of my bunk, ready to strike. My
eyes, now accustomed to the dark, studied Ivan's every move. At the
right moment, if necessary, I planned to hurl myself like a human
cannon ball at his torso. On any other train journey, my contemplated behavior would have been unthinkable. But now I was
infused with the will to survive. Like a marathon runner who had
just endured the first twenty-five miles of the race, I was deter-
mined to cross the finish line. That meant — at least, in the part of
my brain still capable of producing rational thought — preparing
myself against any possibility. I would leave nothing to chance.

The big man seemed uncertain, confused by the darkness.
Gingerly, he took one step into the room. One more step forward,
and I vowed to attack. Ivan paused as if he had perceived my
threat, then turned toward his bunk. For a long moment his body
seemed to sway ever so slightly, as if nudged by a breeze. Then he
quivered and collapsed onto the bunk. His snores began to come in
fitful bursts.

I uncoiled, arose, and examined the prone body. He was out cold, probably in a drunken stupor. When I turned to my own bunk, I could not flip on the reading light because it was shaking. Then I realized that the switch was still; I was the one trembling. Sitting down, I realized the ugly incident that could have transpired. I envisioned bleary-eyed passengers untangling us as we writhed on the floor in a wrestlers' embrace, with Ivan's shouts of "Zorro is loco" drowned out in the confusion. What was I thinking? What kind of beast had I become on this last night of a long and difficult journey? I glanced at my watch. It was 5 a.m. The trip was almost over. The danger had passed. Calm down, I told myself, try to get some sleep.

It seemed as if I had just drifted off when the compartment door slid open again. The pale predawn light revealed the conductor, looking as cheery as she had the previous day. She carried a tray with a steaming cup of tea. Great, I thought as I lay in my bunk half-asleep, room service on the last morning of the trip. But the tea wasn't for me. To my astonishment, she knelt next to Ivan and shook him gently on the shoulder. She whispered sweetly in his ear. The big man stirred groggily and groaned. She lifted the teacup to his lips, gently urging him to drink.

I was incredulous. This couldn't be happening, not after what I heard last night. But then I remembered where I was.

After the conductor left, I dressed and left the compartment. Outside, a brilliant sun rose over a vast marsh. On the horizon stood stark brown mountains. The train came alive for the last time. Men in sleeveless undershirts and blue sweatpants emerged wearily from their compartments and stumbled to the bathrooms at the ends of each carriage. A woman filled a jug with steaming hot water from the samovar. The head conductor walked briskly along the corridor, reminding passengers that Khabarovsk was the next stop.

When the train rounded a curve, golden rays of sunlight burst into the carriage, infusing me with joy. I stood in the corridor allowing the warmth to penetrate. Rossiya had taken me to places far beyond the thin black line that stretched across Siberia. She had tested my mettle, and triggered a spiritual journey that would continue long after I left Siberia. True, I was not a Marco Polo-type person, not even close, but I had managed to survive and to remember something important. The cultural interactions came without pause and at unpredictable times. Through these encounters, along with the backdrop of stark landscapes, gray shadows, and weak light that the days seemed to dole out only grudgingly, Rossiya had helped reveal a small part of who I was. It hadn't been easy, and I probably would not have embarked on the trip if I had known what I knew now. The best travel, I now could confirm, was a process of ordeals, endured at the time and embellished later in the comfort of familiar surroundings.

I made one last trip to the bathroom to shave and wash. Looking into the mirror, I was again shocked by my appearance. The gaunt face staring back looked like the countless faces of New World immigrants trudging off ships at Ellis Island long ago. I thought that's what my immigrant ancestors must have looked like when their ship steamed into New York harbor past the Statue of Liberty.

The long journey had also taken a toll on Rossiya. As I turned the handle to wash my toothbrush, the faucet plopped into the basin. The light in the room flickered, creating a strobe effect. Suddenly remembering what had happened to the lost Swiss Army knife, I dug for it in my pocket. After prying open the knife's screwdriver, I tightened the bolt that secured the faucet. I then removed the covering from the light fixture and tightened the bulb. The flickering stopped.

> *It's the least I can do for you old girl, I thought. At least, I get to go home, but you'll make this journey over and over through the same timeless landscape, listening to the heartbeat of the people. I guess that isn't such a bad fate after all. That's what trains do.*

Back in my compartment, I packed my bags for the last time. Pages of the phrase book littered the room, but I retrieved each one, gently placing them back in order into the broken spine. I still had a few days left in Soviet territory. I might need a phrase for something like "the play is enthralling."

For the last few minutes of the ride, I stood in the corridor watching the scenery. Rossiya crossed an enormous river, the Amur. On its banks, men sat on stools holding long rods that dangled fishing lines into the open water beyond the rim of ice that clung to the shore. In the middle of the channel, a tug belched thick black smoke as it pulled a barge loaded with coal. I watched the scenery from the corridor a few doors away from my compartment. Out of the corner of my eye, I saw the weasel ease into the compartment and remove the parcels that were stowed under my bunk. Ivan emerged. He appeared smaller in the morning light, less menacing. We made eye contract. He smiled lamely.

"Business," he muttered.

The Khabarovsk platform came into view, showing the usual assortment of pale Soviet citizens clutching worn bags and parcels. I was about to shoulder my pack and make my way to the end of the car, when someone tapped me on the shoulder.

"Do svidaniya," said Ivan, warmly. Surprised by his sudden gesture of friendliness, I could think of nothing to do other than to return the greeting. Then he was gone, another enigma tottering down the corridor and disappearing into the mass of passengers. The weasel struggled behind him, lugging the contraband boxes.

With a screech of wheels, Rossiya ground to a halt. As I poked my head out of the carriage to survey the crowd, I noticed a tall, fair-skinned man in a fur cap and a real leather jacket straining as if searching for someone he had never seen before. This had to be my Intourist guide. I knew the routine. I felt as if I was coming home.

When he saw me, he immediately headed in my direction. As I reached the bottom rung of the steps, he grabbed my pack, then shook my hand.

"We were expecting you," he said. His English was excellent.

"Are you sure you are looking for me?"

For a moment he looked uncertain.

"I assumed you were the gentleman from Finland," he said. "Mr. Goldstein. They said you would be in wagon seven."

"You have the right guy," I replied. "I am, indeed, the gentleman from Finland."

Epilogue

Months later, after I returned home, I asked my father about his grandmother, the mystery woman who hid Bubba from the Cossacks. He could not remember where she was born, or even what her name was. My Aunt Frances had heard a rumor that my great-grandmother was from Finland, but she could not confirm it.

This was not enough confirmation. I started to write about the trip, but could not get past the first couple of chapters. The book languished. Other life events overtook me, as they did the country I had visited. I began a new career and was soon consumed by the minutiae of government management. Meanwhile, the Soviet Union collapsed. Years rolled by. When I resumed the narrative a decade later, I once again wondered whether the dream was based on reality. I asked my father one more time to search his memory.

"Yes, I've heard that she was from Finland, but I don't know if it's true," he told me. He urged me to call Uncle Bernie.

"You mean he's still alive?"

"Yes, he's the last one alive who would know," said my father. "Bernie is sort of the family historian."

Bernie was one of the last direct descendants of the original immigrant family. He was the son of one of the young men in the old family photo that had triggered my inquiries about my ancestors. At 80, he and his wife now spent the winters in Florida. I wrote him a letter reintroducing myself and asked if he remembered the name and origin of my great-grandmother on the Rubin side of the family. I told him I would call him in a couple of weeks. One night about two weeks after I sent the letter, the phone rang at my Seattle home.

"I wanted to call you first because I'm hard to get hold of," said Bernie, his voice booming with a thick Lower East Side New York accent, just like in the dream.

"Your great-grandmother's name was Masha, Masha Raisal. She came to the village to visit a friend. Then she met your great-grandfather, Abraham."

Bernie said the village, called Anatol, was located near the Russian-Polish border between Grodna in Belarus and Bialystok in modern-day Poland, but was part of the Czarist Empire at the turn of the twentieth century. Masha and Abraham eventually were married and lived on a farm at the fringe of town. They had four sons, one of whom was Henry, Bernie's father, and two daughters, one of whom was Ethel, my grandmother, whom we called Bubba.

"I remember my father saying that they lived in a small house with a barn. There was a milk cow and a horse, and a small wagon that Abraham loaded up with vegetables to sell in the area. Did you know that Abraham had two thumbs on one hand?"

Before he got sidetracked on Abraham's thumbs, there was one last detail I needed to get straight. I described the trip, the dream, and the circumstances that caused the Soviet authorities to insist that I was from Finland.

"Of course, that makes perfect sense. Masha was from Helsinki. We probably still have distant cousins living there. You are part Finnish, you know."

End

End Notes

Chapter 2

[1] The June 29, 1902, edition of *The New York Times* (p. 5) reported that "eminent French engineer Loicq de Lobel" was lobbying the Czar to approve the $100 million project that would connect from Cape Prince of Wales westward and up the Yukon to Eagle City, eventually connecting with a projected American railroad that would reach Valdez. The Bank of France proposed to back the venture.

[2] Ebenezer J. Hill, "The Siberian Transcontinental Railroad," *National Geographic,* Vol 8, No. 4 (April 1897), pp. 39-45.

[3] Michael Shimkin, "Eastward Ho! Siberia to San Francisco," *The Californians,* Vol 1, No. 1 (May/August 1991), p. 34.

Chapter 6

[1] Burton Holmes, *Burton Holmes Travelogues,* Vol. 8 (The Travelogue Bureau, Chicago and New York, 1902), pp. 227-300.

[2] Harry De Windt, *From Paris to New York by Land* (New York: Frederick Warne & Co., 1904), pp. 1-12.

[3] See previous note on Hill.

[4] See previous note on Holmes.

Chapter 7

[1] "Kalinin's Wife Runs Big Siberian Farm," *The New York Times* (February 6, 1932), p. 11.

[2] See previous note on Holmes.

Chapter 8

[1] Michael Myers Shoemaker, *From St. Petersburg to Peking* (G.P. Putnam's Sons, 1903), pp. 38-39.

[2] *Fodor's Soviet Union 1987* (Fodor's Travel Publications, Inc., 1987), p. 406.

Chapter 13

[1] *Fodor's Soviet Union 1987* (Fodor's Travel Publications, Inc., 1987), p. 402.

Chapter 22

[1] C. G. Fairfax Channing, *Siberia's Untouched Treasure* (G.P. Putnam's Sons, 1923), p. 130.

Further Suggested Reading

The following list includes other works written about the Trans-Siberian Express that were not included in the end notes, but that may interest readers.

Higginbothan, Jay. *Fast Train Russia.* Dodd, Mead & Company, 1983.

Newby, Eric. *The Big Red Train Ride.* Penguin Books, 1978.

Strauss, Robert. *Trans-Siberian Rail Guide.* Bradt Publications, U.K., Hunter Publishing, U.S.A., 1987.

Theroux, Paul. *The Railway Bazaar: By Train Through Asia.* Houghton, Mifflin & Co., 1975.

Tupper, Harmon. *To the Great Ocean: Siberia and the Trans-Siberian Railway.* Little, Brown and Co., 1965.

About the Author

Robert Goldstein was born in Los Angeles, but grew up not far from the train tracks in Santa Clara, California. After graduating from Oregon State University with a degree in technical journalism, he worked as a newspaper reporter for *The Walla Walla Union Bulletin* and *Bellevue Journal-American*. In the late 1980s, his career took a different direction after he received his master's degree in public administration from the University of Washington. Since that time he has held a variety of administrative posts in California and Washington state. He has traveled extensively, and has published articles on Nepal, the Soviet Union, Israel, Bhutan, China, and the Arctic. Currently, he is the chief financial officer of The Seattle Public Library. He lives in Seattle.